TENNESSEE Wishes

Melissa Roos

Tennessee Wishes

ISBN: 978-1-966839-03-3 eBook

ISBN: 978-1-966839-04-0 Paperback

ISBN: 978-1-966839-06-4 Hardcover

ISBN: 978-1-966839-07-1 Large Print

Edited by: Delaney Roos

Cover design: Melissa Roos

TENNESSEE WISHES

Dare them to come true.

Books by Melissa Roos

You Can Hide

In the Shadow of the Black Moon

Cherry Hollow

The Further I Fall

Dedicated to:

To anyone who has ever wished on a dandelion
and fought like hell to make those dreams come true.
This is for you.

Joshua 1:9

ONE

Nashville, Tennessee

(Present Day)

The large alabaster moon shone like a spotlight on stage, illuminating the streets in an enchanting glow. This was Dorthea's favorite time when almost everyone was tucked in safely for the night. The city was subdued—neon stopped flashing, and lights winked out all over the high-rise buildings. The city was now more like a sleeping giant than a buzzing hive.

The twang of music no longer carried in the air, nor did the constant hum of traffic from automobiles or pedestrians. The day's stifling heat finally yielded, giving up its stronghold on the urban jungle.

She slowly wandered through the empty streets, past the small encampment of street people hunkered down by the abandoned warehouses. As she rambled by, one lone hand raised in her direction, a silent salute meant to include her. She knew she could join them. There was safety in numbers, especially since there was a killer on the loose, but she craved solitude. Her aching body craved rest, and her mind desired peace, which she wouldn't find among those chatterboxes.

Instead, she followed the narrow streets leading away from them and the structure. Slipping through the almost invisible opening in the ten-foot-high fence, she entered the maze of the abandoned plant. She picked up the pace, glancing nervously over her shoulder until she had successfully worked her way across it and came to the river. Seeing the river, she relaxed and meandered down by the edge.

Here, man-made sounds faded away, replaced by the croak of a frog, the lap of water, and the steady buzz of insects. The aroma of damp earth replaced the smell of hot asphalt. She was close now. She slipped off her worn shoes and dirty socks, letting her aching feet feel the cool of the grass.

Her mind tried to fathom how man had attempted to contain the mighty Cumberland River in the confines of downtown Nashville with elements constructed of wood, metal, and concrete. Despite that, the river still twisted a long, lethargic line of dark cobalt through the city, shrouding the edges from view, disappearing under bridges—her bridge, the one she called home —only to reappear on the other side, as if unchanged.

She found her place under the bridge's shadow and wiggled into the crevice. It was where the dark of night met the water, where civilization met nature. The edge of her spot was jagged from natural erosion and the ebb and flow of the steady current of the dark water.

Nestled into her sanctuary, hidden from sight by the long grass, she let down her guard and closed her tired brown eyes.

Instantly, her eyes flew open at the unusual way the grass whispered. That swish of blades was meant to sound like the wind, a melody lingering in the air, but she knew better. She'd heard it before.

Under her bridge, shadows fell dank and dark, and life met death. Water pooled in nooks and crannies, mosquitoes teemed, and a body was slipped slowly under the inky surface. The Cumberland Killer had struck again.

TWO

Ava Morgahn

Ava stood in the backyard beneath the towering maple tree, absorbing every detail of the moment as if it were the last.

Today marked the beginning of a new chapter—an adventure that would shape her future in ways she could only begin to imagine.

The sun had only just begun to peek over the horizon, casting a soft glow that kissed the earth. Birds flitted from branch to branch, their constant chatter piercing the morning air. The world felt alive and full of promise, and Ava was ready to step into it, leaving behind everything she had ever known.

"You coming?" Her mother called from the driveway.

"I'll be right there," Ava answered, spotting a dandelion. Her voice dropped low so only she could hear. "After I make a wish."

The weed, with its white, fluffy bloom, was simple and beautiful to her. The delicate globe of white was so tempting. She knew she could send the tiny seeds dancing in the wind with just one small breath—after all, she'd been wishing on dandelions as long as she could remember. It was one of the rare memories she had of her father—his large, strong hand enveloping hers, his voice steady as he urged her to make a wish. If only she'd known about the cancer, she'd have wished that away too.

She plucked the stem and delicately pinched it between her thumb and forefinger and tucked the memory safely back in her heart. She scrunched her eyes closed, held her breath, and made her wish.

With one large exhale, she sent a myriad of miniature parachutes dancing on the wind, dispersing through the warm air. Caught in the late spring breeze, they rose, spreading on an updraft, carrying her wish away. Seeing those seeds scattered gave Ava a sense of contentment, hope, and a determination to make that wish—a wish she had wished a thousand times before—come true.

When she could no longer see any seedlings, she rounded the corner of the house and found her mother standing by her car, scrolling through her cell.

Kelleigh held out the phone for Ava to see. "Here's another article about the Cumberland Killer."

The words in big, bold letters jumped off the screen at her: 'Nashville Residents Shaken as the Body Count Climbs.'

Ava glanced at it but only shook her head.

"I don't know Ava. Maybe you should rethink this whole thing," Kelleigh said as her voice cracked and her face was drawn tight with worry.

"Mom," Ava snapped, her patience gone. "Please, don't start. The cars are packed. I've signed a lease... I'm going."

Kelleigh's voice dropped, "There's three bodies now, Ava."

Ava stiffened, the weight of her mother's words pressing on her. She was well aware. She'd been watching the news herself, but pushed it aside. She wanted this opportunity so badly.

She pulled out her keys and connected her cell to the car. As she punched in the address, she glanced over her shoulder. "Come on, Mom, it'll be fine."

Ava could see Kelleigh purse her lips together, the tension in her face unmistakable as she fought the urge to speak. Ava didn't flinch. She held her ground, started the car, and silently willed her mother to get in her vehicle.

To her surprise, Kelleigh did.

Before she knew it, they were out on the interstate, the horizon unfolding before her. The sun was rising quickly now, painting the sky in vibrant hues of orange and pink as they cruised southeast toward Tennessee.

This wasn't just any road trip; it was a chance to turn her wishes into reality and her passion into opportunity.

Her friend Molly had paved the way for this adventure, moving to Nashville a few weeks prior to work for Cognac Creek. Like Molly, Ava had secured her place in the heart of it all.

Excited, Ava could already picture songwriting sessions, open mics, and recording studios.

As Ava drove, she glanced at the address from the "roommate wanted" ad Molly had texted. It was a lifesaver—a furnished apartment, a non-smoking female with no pets, and a price that fit her budget. After texting the number on the ad, Ava had crossed her fingers and was relieved to get an immediate reply. They had quickly set up a call, and to her surprise, they clicked. The conversation was brief but enough to sort out the details.

With hours stretching ahead, Ava wasn't quite ready for her audiobook. Instead, she decided it was the perfect time to catch up on video messages from her friends, which she hadn't had time for the past few weeks.

One hand on the steering wheel, Ava adjusted her phone with the other, and the familiar app lit up with notifications.

Her eyes trained on the road in front of her, she hit record, her voice lit with excitement. "Hey, Ladies! I decided to do it. I'm on my way to Nashville! I landed a job at Cognac Creek, too."

For her, Cognac Creek was an undeniable opportunity. Though her primary job there would be waiting tables —something she'd done throughout college—it didn't bother her. The venue was known for promoting local talent and offering stage time to those who paid their dues. It was a hotspot that combined a fiery country vibe, passionate music, and mouthwatering food. It was the perfect mix of unforgettable experiences and a spotlight for rising talent. Ava couldn't be more excited to do just that.

"I didn't want to tell you guys if I couldn't make all the logistics work. But thanks to Molly helping me work out some important details, like finding a great apartment, which happened to be available immediately—I'm on my way!"

"And before you ask, yes—I caved and let my mother tag along, too." As soon as the words left her mouth, she couldn't help but laugh at herself. Having her mother with her was a source of contention, something Ava had vented about more than once to her friends.

Her mother was over the moon when Ava got the chance to move to Nashville. But she wasn't pleased when the details came out—when she learned she'd spend the summer waiting tables instead of using her degree. To add to it, Nashville had been in the world's news lately with a string of unsolved murders rocking the city—needless to say, her excitement quickly turned to concern.

The tension simmered between them. Every conversation felt like a tug-of-war, just like this morning.

It wasn't until Ava had finally softened, trying to appease her mother, "What if it was temporary?"

"How temporary?" her mother had asked.

Thinking of the job she already had as the high school music teacher for the coming fall, she said, "Like three months. That would give me the summer. Will you come with me? Help me move in? I want you to see where I'll be living and working—see for yourself that it's safe and that I'll be okay." With that, they reached an uneasy understanding.

As she finished her message, a smile tugged at her lips at the thought of her friends watching it later.

She settled back into her seat, touched a blinking icon, ready to listen to her friend's messages. Molly's was the most recent post.

Ava pressed play and glanced at the screen, seeing it light up, revealing Molly's familiar smile. Her wild, dark brown hair was a little messy, falling into her eyes, and she absentmindedly pushed it back. Behind Molly, Nashville's vibrant streets hummed with energy.

Ava turned her attention back to the road, ready to listen.

"Hey, gang! Greetings from Nashville! I met a guy at this great place on Broadway!" She blurted out. "I can't believe I just said that out loud. Forget I said that. I've only been here a couple of days. I don't want to jinx it." Molly's voice bubbled with enthusiasm, instantly warming Ava's heart. "I started my job on Monday at Cognac Creek! It's a great place."

"Ava, you just have to come! I'm sorry I haven't had a chance to call, but between work and this new guy..." She blushed red. "Convince your mom, or I will! You're going to love it! The vibe is incredible, and there are so many places to play. You have to check out this little coffee shop on Music Row."

Ava could practically feel Molly's excitement radiating through the speakers. She couldn't help but smile, imagining them exploring the city together.

With Molly's energy and words lingering, Ava watched the open road stretching, endless possibilities waiting. She took a deep breath, feeling the thrill of the unknown wash over her. Nashville was calling, and she was ready to answer.

THREE

Detective Wyatt Lockhart

Bodies. There were always dead bodies floating in his river, the Cumberland River, which he'd grown up on, fishing, swimming, and skinny-dipping in. Now, though, he was doing an entirely different kind of fishing.

Disgusted, Detective Sergeant Wyatt Lockhart ran a sturdy hand over his polished bald head, bronzed to perfection from the Tennessee sun. Tucking both hands into the front pockets of his Levi's, he tried to relax. The sleeves of his once crisp, white shirt were rolled up to his elbows, and the taut muscles in his forearms twitched with anticipation. The shirt stuck slightly to his skin as sweat beaded and dripped down his back, his body's attempt to keep him cool in the oppressive Tennessee heat.

Tall and brooding, his shadow fell across the long, damp grass as he waited for the body to be extracted from the murky edge of the river. Concealed behind mirrored sunglasses, his dark eyes scanned the bank.

Instinctively, he knew they wouldn't find anything here. The deceased most likely had entered upriver. The question was how far up and how long the body had been submerged in the water.

Wyatt scrubbed his hands over his face. This was the fourth body pulled from the river in less than six months. It was like clockwork. Every six weeks, one surfaced in approximately the same vicinity along the bank of the Cumberland. This trek of the river was shallow, and the bend tighter, which tended to collect more debris. And more bodies.

The uptick in random homicides had him concerned. Very concerned. After the second victim had been pulled from the river, the media had dubbed the murderer as the Cumberland Killer. He could only imagine what the headlines would be tomorrow when word got out that there was another body.

He walked over as they laid the corpse on the ground, noticing the supervising Field Training Officer, FTO Darwin Ransick, standing nearby, flirting with one of the young, very pretty techs on the scene.

Wyatt acknowledged him with a jerk of his head. "What do we have?"

"Looks to be a Caucasian woman in her early twenties,' Ransick responded. "Probably another new transplant. The city is being overrun by thousands daily."

Wyatt stepped closer, squatted, and noted the pruning of her hands, the bloated body, abrasions on her exposed appendages, and the bluish tint of her skin, marked by the dark lividity pooling at her extremities. Her once blonde hair was tangled and matted with debris. He slipped on a glove and carefully picked up her left hand, turning it slightly to see her palm, preparing himself for the inevitable. The faded black number in marker jumped out at him like a scarlet letter. Branded with the number four, Wyatt knew without a doubt she was his fourth victim. The real quest on was—how many did the Cumberland Killer intend to have?

His nose wrinkled ever so slightly as he shook his head in disgust. "Let's get her bagged and out of here before this ninety-five-degree heat and the merciless sun beating down on us does anything to move along the postmortem."

"Yes, sir," the young technician said.

Detective Lockhart barked orders to the nearby forensic team.

"I want the temperature of the water taken and the rate it's moving."

Ransick signaled a couple of men.

"Once we have an idea how long the deceased has been dead, we can backtrack and trace her path along the river. See if we can pinpoint where she went in."

"Any ideas on how this woman died?" Ransick asked, shifting from one foot to another on the rocky ground, waiting.

Ransick was like a two-year-old, Wyatt thought, always underfoot and asking questions. He ignored him.

When Wyatt remained silent, Ransick offered up a suggestion. "Looks to me to be about the same age group as the others. Pretty, young, Caucasian. On the surface, there doesn't seem to be any trauma."

"You mean except for the fact that she's dead? Or the rope burns around her wrists and ankles. I'd say that was some serious trauma," Wyatt responded gruffly. He cursed under his breath. The FTO was a decade younger than him and did sloppy work. Always taking shortcuts. Wyatt didn't deal well with incompetence. Yet somehow, Officer Ransick always seemed to skate by on his good looks and southern charm.

Wyatt shook himself inwardly. He didn't want to get sucked down into that rabbit hole again. He cleared his throat. "I don't want to jump to any conclusions just yet. Collect the evidence per basic procedure. Follow the book. No cutting corners." Wyatt ticked off items. "Get the body to the coroner's office for the autopsy report. Have the water temperature and velocity measured ASAP. Then we'll talk."

Wyatt saw Ransick's jaw clench.

"What's the problem, Detective?" Ransick asked in a derogatory tone. "Can't we even speculate? Or are you too worried about your reputation to make an educated guess? I'd even go so far as taking bets that the deceased has the same MO as the other women."

Wyatt knew that Ransick was trying to get under his skin. As the number of bodies being pulled from the Cumberland River increased, so did the pressure from higher up and below. He'd heard through the grapevine that Ransick was after his job.

Six months, every six weeks, three bodies. No four, he corrected as he witnessed the team slowly zipping up the black body bag. He tried to keep himself detached as he watched the long, dirty hair get tucked in, so it wouldn't get caught in the zipper.

Four bodies, he repeated. In his gut, he knew she was like the others—he didn't need it officially confirmed. The number written on her palm had been enough. He assumed what the autopsy would find. Drowned. Excessive sleeping pills in her system. If he was a betting man, which he wasn't, he'd take that bet.

Four women, four drownings, and they were no closer to finding the killer. No closer to solving the case. His blood pressure spiked. Wyatt turned on his heel, disgusted. What a waste.

"Don't speculate. Don't make wagers. Just do your damn job. And," Wyatt looked directly at Ransick. "It's Sergeant to you."

Wyatt climbed the bank of the river back toward his car, still within earshot, he swore he heard . . .

"Not for long."

FOUR

Owen Layne

The hot southern sun rained down on them as they carried their equipment along the baked concrete of Broadway in downtown Nashville. Owen Layne switched his guitar to his left hand to adjust his backpack, maneuvering himself, his equipment, and the dog, weaving in and out of the crowd of tourists headed to his evening gig.

The vibrant streets buzzed with energy, the air thick with the sweet scent of fried chicken and the distant twang of a fiddle drifting out from a nearby honky-tonk. Neon signs flickered overhead, beckoning pedestrians to step inside for a taste of live music and cold drinks. Tourists snapped photos in front of iconic venues like the Ryman Auditorium, Tootsie's, and Ole Red.

As Owen navigated the crowd, he caught snippets of conversations, laughter, and the occasional off-key singing, each note a reminder of the city's heartbeat.

The buildings cast long shadows as the sun dipped closer to the horizon, painting the sky with hues of orange and pink. He could feel the excitement building; tonight, the stage awaited, and he was ready to perform. He was eager to immerse himself in the heart of Nashville's vibrant music scene, hoping to forget his troubles.

Toby Rauchert, his drummer, walked several steps ahead, releasing a low whistle as he turned his head to watch a bachelorette party parade by.

The women were dressed in tight, matching pink T-shirts. The smell of sweet perfume and tequila clung to their skin, drifting toward them as they passed.

"I think I'm in love," he said, clutching his chest as a pretty redhead returned his smile.

"You're always in love," Owen said, weaving to avoid a cameo in a tourist's selfie.

"Of course I am. What's not to love about love? And women?" Toby winked at a different woman coming toward him. When she blushed, he tipped his black Stetson in her direction.

The two of them and the dog paused at the corner of 3rd and Broadway and waited for the light.

"The problem with you is you'll fall for anything with pretty eyes and a smile," Owen grumbled.

"I'm sorry that I'm not cynical like you." Toby jerked a thumb at him. He glanced down at the German Shepherd that trotted alongside Owen. "Even Gunner's more upbeat than you. And that's saying something. Although Stella won't be happy, you brought him again."

"You know I can't leave him home alone. He goes crazy by himself," Owen said, as if Toby needed reminding. He tightened his grip on the leather strap on the dog's tactical vest as they maneuvered around the homeless in the middle of the sidewalk, holding up their signs, eager to attract attention.

"That's an understatement," Toby continued without missing a beat. "The damage he did to that last crate—bent the metal like he was Superman. He chewed up the cushions on our sofa and the woodwork by the front door."

"I know. We can't afford to leave him home. Too much collateral damage. And my mother isn't an option tonight."

"Well, if we get booted from this gig because of him, I'm gonna . . ." Toby's voice trailed off.

Owen stopped abruptly in the middle of the sidewalk and faced his friend. "You're gonna what?"

"Nothin'," Toby backtracked, his southern drawl evident in that one word.

Owen knew Toby was all talk when it came to the dog.

"We just can't afford to lose this gig. We've worked too hard."

"We're not going to lose it. Stella won't even know he's there." Owen glanced down at the animal in question. "Will she?"

The German Shepherd cocked his head and stared back, focused on Owen with those soulful brown eyes, the pain of loss shining out of them like a haunting echo that refused to fade.

Owen swallowed hard. He could only imagine what those eyes had seen, what that dog had been through. The loss was so significant, the price so high—Owen felt it too, all the way down to his core. "It'll be fine," he said, not only to reassure Toby but himself.

They ducked into the alley at the rear of the building and opened the back door. Country twang poured out, along with the smell of barbeque, burgers, and beer.

"Ahh, now that's a smell like home," Toby said, breathing deeply.

No sooner had they walked through the door than the bar manager greeted them. "Thank God you're here," Stella Doyle said with a sigh of relief.

"Well, that's a nice greeting," Toby chuckled. "I always knew we were your favorite band."

"Today you are," Stella agreed.

"Since when are you this happy to see us?" Owen questioned. "I thought you didn't have favorites?"

"Since about twenty minutes ago, and I haven't." Stella smoothed her white button-down shirt and neatly tucked its tail into her 501s. Her brown leather boots clicked against the hardwood floor as she took a few steps closer. She cut straight to it. "My main act canceled. I'm bumping you to the rooftop tonight. Think you can handle it?"

"The rooftop?" Toby questioned with an edge of awe in his voice.

"Of course we can," Owen nodded, accepting the challenge.

"Good. Wait. What's he doing here?" Stella frowned, a deep crease forming between her eyes, pointing at the dog. "I thought we agreed you should leave him at home."

Owen and Toby exchanged a worried glance.

"You're right, we did," Owen agreed to try to deflect.

"But Stella, have a heart." Toby draped a friendly arm over the manager's shoulders. "He's still grieving the loss of Owen's brother. He can't stand to be home alone. He won't be any trouble, we swear. You can't ask for a better-trained dog," he soothed.

Stella sighed heavily. Suddenly, she looked her full fifty-three years. The small crow's feet at her eyes and the lines etched around her mouth seemed more prominent than a moment ago. She yanked the elastic band from her jet-black hair, ran her fingers through it, refastened it, and smoothed the ponytail. "Fine. I need you guys in the worst way tonight. So, he can stay."

"Thanks, Stella. He won't be any trouble," Owen promised.

"If he so much as looks at a customer sideways, he's out. I will personally drag him to the basement and lock him in the storage closet, and you will be permanently behind the bar instead of on the stage. Do you understand?"

"Yep." Owen put his palm on the dog's head. "He'll behave. I promise." He prayed he could keep that promise.

"Alright. Go. Off to the third floor with you. I'll send the rest of the band up as they arrive. Twenty minutes to sound check. Thirty to showtime."

FIVE

Ava Morgahn

Sweat ran down Ava's back and pooled at the top of her cutoff jeans as the hot Tennessee air curled around her. She lugged the last box up the stairs with her guitar strapped over her shoulder, bouncing off her back as she took the steps to her second-story apartment. She used her elbow to open the door, slipped in, and pushed it shut with her foot.

"This is the last one," she called out to her mother as she placed the box on the kitchen counter and shrugged off her guitar.

"It's about time," her mother said, emerging from the bedroom on the right. "I didn't think we brought much, but going up two flights of stairs made me second-guess what we did bring and if you need it all."

"Thank goodness the place was furnished," Ava said as she flopped on the leather couch. "I don't know what we would have done if we had to drag a dresser and a mattress up those stairs. They are steep."

"You're not kidding." Kelleigh sank onto the sofa next to her daughter and leaned back. "That's bonus points for Molly. She was thinking when she found this place."

"From what Molly said, not many places have become available in this area at this price."

"It was a good find," Kelleigh agreed.

The gentle strum of a country song from Ava's playlist drifted from her phone, filling the air with a warm, inviting melody. The music wrapped around Ava like a comforting embrace, making her feel like she was already at home in the apartment.

"What are you thinking?" Ava asked her mother, wanting her to feel the same level of comfort in the new environment as she already did.

Kelleigh furrowed her brow. "This is an amazing opportunity. I'm sad knowing you'll be over ten hours away, but I'm also genuinely thrilled that you're excited to start this new adventure." She took a deep breath, gently placing her hand on the side of Ava's face, "How could I possibly be upset with you getting this chance? You've earned it. After everything you've put into your dreams these past years, you deserve every opportunity that comes your way. And if it doesn't work out for some reason," she shrugged, "or you don't like it, you have a great job to return to in the fall."

Ava felt a faint blush creep onto her cheeks. She had accepted the teaching position for the coming fall, but let's face it, playing and singing music in Nashville is what she wanted to do. This was once in a lifetime. So what if it was all hinged on a waitressing job at Cognac Creek? There was potential to make good money over the summer and have access to the stage. It was a rare chance to pursue her dreams and still have a safety net to fall back on. At least, that's what she let her mother believe. Now that she was here, Ava had no intention of leaving.

"Since the car is unpacked, we should get something to eat," Kelleigh said, breaking into Ava's thoughts. "I'm starving."

"Yeah, me too."

"We could grab fast food or do you want to sit down somewhere?"

Ava perked up at the thought. "I would love to go downtown Nashville, to Broadway," she suggested, her eyes lighting up with excitement. She imagined the two of them strolling along the bustling streets, taking in the sights and sounds of the honky-tonks, stopping to listen to a local band, and maybe scoping out places to play.

"That sounds fun," Kelleigh agreed, her enthusiasm matching Ava's. "Your roommate won't come home until tomorrow, correct?"

"Yes, that's right."

"What was her name again?"

"Cara McCray."

"Right." Kelleigh reached for her purse. "And Molly?"

"I haven't been able to reach Molly by phone or text. I'm sure she's busy. I'll catch up with her after you leave."

Kelleigh nodded. "Do you have a specific place in mind to eat or want to decide once we're downtown?"

"If you don't care, I'd like to go to Cognac Creek. Get a feel for it before I start work on Monday. They have five-star burgers and the best live bands with rooftop seating," she suggested, already picturing the view of the skyline. "And maybe Molly will be there working."

"It would be great to see Molly." Kelleigh smiled. "Burgers, music, and a view of the city. Sounds like a good combination to me."

Kelleigh stood still for a moment and let her gaze drift over Ava.

"What?" she questioned.

Kelleigh shrugged. "I just wish your dad could have seen this. How talented you are, how confident and beautiful you've become." She sniffed. "He would be so proud of you if he were still alive."

Ava leaned in and gave her mother a hug. "Thanks, Mom."

Kelleigh wiped a tear. "He's missed so much."

"I believe he's seen it all."

SIX

Owen Layne

Owen glanced at the dog lying at his feet as the first set ended. The German Shepherd sprawled across the stage, his head on his front paws, unmoving. Only his eyes flicked from side to side every once in a while.

Owen knew the stimulation of the people, lights, and loud music was a lot, even for a police-trained German Shepherd, but so far, he'd been well-behaved. Owen didn't want to push his luck, though. The dog needed a break. He signaled to the band as the last chord faded on the set.

"Ladies and gentlemen, we will take a ten-minute break." He made the announcement and then turned off the mic. He mouthed, "Taking the dog for a walk," to Toby, then bent down and took his leash. The German Shepherd stretched and looked at him. If dogs could look humiliated, that's how he looked at that moment.

They both knew he didn't need a leash. He wouldn't run, he wouldn't wander, he didn't need to be restrained.

Owen was under no delusion that he would be able to stop the dog with physical restraint if he did decide to take off. The leash and the tactical vest were for the people around them. The pure pretense that Owen had control. It made strangers—people around them feel more at ease to see a dog like Gunner on a leash.

Owen lifted the leather strap and shrugged. "I don't like it any more than you do, buddy."

The German Shepherd blinked at him with indifference as if to say, "You're not my buddy, not even close," but obediently waited for the command to jump off the stage.

"Let's get you outside," Owen said to the dog.

Once down, the two of them maneuvered their way through the crowd and headed for the service elevator. Owen stopped to autograph a napkin and take a photo with yet another bachelorette party but managed to move on quickly, wanting to get the dog outside.

Stella was waiting for him by the elevators with a bottle of water. "Great set," she said, handing it to him.

"Thanks."

"Got two more in you?"

"We do."

"Keep it up, and you just might be my feature band every weekend." Stella glanced down at the dog. "Think he will behave that long?"

Owen bristled. "It was one time, Stella. Right after... that was months ago." He scowled at her. "When are you going to let that go?"

"One time too many, if you ask me. And maybe never."

"Good to know you don't hold a grudge. I'm going to take him out."

"You do that." Without saying anything else, she pushed the elevator button, and the doors parted for them.

Owen stewed on the way down. He didn't bother looking at Gunner. "You knock down one person by accident, who was already so wasted and acting sporadically, catcalling and swinging at women with fits and starts of rage, he could barely stay on his own two feet. How quickly she forgets that we squelched that situation before it could escalate." He huffed and fell silent as the elevator dinged, and the door glided open.

On the main level, Owen shoved hastily through the metal service door, and they emerged into a crowd of people. He was elated at Stella's comment about them becoming the main band but knew better than to get his hopes up. In this town, nothing was a sure thing. One false move, and he could be stuck behind the bar permanently. He didn't even want to think about it.

The streets were teeming with tourists, and his already furrowed brow deepened. This wasn't the relief he sought or the space Gunner needed.

"Let's go around to the alley." Owen turned hastily, saw a blur of green and ran smack into a woman. "Son of a—Watch where you're going!" he spewed gruffly.

"Excuse me?" a female voice questioned. "You," she jabbed a finger at his chest, drilling into Owen, pushing him back slightly, "ran into me."

His vision cleared. He focused on her face, and the smart-ass comment he wanted to say instantly died on his lips. "I ... I," he stammered. The aggravation he had felt from the collision drained from him. His brain took a one-eighty. "You're right, I did."

She scrunched her eyebrows, looking like she was ready to argue. "Is that a trick? By agreeing with me, you're just going to walk away unscathed? Oblivious to the venom you were about to spout off to a total stranger?"

He couldn't help but smile. She was cute—not in the made-up way that girls post on social media with various filters to gain more followers or likes. No, this was all natural. Her hazel eyes, encircled by dark lashes, glimmered against her soft, honeyed skin. Dark, cocoa brown hair, streaked with copper and gold highlights, framed her captivating, oval face. And that voice was like... like liquid gold despite the edge to it. He was immediately charmed.

A small, insidious feeling settled in the pit of his stomach, a sharp pang. At the same time, something inside him, something solid, fractured deep within the wall he'd painstakingly built around his heart. For a moment, his guard faltered, slipping just a fraction. But instinct kicked in, and with a cold, deliberate motion, he rebuilt it—slamming another brick into place in his invisible fortress, higher and stronger than before.

"Simmer down," he scanned her, looking for something, anything to latch onto. He needed a sarcastic comment or a good retort to even the playing field. He wasn't used to being caught off guard. That's when he noticed the pendant on her necklace.

"I State?" He questioned. "What are you from Idaho or something?"

"Idaho?" She cocked her head. "Why would you think that?"

He pointed at her chain. "Big I, little state."

"Oh." Instinctively, her hand went to her necklace and fingered the pendant. "The I is for Iowa."

"Right, the land of Lincoln."

"That's Illinois," she corrected him with a roll of her eyes.

"My bad. Iowa—you grow potatoes." He could see her bristle and inwardly congratulated himself. Better.

"That's Idaho. Try cracking a book sometime." She looked down at the dog. "He's beautiful. May I?"

"Be careful. He doesn't usually like strangers, especially ones that go 'round poking people."

"Funny," she said dryly.

"Go slow. He doesn't usually like strangers."

"You already said that."

"Did I?" he questioned. He had. She had him slightly rattled. He wasn't on his best game.

Turning her attention to the German Shepherd, she reached out slowly. "Well, hello, handsome," she all but purred. "What are you doing hanging out with the likes of him?"

"Ouch. You're mean," he said, trying to keep his mouth from twitching into a smile. If he was looking for a response from her, he wouldn't get one. She was too focused on the dog. And damn if he didn't want her attention too. He felt a brick in that protective wall crumble.

The German Shepherd looked at her with those soulful eyes. She reached out and rubbed his head. He thumped his tail like a puppy. Owen stood baffled at the out-of-character reaction the dog was having to her. He wasn't a puppy or an average dog, for that matter, but he was acting like one. No, he was a full-fledged tactical dog. A broken one. A retired one. And Owen had never seen the German Shepherd look at anyone like that, not even his brother.

A pang of loss shot through his gut. He securely reinforced the crumbling brick, lodging it in place. He cleared his throat. "I'm sorry to cut this little love fest short, but we need to get back."

"That's fine. I'm waiting for someone anyway." She gave the dog a last rub and brushed her hands off on her jeans. "There she is now. Mom!" she called out. "Over here." She stuck her arm in the air and waved.

That was his cue. "Later, Hawkeye." He gave the command, and they moved as a unit.

They were rounding the corner of the building when he heard her call out, "The Hawkeyes are the University of Iowa, not Iowa State."

He didn't turn. He knew damn well Iowa State was the Cyclones. After all, he went to Kansas, and he was a Jayhawk. Kansas was in the Big 12 conference with Iowa State. But he didn't need her to know that he knew. Then again, why did it matter? He'd probably never see her again. She clearly wasn't a local. She was on Broadway on a Saturday night with her mother. She was most definitely a tourist.

He let the dog off-leash. "Free," he said with a flick of the wrist. The dog moved down the alley leisurely, stretching his legs and surveying his surroundings. The thought niggled at Owen as he watched him. Why did it matter that she had gotten under his skin in such a short amount of time? Because... because it did. He'd felt... something.

He hadn't felt anything for months. Not since the officers had shown up to inform him of his brother's death. His older brother, Dylan. His only brother. And he was left to care for his injured dog. He was numb. Hardly anything phased him anymore or stirred him except his music. And sometimes, that didn't even do it.

He hadn't even registered the moment his girlfriend of three years burst into tears and ran from the room. The sound of the door slamming barely pierced through the haze of his thoughts, he'd been on autopilot, just going through the motions. But what came next shattered every illusion.

She returned, eyes red, voice trembling, and she told him the truth without hesitation. She wasn't in love with him, never had been. The secret she'd kept for so long—her heart had always belonged to Dylan. She'd explained that she told herself she could wait, that if she were patient enough, Dylan would notice her, or that maybe her singing career would take off and change everything. But the truth was undeniable, she said—Owen was already a washed-up, wanna-be country singer at twenty-seven, and he wasn't the one she loved.

The joke was on her. Dylan would have never picked her over his younger brother, and the reason she couldn't make it in the music industry was because she always sang as if she were slightly drunk at a karaoke bar, off-key and loud.

He shook his head at the memory, the loss, and the irony that had freed him from her but stuck him with the dog—one leash for another.

Mentally, he tried to shake it off, refusing to get sucked back into his funk. Thank God they still had two more sets to play. Music was the only thing that helped, the only thing that made him feel.

Except her.

The thought rang through his mind uncensored. His brow furrowed. It could have been a fluke, he told himself, still feeling high from the set. Yeah, that was probably it. Guess he'd never know since the chance of seeing her again was slim to none.

He signaled for the dog, ready to head back inside, when he noticed the older woman leaning against the brick wall.

She wore baggy pants and an oversized gray T-shirt that swallowed her tall frame, a worn military-grade green backpack slung over her shoulders, with a fluorescent pink rabbit's foot dangling from the strap.

Homeless—echoed through his mind.

"Are you alright, ma'am?" Owen asked.

Her bronzed face creased into a tiny frown, the years etched into it from weathering the elements. She glanced over her shoulder as if double-checking he was speaking to her.

A gnarled finger extended. "You talkin' to me?"

"I am."

"You see me?"

Owen's lip twitched up into a small smile. "Yes."

"Oh." She hesitated, then shot a suspicious glance around, her posture stiffening. "I'm not used to people seein' me. Usually look right past."

"Well, I see you. And I'm askin'—are you alright?"

"Just tryin' to stay cool. Dreadful hot today," she answered curtly as if the conversation was already over.

"Yes, it is." Owen signaled for the dog and realized he still had the bottle of water in his hand. Unlike the homeless that he usually walked by, who stared off into oblivion or wanted his money, she stayed back and seemed as if she had all her faculties. He noted she watched him under a reserved mask.

"Would you care for a bottle of water?" He held it out to her. "It's unopened."

She hesitated. "I ain't fixin' for a handout."

"It's not a handout. It's a friendly gesture, that's all. From one human to another."

She reached out a tentative hand. "If you're sure?" she questioned.

"I am." He moved it closer to her. "My name is Owen."

"Bless you, Owen," she said, softening, taking it from him. Immediately, she stepped back, twisted the top, and took a long drink, watching him over the bottle. She screwed the top back on and dried her mouth with the back of her hand. "Name's Dorthea. But everyone I know calls me Dot."

"Nice to meet you, Dot."

"Likewise." With a tilt of her head, she gestured back toward the bustling street. "Don't run into girls like that too often, now, do ya?"

Owen laughed. "You saw that, huh?" Had she been standing there this whole time?

"I did," she said knowingly.

"I guess not." He hooked a thumb over his shoulder. "We need to be getting back in. Have a good night, Miss Dorthea."

Without looking back, they disappeared inside, and Owen wondered what else the woman saw while she went unnoticed.

SEVEN

Ava Morgahn

"I love this. It's so much fun." Kelleigh waved her hands in the air, encompassing the whole bar. "And the atmosphere. Just look at this place!"

Her mother was right. The bar was gorgeous, with its rough, unhoned wooden rafters, wide planked floors, and warm earth tones. The rooftop was covered, where the band played, the dance floor, and a good portion of the seating area.

However, the double-sided bar was partially open to the elements, opening to a large balcony filled with tables. The massive beams jutted out over the balcony, cantilevering, providing some shade in the afternoon, while strings of small globe lights swayed in the air, setting a dreamy mood.

The glassware and bottles behind the bar sparkled in the soft lighting and the sun's slanting rays. The warm summer air poured in as the air conditioning and music flowed out. Large planters filled with grasses, Hostas, and wildflowers softened the edge of the brick building.

They had been lucky to get a table because both sides of the bar were brimming with people. Snippets of conversation could be heard over the backbeat of the bass guitar, but when his voice rang out, Ava couldn't focus on anything but him.

That voice—low, deep, and seductive—had a rasp that was pure gravel yet smooth like hot buttered rum. It sent a delicious curl of desire through her.

She'd know it anywhere.

Even though she had only heard it for the first time less than thirty minutes ago, it was lodged in her heart and anchored in her soul.

She was good at recognizing voices, sounds, lyrics, and melodies. It was her gift, and that voice was his.

Oh, how she longed to sing with him, to harmonize, match her voice to his, and lose herself in a magical duet that would bind their voices together in a perfect, unforgettable melody.

Ava leaned forward in her seat, trying to get a better view of him. He strutted across the stage like he owned it, cocky, confident, and charismatic. She'd seen a glimpse of that attitude out on the street when he ran into her. But on stage...he was all that and more.

And for the record, *he* had run into *her*—it was inevitable. She couldn't have avoided him even if she tried. The moment she saw him step out from the building amidst the bustling crowd, she felt it. The undeniable pull. Their paths *had* to cross. It was as if he were a magnet, a force she couldn't resist, drawing her in with a power so intense she couldn't look away.

The dark hair, the five o'clock shadow, and the hint of dimples in both cheeks etched on that rugged face had made her heart skip. But the way those denim blue eyes flashed as he scanned the street was so intense that her body was immediately on high alert. She froze for a split second, just long enough to change her direction, her intentions of avoiding the collision gone.

He had flipped his backward baseball cap around to shield those eyes from the sun and made the turn into her—according to her plan. He had been a solid wall of muscle with a deep, dark, seductive scent lingering in the air just inches from his skin.

The conversation hadn't been planned, though. She hadn't had time to think that through. It annoyed her slightly that he hadn't or didn't have a clear conception of Iowa State, her alma mater.

"What in the world are you doing, Ava Lynn? You lean over much further, and you will fall right out of that chair," her mother commented.

"What?" Ava asked, bringing her attention back to the here and now. She shifted in her seat, realizing her mother was right. She was dangerously close to tipping over.

She righted herself as the appetizer arrived and was sampled while Kelleigh chatted away, oblivious to Ava drowning in the wake of a country cowboy.

She knew she should be listening and enjoying what little time she and her mother had together, but she couldn't focus. In approximately 48 hours, she'd be on her own. Her mother headed back to Des Moines, some ten hours away.

It would be hard because they were close and had been since her father passed away when she was little. But once her mother left, she'd be alone after all these years.

That wasn't entirely true, she corrected. She had Molly and her new roommate, or so she hoped. It surprised her when Molly didn't acknowledge her arrival, but she knew her coming had happened quickly. The last time she and Molly spoke, it didn't look like she could make it work. So how could she have expected Molly to drop everything and be here when she arrived? She couldn't, but since she hadn't been able to reach her, Ava hoped she might run into her here at the bar.

When she asked if Molly was working, they told her no. She was probably out with her new guy. It wasn't a big deal. They'd hang out soon enough. She had to stay hopeful that the music industry bigwigs would take notice of her, too. She was in this for the long haul—these first few days without Molly would soon be nothing more than a distant memory.

One way was to capture the moment so it wasn't all a blur. Ava grinned and raised her phone high. With a quick tap, she hit record, eager to share the moment with the girls and later with her followers. She angled the camera to catch the glowing Cognac Creek logo, the energy of the place buzzing around her.

"Hey!" she called out, her voice full of excitement. "I made it! We arrived late this afternoon, hauled everything into the apartment, and now we are in downtown Nashville, hanging out at Cognac Creek. We're about to eat these delicious burgers." She panned down for a quick sweep of her meal and her mom. "Say hi to everyone, Mom."

Kelleigh gave a little wave to the camera.

"I hope you can hear this music." With a slow scan of the stage, Ava was quiet for a moment, letting the band play, leaving the camera linger a little longer than necessary on Owen Layne. She spun the camera for a quick, dramatic sweep of the bar, the string of delicate globe lights reflecting the pulse of the music. "I'll keep you in the loop as to what's happening. Now that I'm here, I look forward to settling in, and hopefully, Molly and I can get together soon. Love you guys!" She hit stop on the recording, her smile remaining.

"I think it's wonderful that you have such a supportive network."

"They encourage me, and in return, I encourage them. It goes both ways," Ava said, typing Owen's name into her search engine. The phone worked its magic, and she scanned the information on him.

"Here's to that!" Kelleigh beamed, lifting her glass.

Ava didn't miss a beat. She lifted her margarita to her mother's and her eyes, looking at the band and Owen Layne. She felt a jolt as their eyes connected. The air sizzled with heat for one brief electric moment as those eyes burned holes through hers. Just when she didn't think she could take the intensity anymore, he looked away, breaking the connection.

"Are you alright?" Kelleigh asked.

"I'm just taking it all in." Ava picked up a fry and held it inches from her mouth. "I can't believe I get to live here. It's a dream come true."

Kelleigh patted her hand. "I know. I'm so excited for you. And to think you get to come to Broadway and listen to live music whenever you want and hopefully sing and play here, too. What a treat." She took a bite of her cheeseburger. "We still have some things to do before you start work on Monday. I want to give that bathroom a good scrub, run a cleaning pod through the washing machine, and ensure you have a fully stocked fridge and pantry before I leave," Kelleigh said, ticking off her mental list. "I wonder when your roommate did that last."

Ava laughed. "We'll get to it, Mom. Just enjoy tonight. We'll worry about that tomorrow."

Their meals were long gone, and their glasses empty as the crowd thinned and the band stopped to take another break.

Ava sat straighter as Owen Layne stepped off the stage. Women flocked to him. She felt a little twinge of jealousy as she watched them run their hands all over him.

Owen didn't bat an eye. He flirted, posed for photos, and laughed at something she couldn't hear. He effectively excused himself from the congregated women, leaving them drooling in his wake, and walked directly over to her with his dog in tow.

Their eyes locked as he stopped at her table. Much to her surprise, he broke the connection and turned toward her mother.

"Excuse me, Ma'am." He stuck out his hand to Kelleigh. "My name is Owen Layne."

"Kelleigh Morgahn," she said, taking his hand. "Nice to meet you." Kelleigh gestured toward Ava. "This is my daughter Ava."

"We've met. Hello again, Hawkeye."

"Cyclone," Ava corrected. "The Iowa State mascot is a Cyclone."

He flashed a smile, so quick and so deep that identical grooves creased the sides of his face.

Oh, boy.

"You've met?" Kelleigh asked, clearly surprised.

"Briefly. Outside—when your daughter plowed into me on the street."

Ava raised an eyebrow. "Plowed into you? I'm pretty sure it was the other way around."

"Let's agree to disagree." He turned his attention back to her mother. "Are you enjoying the music?"

"Yes. You and the band are quite good."

"Thank you." He cleared his throat, and that gravelly voice asked, "Would it be rude of me to ask if we could buy you a drink?"

"That's not rude . . ."

"More like presumptuous," Ava finished for her mother.

"What my daughter means is that would be very kind. But I must ask—who is we? You and your beautiful dog?"

"Us and my guy, Toby, over there." Owen turned and pointed at the drummer. On cue, Toby looked over and smiled widely, tipping his hat in their direction. "Wanted to buy you a drink."

Kelleigh laughed. "Now, isn't that just the sweetest?"

"Is that a yes?" Owen asked.

Ava watched the exchange, curious about where this whole thing was going.

"It's up to my daughter if she'd like to stay longer."

Owen pinned her in place with his eyes, challenging her with a look. "Well? How 'bout it, Hawkeye?"

She wasn't sure what he was up to. If this was about her mother or not. Regardless, she wasn't about to back down from a challenge. She leaned over and gave the German Shepherd a quick rub, stalling. "I guess we could stay for one more drink." She shifted in her chair looking directly at him.

Owen snagged a chair from the table next to them, dropped the leash, and let the dog crawl under the table. The bar's automated playlist started, filling the room with music. Owen signaled for a server as Toby sidled up to the table.

"Ma'am." Toby tipped his Stetson in Kelleigh's direction. "Got room for one more?"

"Of course." Ava gestured. "Pull up a chair."

"I would," Toby offered, hesitating, clearly changing his mind. "We only have ten minutes until the next set. If I'm going to make my move, I need to do it quickly."

"Your move?" Kelleigh asked, taken back. "What move would that be?"

"It's not a live band or us," he waved his hand between himself and Owen. "But the playlist here is pretty good." With a smile as wide as Old Hickory, Toby held out his hand as the next song started. "Can I have this dance?"

Kelleigh laughed. Then, flushed a shade of red. "Oh, you're serious?"

"As serious as a runner doing the stairs at Percy Warner," he said without his smile dimming.

"I'm not sure what that means, but," Kelleigh glanced around, noticing a few others still on the dance floor. "Why not? I'm in."

Toby took her hand and pulled her up and out onto the floor, giving her a quick twirl.

Owen abandoned his chair and slid quickly into her mother's vacated one across from Ava.

He watched them gracefully glide across the dance floor, their movements perfectly in sync, and a faint smile tugged at the corner of his lips. "They really can dance, can't they?" he remarked, his voice casual, but the admiration in his tone was clear.

Ava, too, couldn't help but be captivated by the way they moved. She nodded, her gaze lingering on the couple as they twirled past. They made quite the pair despite the age difference. Toby was young and lanky, but apt and confident as he led her mother around the dance floor. "Yeah, they can," she agreed, her voice soft but thoughtful.

Owen turned to face her, his expression shifting just slightly, as if a spark of something mischievous danced in his eyes. "What about us?" he asked, his tone playful yet laced with something more, a challenge beneath the surface. "Want to see how well we fit together on the floor?"

She leaned forward and looked at him intently. "I'm more interested in knowing how someone who claims to have graduated from Kansas doesn't know the difference between Iowa State's mascot and the University of Iowa's."

He chuckled, caught. "You Googled me."

She shrugged and ticked off items: "You had a full ride to play basketball for the Jayhawks, your number was seven, and you majored in music. I could go on, but there's not much after that. Maybe a co-written song or two in there."

Leaning back, he acted casual, draping one arm over the empty chair beside him. "I'm impressed."

"You shouldn't be." She leaned back, mimicking him. "I didn't spend much time on it. It took me all of two seconds to find you and read everything there was to know."

"But you did find me."

She cocked her head knowingly. "I did."

EIGHT

The night was dark, the road curvy, and that last glass of whiskey wasn't sitting well. The road's markings zoomed by, yellow dashes, turning into a blur and making them seem like a solid line. The gas pedal was pressed to the floor. The car was accelerating. Too fast. The curve was tight. The shoulder was narrow. The car drifted toward the center and over. Gripping the steering wheel, hands jerked to avoid a car as the vehicle flew past in the opposite direction. Veering toward the shoulder there was a second of recognition. A man. A dog. Too close. The wheel jerked. The brakes locked. A dog barked.

He came up over the hood. The windshield cracked. Split like a web. For a fraction of a second, their eyes connected. Pain and panic. And then he was gone. A thud registered. The thump was palpable as the screech of tires rang out into the darkness. The smack of flesh on the wet pavement echoed through the dark, and the dog began to howl.

Jolted awake, gasping for breath, eyes shot open in the darkness. Sweat clung to damp skin. Hands fumbled for something familiar, something safe… the edge of the bed, the blankets, and a pillow gave some comfort. *It was a dream. A nightmare.* It had been six months, but the impact of that body, the fear in his eyes, the mournful call of the dog—still haunted.

NINE

Ava Morgahn

"Knock, knock! Anybody home?"

There was a commotion just outside the door.

"Oh, my word!" Kelleigh exclaimed. "What in the world is happening out there?" Ava quickly went to the door, peered out the peephole, and opened it.

"Hiya!" the little blonde at the door exclaimed. "I'm Cara, your roommate. The Uber dropped me off. Thank you for opening the door. My hands were full, and I couldn't open it." She plopped down a suitcase, shifted a purple duffel bag higher on her shoulder, and stuck out her hand. "So glad to finally meet you face to face."

"Likewise," Ava said. "Here, let me help you." She reached for the suitcase. "Do you have more downstairs?"

"Nope, this is it," Cara said, edging past her into the apartment. "So glad you're here!"

"Thank you. I'm excited to be here, too."

"Cara, this is my mom, Kelleigh."

"Hiya," she said again, her smile spreading, stretching the sprinkling of freckles across her face.

"Where were you coming back from?" Kelleigh asked.

"My mom's," Cara laughed. "I like to pop home when I have a break in my schedule. But aren't you just the prettiest," she commented, giving Ava the once over. "The camera on your laptop didn't do you justice. We'll have to beat the cowboys off with a stick."

Kelleigh laughed. "That's the truth. You should have seen them falling all over her at the bar last night."

"Really?" Cara wiggled her eyebrows. "In town for one day, and you already have an entourage of admirers? I'm not surprised."

"I would hardly say that. My mom likes to exaggerate."

"But there was at least one?" Cara prodded.

Ava lifted a shoulder in a small shrug, unable to contain the slight rise in heat to her face as Owen filled her mind. "Maybe." She shook herself. She couldn't let herself think about him, not the way he twirled her around the dance floor or the sexy rasp of his voice.

"Let me help you get this to your room," Ava said to Cara, lifting the suitcase.

"You don't have to do that. I'll unpack later," Cara said, dropping her duffel bag near the bedroom door. "I want to get to know you first. That's more important in my book."

In the living room, Kelleigh sat on the sofa. "Tell us everything. How long have you lived here?"

"About a year now," Cara said. "I'm so excited to have a roommate again. I couldn't stop chatting about it with the guy next to me on the airplane. I think he was relieved when we pulled up to the gate." She laughed and bounced slightly on the arm of the chair. "I tend to talk a lot when I'm nervous or excited."

"I'm so glad you're here. It makes leaving on Monday a little easier, knowing you already have each other to rely on."

"My mom's a little overly protective." Ava rolled her eyes at Cara.

Kelleigh swatted at a tear that was ready to fall. "Oh, look at me!" she said unabashedly. "I'm already tearing up, and we still have the whole day ahead."

"You have a car, right?" Cara asked.

"I do," Ava acknowledged.

"Great!" Cara stood, brushed her hands down her capris, and smiled. "Ladies, grab your purses. I need to show you around Nashville."

"That sounds like fun!" The buzzer went off in the laundry room. "Just give me a minute. I want to grab my clothes out of the dryer." Ava got up and crossed the room. "I hope you don't mind, but I ran a load this morning to get a few wrinkles out of my clothes."

"Why would I mind?" Cara asked. "This is your place too."

"I'll just be a minute."

Ava stood in the laundry room, absentmindedly unloading her clothes from the dryer while her mom and Cara chatted.

She pulled out her garments, folding them as she went, and noticed a hoodie that wasn't hers.

She held it up—black, soft, and the word 'Tennessee' written in bold letters across the front.

It looked like something she or even Molly would buy. Now, standing in the quiet of the laundry room, she pulled the hoodie tighter.

"What's taking you so long?" Cara questioned, popping her head around the corner.

Ava held out the sweatshirt. "Is this yours?"

Cara grabbed it from Ava, and her cheeks turned pink. "There was this guy..." she explained, and the slight flush went from pink to crimson. "He spent the night..." she continued in a hushed voice. "He left it behind, so I thought I would wash it..." her voice trailed off. She shrugged and pursed her lips together, not saying anything else.

"I'm sorry. I didn't mean to pry."

"You didn't. Just one-night stands can be a tad embarrassing. I'll throw this in my room, and then we can go."

"Sounds good," Ava agreed.

They started by driving past celebrity homes. They caught glimpses of a wide variety of stunning architecture neatly tucked behind gates with well-manicured, sprawling lawns hinting at the lives of the stars who called Nashville home.

After being in the car, they decide to walk around Centennial Park and stretch their legs. The park was lush and green, filled with flowers and winding paths. The centerpiece was a full-scale replica of the Parthenon. Its white columns gleamed under the bright Tennessee sun.

Cara enthusiastically pointed at everything along the way while chatting a mile a minute, her animated stories blended seamlessly with the lively atmosphere around them.

Finally, they wrapped up their day at a local honky-tonk.

"What do you think?" Cara asked as they slid into a booth.

"I love it! I definitely want to ride one of those Pedal Taverns before the summer is over. You'll go with me, won't ya?" Ava asked.

Cara laughed. "Sure. Why not? I haven't had a chance to do that myself. We will need to check out the John Seigenthaler Pedestrian Bridge on another day, too. There's a breathtaking view of the skyline with the river below."

"I think it's all wonderful and confusing," Kelleigh answered. "My head is spinning from the traffic, and the number of people. I don't know how you girls will ever get around."

"That's why we have this wonderful invention called the GPS, Mom," Ava reminded her. "And Cara knows her way around; she's been here for over a year."

"Exactly," Cara agreed. "Let's order."

They ordered, and Ava leaned forward. "Cara, you mentioned on the phone that you are in real estate?"

"I am. I'll warn you, I tend to have weird hours, a lot of evenings and weekends. But I have to go in bright and early tomorrow since I've been away for a few days."

Kelleigh settled back against the booth. "Do you sing too? I noticed a guitar in the living room."

Cara laughed. "That's more of a decoration. I sing but I can't play. I want to learn, though."

"It's never too late to learn," Kelleigh added. "Didn't Molly take a job in real estate as well?"

"She was going to, but she ended up getting the job at Cognac Creek," Ava acknowledged.

"I'm surprised you haven't heard from her since we arrived," Kelleigh commented.

"I listened to her latest message on the drive down. I'm sure she will be around sometime tomorrow to meet me after work if she can." Ava directed her attention back to Cara. "Have you been to Cognac Creek?"

"Yeah, I've been there a few times. Good food, great live music."

"That's where I'll be working as well."

Oh!" Cara exclaimed. "I'm a little jealous. It's hard to get a job there, I've been trying for months."

"It wasn't easy, but I'm thrilled to have gotten in. I've been following them on social media, and we went last night. They have such a great atmosphere and a cool country vibe," Ava commented, running a finger down her glass.

"They do." Cara took a dainty sip of her iced tea, leaving a faint pink lip print on the rim. She picked up a packet of artificial sweetener from the glass container on the table and dumped the contents into her glass.

Their meals arrived.

"Enough about work stuff," Cara said, changing the subject. "Kelleigh, what time are you planning on leaving tomorrow?"

Kelleigh sank her fork into the pasta. "I'll leave after you girls go to work. I want to see Ava off."

Ava felt her phone vibrate. She slipped it out of her pocket and peeked at the message. It was from Owen. Ava felt a delicious uptick in delight that shot down to her toes. She'd been thinking of him too.

Owen: I know you're out and about. I hope you're having fun. If you're in the area, stop by Cognac Creek.

She squashed a smile that played on her lips. There was no sense tipping off Cara that her cowboy—was he her cowboy? As Cara had not so delicately put it—wanted to see her. She pushed the phone back in her pocket and focused on the conversation, all the while images of Owen danced through her head.

TEN

Detective Wyatt Lockhart

Twisting the top off of a Dr. Pepper, Wyatt swallowed the ice-cold beverage as he walked down the hall toward his office. He stopped short when he noticed the door was ajar. He scowled as he peeked around the corner and saw FTO Ransick leaning over his desk, sneaking a look at his notes.

Wyatt kicked the door with the toe of his boot. It hit the wall with a loud bang. Ransick jumped, and Wyatt smirked with a smug sense of satisfaction.

"What the hell are you doing in my office?" Wyatt demanded.

Like a kid caught with his hand in the cookie jar before dinner, Ransick stepped back from the desk. "I came to bring you the coroner's report for the last victim we pulled out of the Cumberland and the newspaper."

"What's it say?"

"Have a look for yourself." Ransick handed him the newspaper.

The headline in big, bold letters read: **Rising Crime in Nashville: The Cumberland Killer Strikes Again**

As the city grapples with an uptick in violent crime, fear looms over Nashville. The Cumberland Killer has claimed yet another victim, sparking widespread panic among residents. With each new attack, people are increasingly afraid to venture out after dark. Authorities are urging citizens to stay vigilant...

Wyatt wadded up the newspaper and tossed it in the trash. "Not that, damn it! The autopsy report."

"My mistake."

Disgusted, Wyatt took the manila folder from the man and flipped it open. Was the guy just trying to get under his skin? He scanned the contents, looking for any consistencies that stood out to him.

Name: Jane Doe

Gender: Female

Race: Caucasian

Age: Mid twenties

Height: 5'5" (165 cm)

Weight: 110 lbs (49.9 kg)

Cause of Death: Drowning   asphyxia: respiratory impairment due to inhalation of water.

Skin: Abrasions observed on exposed limbs. Concentrated abrasions around wrists and ankles.

Toxicology Report: Elevated levels of antihistamines detected, including diphenhydramine and doxylamine succinate. The concentration of these substances is consistent with the dosages found in over the counter sleep aids, aligning with findings in other victims' cases.

Notable Observations: (Unusual Findings) Laryngitis found in the victim and extreme inflammation of the larynx (voice box). Possibly caused by viral infections, overuse of the voice, irritants like smoke or allergens, or bacterial infections.

Once again, Wyatt thought, this woman took a heavy dose of sleeping pills either by choice or force. Or maybe even without her knowledge. She could have been drugged and wholly unaware, and either walked or was carried to the river's edge. Then fell in or was pushed. Regardless, in her deep sleep, once submerged under the water, she drowned quickly. He shook his head in disgust.

It was estimated the body had been in the water for approximately ten to twelve hours before being spotted entrapped in the rocky edge of the bank.

His gaze traveled further down the report. He flipped the page and noted the river's water levels and the rate at which the water flowed.

He did a quick calculation and estimated how far the body had traveled.

"Well?" Ransick asked.

Wyatt looked up. He had forgotten that the man was still there.

"I'm thinking," he answered gruffly. He turned on his heel and walked across the room to the map of Nashville he had fixed to the wall. He had already marked the point at which they had found the woman's body with a pink pushpin and the number four. His brow furrowed as he took in the other pink pins.

Shoving the victims to the back of his mind, he ran his finger up the map along the river, estimating the mileage. Sure enough, when he stopped counting, he was again in the center of the other pins.

His brow creased. The body had to have been dumped in the river in close proximity to the others.

Wyatt had been to that part of town enough times to know there were no cameras and little security—the perfect spot to slip a body into the river.

Ransick quietly stepped beside him, tilting his head as if contemplating the map. He didn't say anything, but Wyatt could hear the click of his jaw as he crunched on a hard piece of candy. When he spoke, Wyatt's nostrils were filled with the scent of peppermint.

"It looks like she entered at about the same spot as the rest of them, don't you think?"

"Looks like," Wyatt grumbled.

"Are you gonna put another pin there?"

Annoyed, Wyatt didn't answer. He picked up the box of push pins on the ledge, shook out one, and stuck it in the map. Then, he reached for his sticky pad of numbers and added four to the pin.

Ransick popped another peppermint. "Such a shame. Four women, and we don't seem any closer to finding the culprit. I can't help but wonder if we had a K9 unit we could put on the task maybe we would be closer."

He knew Ransick knew as well as he did that they didn't have the funds right now.

"It's only a matter of time. We will find something that connects them." Wyatt rubbed a hand across the back of his neck, trying to work out a kink and not react to Ransick's last comment. He knew it was a dig on his leadership and the great loss the department had received months earlier. "Don't you have something better to do than stand here staring at the map and annoying me?"

Ransick shrugged and pointed to the map. "Want me to run out that way and see if I can find anything?"

"Yes," Wyatt agreed quickly. Ransick wouldn't be underfoot if he were out on the beat. "Go. Take the rookie with you. Knock on some doors and talk to anyone with a heartbeat in a six-block radius."

Ransick nodded, walking backward toward the office door. "On it."

"Ransick," Wyatt called after the FTO as he ducked out the door.

"Yeah?"

"Come back with something."

Ransick hooked a thumb back at himself and said, "I won't let you down." Then he disappeared around the corner.

"That's debatable," Wyatt muttered.

ELEVEN

Owen Layne

Owen felt the air leave the room as soon as she entered. It was like being sealed in a snow globe, and someone suddenly turned it upside down. The air around him tumbled and tossed, leaving him in turmoil, unable to catch his breath.

Their eyes locked. The room shifted, and slowly, the world around him settled. Ava gave him a little wave as she, her mother, and another woman walked across the bar and headed for a booth.

It was a kick to his gut and a shot to the heart that she could unknowingly have that effect on him. He'd have to do better, he berated himself. The first pretty girl to turn his head in years, and he was acting like a love-sick, angsty teenage boy. He was twenty-seven, for Pete's sake.

He shook his head as if trying to clear cobwebs from it and really looked at her. She was pretty; a few men turned to watch her walk across the room, but if he was honest, she wasn't drop-dead gorgeous. Yet, there was just something...

She filled out her jeans nicely, and that simple, white tank top revealed golden, sun-kissed skin. Her long dark hair hung like a satin curtain, loose down her back. He saw the glint of a chain in the lights and wondered if it was her Iowa State pendant.

Owen stumbled over the lyrics and had to force his eyes off of her before he made a fool of himself.

What was happening to him? He hadn't felt this way in—he

racked his brain— like four or five years or maybe ever.

Laura, his ex, had always been a flirt, full of energy and effortlessly drawing everyone's attention. She was a friend of one of Dylan's close friends, and after a double date, he and Laura had instantly hit it off. From that night on, their connection had grown with their shared love of music, they quickly became inseparable, but... She had never made his heart pound like it did now.

That should have been the first sign, he thought, bitterly aware of his oversight. But he hadn't seen it—not then. He'd been too wrapped up in chasing his career, and she, ever supportive, had urged him to go out and seize opportunities, even though it often meant leaving her behind, either alone or in the company of his brother. Now, the pieces fell into place, clear as day, but back then, he'd been blind to the truth. Hindsight, of course, was always difficult to swallow.

That was Laura, and she was in the past. This was Ava. She was different. And she could be... STOP! He scolded himself. Don't go there. But he couldn't help it.

He couldn't wait for the set to be done. He wanted to go over and sit next to her, lean in, and see if she still smelled like jasmine on a hot southern night like she had the night before.

They reached the end of the song, and mercifully, the last chord died out. He signaled for the band to take a break. Technically, they should have played for five more minutes, but he didn't have it in him now that she had arrived.

He thanked the crowd, announced the break, and unstrapped his guitar.

"You okay, man?" Toby asked, coming up to stand next to him. "You screwed up the chorus."

"I know," Owen muttered apologetically. "I'm sorry. I need a break."

"You never miss the lyrics on that song or any other. What's goin' on?" Toby followed Owen's gaze as it shifted slightly to the left. Spotting Ava, he gave a discreet head bob in her direction. "Ah, so that's it. You got it bad."

"No, I don't," Owen argued, scowling back at his friend.

"Yes, you do." Toby's mouth widened into what Owen could only describe as a shit-eatin' grin.

Toby clapped Owen on the shoulder. "Wipe that scowl off your face. There's no need for it. This is a good thing."

"How's that exactly?" Owen asked, reaching down for the dog's leash.

"Because you haven't had anything for anybody since you kicked out that no good, two-timing bitch of a fake girlfriend."

Owen knew he was right. Ava stirred something in him, but he wasn't ready to admit it to Toby and hardly himself. His guard was still up, but he tried to relax his face. After all, people were in the bar, and scowling at the customers wasn't good for tips.

As if reading his mind, Toby said, "It's alright if you're not ready to admit it. Heck, I get it. This is all pretty new." He glanced from Ava back to Owen. "Since we only have ten minutes, do you want me to do you a solid and take Gunner out?"

"Would you mind?"

"Nope," Toby's grin flashed back into place. "I'll add it to your tab."

Owen stepped off the stage. "What tab?"

"The favors tab. There's quite a string of tallies."

"What the hell?" Owen held out his hand. "Let me see it."

"Can't."

"Why not?"
"Cuz, it's locked away in the vault." Toby tapped the side of his head. "Right here."

Owen visibly shuddered. "I bet it's dark and scary in there."

"Can't argue with that." His head jerked in Ava's direction again. "Looking at her makes me think you'll be making regular deposits on that tab. You'll be rackin' 'em up pretty quickly, and I'll store them away." He paused for effect, the shit-eatin' grin back in full force. "Saving them for a rainy day."

"Don't count on it," Owen said, but he wasn't so sure. He strolled backward to the booth. "I got a list of my own." He pointed a finger at Toby and mouthed, 'For you.' He turned on his heel and faced the booth. "Hello, ladies."

Ava looked up at Owen with those hazel eyes, and he had to swallow hard to force down the lump in his throat.

Including Mrs. Morgahn and the blonde who sat at the edge of the curved booth, he asked. "Mind if I join you?"

"Please," Ava said, indicating the bench beside her. "Have a seat."

Instead of sliding in next to her like he desperately wanted, he slipped in beside the other woman and surprised them both. He wanted so badly to be next to her, but he wanted to look at her even more.

He flagged a server down. "Can I get anyone anything?"

"We're good," Ava said evenly, watching him.

Owen ordered a glass of ice water with lemon and a cheeseburger to have ready at the end of the last set. He didn't trust himself with alcohol at the moment. He needed all his wits about him to stay on top of his game. Once he had his footing, he might consider a drink.

"Do you have another set?" Ava asked, swirling what was left of the liquid around in her glass.

"Yes, one more tonight."

"You must be exhausted after playing the last three nights," Kelleigh commented, shifting in the booth to look at him.

"Four-day gigs are always a whirlwind. They're a lot of fun but exhausting."

"I can tell. Kinda screwed up the chorus of that last song, didn't you?" Ava asked, calling him out on it. A smile played around her mouth.

"Ava Lynn," her mother scolded. "That wasn't very nice.'

"Maybe not, but," she shrugged. "It's the truth."

Owen laughed. He could see she was going to keep him on his toes. "Noticed that, huh?"

"I did."

"Oh, now," Kelleigh tsked, trying to gloss over it. "You didn't miss a beat."

"Not a beat, but a word. More like a whole string of them."

She had him there.

"What happened?" She leaned in, intrigued. Those eyes locked on his, daring him to answer.

That lump that he had pushed down when he had first walked over retaliated and lodged in his throat. How was he supposed to answer the question when she was the reason? What had happened to his ability to supply quick comebacks? Somehow, she must be able to kill off a few of his brain cells every time she looked at him. Otherwise, he didn't have an explanation for what was happening to him.

She raised her eyebrows and waited for the waitress to place his water on the table, not letting him off the hook. "More importantly, how often does that happen?"

That he could answer. "Very rarely. Tonight was a fluke thing. I'm just exhausted tonight." It wasn't a lie. He was tired. It had been a brutally hot couple of days, schlepping equipment to and from the bar and playing late. Then there was the dog—whining at odd times of the night, waking him up and demanding attention. Not that he could blame it all on the dog. He'd had his own fits and starts as his mind played through visions of her.

Kelleigh reached across the table and patted him on the arm. "That's understandable. I'm sure this isn't easy. It seems like a very demanding job."

"It is," he answered truthfully. "But I wouldn't want to do anything else."

There was a small giggle from the blonde.

"Oh, forgive my manners. Owen, this is Cara, my roommate," Ava said to include the other woman in the conversation.

"Nice to meet you."

"Hiya!" Cara chirped like a little bird in awe.

Toby walked up to the table, returning the German Shepherd. "Good evening," he said, addressing the women. "Nice to see you again." He gave Kelleigh a wink. He handed the leash to Owen. "The deed is done."

"Thanks, man," Owen said.

The dog let out a low growl.

"Heel," Owen scolded.

Immediately, the dog stopped. "Sorry about that. I'm not sure what got into him." Owen gave the command and the dog laid down without any fanfare. He felt a wave of discomfort wash over him. *Great, just what I needed.* He shot Gunner a sharp look, hoping it hadn't caused too much of a scene. Owen hated when he acted up in public, especially at work.

"Are you going to join us?" Ava asked Toby.

"I would, but I need to do a few things before the next set. Ladies, if you'll excuse me."

"Of course," they chorused.

"So what's his name?" Ava asked. "You never told me."

"Dog," Owen offered, then heard how cold that actually sounded, even to his own ears.

"Really?" Ava asked. Her brow furrowed slightly.

Owen lifted a shoulder. "His name is Gunner."

"Gunner? I like that. It suits him. Can he sit beside me in the booth? The floor is kind of dirty," Ava said.

"He could, but my boss won't like it. Besides, he's very structured. The floor doesn't bother him."

"Can I pet him?" Cara asked, reaching out a tentative hand.

The German Shepherd lifted his head, released a low rumble from his throat, and bared his teeth.

Cara quickly retracted her hand. "Oh, my!"

"Heel," Owen commanded. "I don't think that's such a good idea. He seems a little on edge tonight. Sorry about that." His blood pressure ticked up a notch. This dog would get him fired yet.

"That's understandable. There are probably too many people for him," Ava said. "Still, he is really well trained."

"He is," Cara agreed.

"How long have you had him?" Kelleigh asked.

"Five months, two weeks, and three days," Owen answered without thinking.

Ava stopped petting Gunner and arched an eyebrow at him. "Wow, that's oddly specific."

Owen played it off. "I'm good with numbers."

"Did you train him yourself?" she asked.

"No, my brother did." He quickly changed the subject. "So, tomorrow is your big day?"

"My big day?" Ava tilted her head.

"Don't you start your job tomorrow?" Owen asked. Now that the initial awkwardness had worn off, he relaxed and settled in. "At least that's what you said last night. But you didn't mention where."

"Oh, didn't I?" She laughed and waved the question away.

It was a warm, fascinating sound that Owen found oddly comforting, and the lump in his throat dissolved completely.

"How could I forget? It's the whole reason I'm here. Well, one of the reasons."

"In this bar?" he questioned, knowing that's not what she had meant.

"No, of course not." She flushed.

He liked to see her slightly off balance. He certainly had been when he sat down.

"I meant in Tennessee. In Nashville."

He heard Kelleigh sniff and saw her lift a napkin out of the corner of his eye. She dabbed at the tear daintily.

"How long are you staying?" he asked Mrs. Morgahn.

"I'm leaving tomorrow."

He saw the pang of sadness in her eyes and saw it reflected in Ava's. He needed to do something quickly before it was too late, and Kelleigh cried. "I'm sure it will be hard for you to leave."

Kelleigh nodded.

"Especially since it's like a thirty-hour drive from here to Idaho."

"Yes." She nodded. "Wait. What? Idaho?" Kelleigh sucked in a breath. "We're not from Idaho."

Ava sniffed. "He thinks he's funny. He knows it's Iowa." But silently, she mouthed thank you as Kelleigh laughed and dabbed at a tear that didn't fall.

With a smile, Kelleigh said, "You'd be surprised how many times a person hears that. Don't they teach geography in school anymore?" The sadness was quickly replaced by pride. "Do you know Ava won the school geography bee in eighth grade?"

"Mom!" Ava hissed. "Don't start that."

"Well, you did," she said, genuinely proud of her daughter. "Even went to the state level."

"Really?" Owen grinned.

"That's fun," Cara chimed in. "Who knew you had so many talents?"

"If it hadn't been for that one question, she could have been the state champ and went on to Nationals."

Looking from mother to daughter, he asked, "What was the question that tripped you up?"

"We don't talk about that. And don't encourage her, Owen," Ava warned. "She'll be here all night telling you stories of blue ribbons, art projects, and wishes."

He liked this mother-daughter team. And that's what they seemed to be. "Not that I don't want to hear all about blue ribbons and art projects, but wishes? I'm intrigued."

"Oh, me too," Cara interjected.

"Oh, it's this list I made. My wish list for my life," Ava explained.

"Well, what are they?" he asked, leaning forward, interested.

"Dreams and goals I'm determined to achieve."

"That's so cool," Cara acknowledged. "I wish I had done something like that."

"You still can," Kelleigh said. "Ava is always wishing on dandelions. Sending them out into the world."

"And Tennessee is on your list?" Owen asked.

"It is," Kelleigh said softly, answering for her daughter. Her words were almost lost in the din of the background music. "Did Ava mention she wants to be a singer?" Kelleigh asked. "That's why she's here."

Owen lifted an eyebrow. "No, she didn't mention that." He studied Ava for a hot second. "Are you any good?"

She shrugged. "I can hold my own."

"I know I'm biased, but I think she's pretty good," Kelleigh answered.

He heard Toby's whistle between playlist songs. He turned toward the sound and saw the drummer tap his wrist. It was time for the last set.

"I'd like to stay and hear more about this list, but I have to get back to the stage." He hesitated, not wanting the night to end without her. "Are you going to stay for the last set?"

Ava looked at the other two women, and both gave their approval. "We are," she assured him. "Go. We will be right here when you're finished. Won't we?" Ava leaned over and gave Gunner a good rub before Owen walked away with him.

He had only taken a couple of steps when he heard Ava say, "Try to remember all the words this time."

"Think you can do better?" he shot back before he could think it through.

She gave him a smile that could melt a thousand suns. "Maybe."

"You may have to prove it, Ava Lynn." He turned on his heel.

"We will be watching and listening for any little mistake," Ava called after him.

He cringed but didn't turn around. The lump that had slowly dissolved in his throat was suddenly back, knowing her eyes would be on him.

TWELVE

Ava Morgahn

Ava shifted in her seat as Cara returned to the booth.

"I just had some guy hit on me on my way to the bathroom," Cara giggled. "He wanted to buy me a drink."

"Was he cute?" Ava asked casually.

"Yeah, kinda," Cara said. "But I told him I was here with friends."

"You girls need to be careful when you're out. Always watch your drinks, especially with this Cumberland Killer on the loose. I can't believe they haven't caught him yet." Kelleigh shivered. "You just never know."

"Believe me, I completely understand, Mrs. Morgahn." Cara leaned over and whispered conspiratorially in Ava's ear. "I figured she wouldn't approve, so I gave him my number instead."

The atmosphere around them buzzed with bittersweet energy as she realized the set was coming to a close and the customers had thinned. She felt a pang of sadness; the night had been pure magic. The soulful notes of Owen's voice had wrapped around her like a warm embrace, and she found herself lost in daydreams of being up on that stage with him.

Owen's voice cut through Ava's thoughts like a spark.

"Thanks for being an incredible audience tonight," he said, his tone warm yet teasing. "We've got one last song for you."

Ava straightened instinctively, her heart racing as their eyes locked across the room. The connection was instant and intense—like the quiet before a storm. She could barely breathe.

Owen's playful grin flashed as he leaned toward the mic. "I just might have a little surprise." He paused, scanning the crowd with a mischievous gleam in his eyes. Then, as if reading her mind, he turned back to her. "If I could get a round of applause, Miss Ava Morgahn," he said with a wink and a finger pointed directly at her so there was no question. "Please join me on stage."

The small group of patrons that were left gave a polite applause, and Ava's pulse quickened. Was he serious? She could feel the warmth of the spotlight calling her, but still, she hesitated.

"Go," Kelleigh encouraged.

As she stepped onto the stage, the spotlight washed over her, momentarily blinding her. Her heart ran wild. She focused solely on Owen, who stood a few feet away, guitar in hand. His eyes shimmered with encouragement and amusement, demanding she accept his challenge. The bass player brought over an extra microphone and placed it before her.

"Are you familiar with Morgan Wallen's latest single?" Owen asked.

She nodded, and after a brief exchange, they quickly settled on the song. Owen turned to the band and announced their choice.

The opening chords filled the air, vibrant and alive. Ava felt an exhilarating rush as the melody wrapped around her. She was swept away with each note as if the world outside the spotlight ceased to exist, and it was only her and Owen. His gaze held hers, intense and unwavering, pulling her into a shared moment filled with electricity.

As they sang together, their voices blended harmoniously, creating a magic that resonated deep within her. She could see the warmth in his eyes. The way he smiled just for her sent butterflies swirling in her stomach. The lyrics flowed through her, telling a story that felt both familiar and new. She lost herself in the rhythm, every guitar strum striking a chord within her soul.

Owen's steady gaze anchored her. Their harmony blended seamlessly as if they had been performing together for years.

As the final notes echoed through the air, Ava's heart swelled. The applause washed over her like a wave, but Owen's gaze held her grounded, steadying her as the world seemed to pause. At that moment, with the last chord lingering in the air, she felt a surge of confidence—a quiet certainty that this was only the beginning of what could be.

The music faded, but their connection remained unspoken yet palpable. As the last of the applause died out, Ava turned to the audience, her voice soft but filled with gratitude. "Thank you," she said, looking over the crowd, her eyes glistening. "Thank you for indulging me with this moment." She turned and waved her hand, encompassing the entire band. "And to this incredible band for letting me join them for the last song. You've made this moment something I'll carry with me forever."

She paused, breathed, then looked at Owen, her smile deepening. "And especially to Owen Layne for taking a chance and letting me sing with him."

Ava stepped off the stage, buzzing from the performance, with the warmth of their shared moment still in her chest.

She scanned the room, her heart still racing, and saw her mother beaming and Cara waiting patiently by her seat. She smiled at the thought of sharing this moment with them.

"That was wonderful, sweetheart!" Kelleigh exclaimed, hugging her.

"It was," Cara echoed. "Who knew my new roommate had such talent?"

"Thank you," Ava said, unable to stop smiling.

As the band packed their gear, Owen picked up his burger at the bar.

With an easy grin, he joined them, Styrofoam container in one hand, dog in the other. "Ready?"

They all walked down the stairs together, the excitement of the night lingering in the air. Owen held the door wide as they stepped outside, the warm night air enveloping them and a hushed stillness settling over the street.

The heat was palpable, but the bar's lively energy had quieted. Only a few cars passed by, and pedestrians dotted the street like distant stars in a peaceful sky. Those still out moved with purpose, returning home after a night of laughter and music. Ava felt a sense of connection, each step carrying the excitement of the evening as they all walked into the calm night together.

How would she ever sleep tonight knowing she had to be back here bright and early for her new job and the possibility of seeing him again so soon? She was still wired from the music and the stimulation of being in downtown Nashville. Not to mention leaving the bar at closing time with Owen and performing the last song.

"Did you park in the parking garage I told you about?" Owen asked, breaking into her thoughts as he turned to face her.

"We did."

"That was perfect. What a lovely night," Kelleigh added. "Thank you."

"Yes, thank you," Cara added.

"You were good," Toby said, lightly punching Ava in the shoulder.

"Thanks for letting me sing. It was so much fun."

"No problem. Anytime. We get tired of hearing Owen's old scratchy voice," Toby joked. "It's nice to change it up. Plus, you're way better to look at."

"Thanks, I think," Ava smiled.

The women turned to go.

"Hang on a minute, and we will walk you to your car," Owen said.

"You don't have to," Ava started to protest.

"I know we don't have to. We want to. Besides, we're all going in the same direction. That's where we park." He looked around. "I just need to check something first. Give me just a minute."

He stepped back into the alley. After a moment, she was curious, so she followed him.

"Dorthea?" he called. He waited a beat. When there was no answer, he tried again. "Dorthea, it's me, Owen."

"What are you..." Ava's voice broke off as she saw a figure barely visible among the shadows.

The older woman emerged—a mere wisp of darkness against the brick wall, her presence initially unsettling.

"There you are," Owen said with a hint of a smile in his voice.

"What do you want?" Dorthea asked, stepping from the darkness and stopping at the edge of the pool of light, which kept her on the rim of obscurity.

Ava could see the whites of her eyes reflecting in the pale light.

"I thought I told you to call me Dot."

Owen chuckled. "That you did." He walked toward her, holding out the stark white container. "I have something for you."

She stepped into the circle of yellow and adjusted her worn green backpack. "What is it?" she asked, trying not to appear too eager.

"A cheeseburger. The kitchen had a few left from the evening rush. I thought maybe you might like it."

Ava stood silently behind Owen, with Gunner at her side, and watched the scene unfold. She knew what Owen said wasn't true. She had watched him order and pay for the burger himself. Her heart gave a little pang at his sweetness as the older woman eyed him a little warily.

"How did you know I was going to be here?" she asked. "Are you stalking me?"

He laughed and said, "I just took a chance."

"Like you did on that pretty girl from the other night?" Dorthea questioned, raising a crooked finger in Ava's direction.

Owen's head turned as if on a swivel. He smiled at Ava. Turning back to Dorthea, he winked. "I guess you could say that." He lifted the container. "If you're not interested, that's okay."

"Now, now. I didn't say that." She moved even closer.

She reminded Ava of a stray cat—curious, cautious, yet hungry, unable to withstand the pull of a hot meal. The delicious burger was a temptation the woman couldn't resist. Then again, so was Owen.

Owen stepped closer, his arm outstretched, not making the older woman come to him.

She took the container from him cautiously. Slowly, lifted the lid and peered inside. "Looks delicious," she said. "Smells even better."

Owen smiled. "They make the best burgers."

"Thank you." Licking her lips, she swallowed hard and closed the Styrofoam lid. Shifting slightly, she cocked her head. "Can I meet your girl?"

Owen laughed again, the sound carried in the empty alley, husky and deep. "Not sure she's my girl, but I would be more than happy to introduce the two of you." Owen turned and motioned toward Ava.

Ava stepped forward with Gunner.

"Ava, this is Dorthea."

"It's so nice to meet you."

"Likewise," the older woman said, looking Ava over. "My, my

there, cowboy. She is a pretty thing."

"That she is," Owen agreed.

"You got lucky."

"I did." He cleared his throat. "Well, it's late, and we need to get home. Are you going to be alright out here?"

"Me?" she asked, then let out a hearty cackle. She cocked her head at him. "I can't remember when someone asked me if I'd be okay."

"Will you?" he asked again sincerely.

"Oh, go to war, Aunt Hanny." She waved him off. "Of course I will. Don't you fret over me." She lifted her hand to encompass the area. "I know these streets like the back of my hand."

"Alright then. You have a good night."

She rattled her container in his direction. "You bet your boots I will."

"Have a good night," Ava added as Owen reached for her arm.

Dorthea croaked something inaudible.

Before they turned the corner, the older woman had melted into the shelter of the shadows and was gone.

Toby, Cara, and her mother waited on the sidewalk just outside the bar.

"Ready?" Owen asked as if the whole thing in the alley hadn't transpired.

"You bet," Toby nodded as they started toward the parking garage.

Ava wasn't sure what to say, but she had to ask. "Dorthea— she's homeless?"

"I assume so," Owen answered. "I've seen her around, but I officially met her the other night when you plowed into me on the street."

"When I plowed into you?" Ava questioned. "As if. I hardly think that's what happened."

"If you don't believe me, you can ask Dot. She saw the whole thing."

"Oh, did she now?"

They walked under a pool of light that illuminated the sidewalk, and Ava could see the ghost of a smile play across his mouth. "How do you know she isn't a little crazy?"

He shrugged. "I don't." Then shot her a smile. "But I do know one thing."

"What's that?"

Owen slipped his hand into hers and intertwined their fingers. Warmth spread from his to hers and up her arm, heading right to her heart.

"I got lucky when I ran into you."

Her heart fluttered. "You're a smooth one, aren't you, Owen Layne?"

He didn't answer, he just let the question drift into the warm summer air.

THIRTEEN

He held his cards close to his chest, arranging them numerically. His heart skipped as he realized he had a Straight Flush. It was the best hand he had so far. But why should that surprise him? It was the seventh hand of the night, and seven was his lucky number. The only thing higher was a Royal Flush. What were his odds?

He took a long swallow of beer. His eyes scanned the other players, trying to read their expressions. From the looks of things —pretty damn good. He tried to suppress the smirk twitching at the corner of his lips. He had this. The odds were definitely to his advantage.

His eyes flicked to the pile of poker chips, the hundred-dollar scratch-off ticket, and the switchblade in the middle of the table. His nerves hummed under his skin. On edge, he glanced at his last few blue and red chips, trying to decide if he should risk it all.

Poker and alcohol were as essential to him as breathing—he needed both to feel alive. His job, however, didn't provide that same sense of fulfillment, at least not yet. To him, poker and alcohol went hand in hand. Unfortunately, both required money, which he never seemed to have enough of.

Poker, in particular, had the power to take and give. There were rules. But those rules were meant to be tested, stretched to their limits. He mused, ever since he devised the plan, just like he was doing now.

And it was working.

He couldn't believe how easy it was to take from another, to feed them lies, and then capitalize. He couldn't believe how gullible some people were, especially women. They would believe anything and trust anyone. If you just waved the right bait in front of them and knew what button to push—they would come crawling for a chance.

He watched the other players call. When it was his turn, he didn't even hesitate. Just like the plan—he was all in. He pushed his chips into the center of the table with a grin. All or nothin', baby.

FOURTEEN

Ava Morgahn

Ava hurried around the small apartment, a little frazzled. "Have you seen my makeup travel kit?" she asked her mother, digging through a cardboard box.

Kelleigh stood beside her, slightly in the way, and leaned over the carton, looking down. With her hands on her hips, she said, "I thought you put that in your backpack with a change of clothes last night."

Ava stopped digging and blinked up at her mother. "You're right. I did." Ava shoved the box aside.

"Why are you taking a change of clothes? Aren't they giving you a uniform?"

Slightly irked that she had to explain, Ava answered, 'They are, but I like to be prepared for whatever. Maybe I'll see Molly or..." Her voice trailed off, thinking of Owen, hoping she might run into him at work or maybe that he would call. And if he did, she wanted to be prepared and have a nice outfit with her so she wouldn't have to come home and change. She knew it was wishful thinking, but still...

"Hmmm..." Kelleigh looked at her, a little skeptical, but brushed it off. "You're just nervous and rushing. Slow down and take a deep breath."

Ava did as she was told, but she was a little irritated with her mother. She inhaled deeply and felt some raw nerves settle.

"Feel better?" Kelleigh asked.

"I do," Ava admitted.

"Good. Now come and have some breakfast. Cara?" Kelleigh called. "Do you want breakfast?

Cara came bounding out of the bathroom. "Definitely!"

"I'm not sure I have time." Ava glanced at the clock on the wall.

"You have at least ten minutes before you need to go. That's plenty of time to get a few bites in."

"I guess you're right," Ava replied slowly, her voice tinged with uncertainty. She felt torn. On the one hand, she appreciated her mother's help in the kitchen, but on the other, having her there proved to be a challenge. After four years of living on her own at college, the sudden closeness and questions felt a little stifling. Still, she reminded herself that tomorrow would be different. Cara and herself would have time and space to find their rhythm.

"Of course I am." Kelleigh stepped around the counter and got out two plates. The toast popped, and she snagged it with the efficiency of someone who had done it daily. Then she placed two more slices of bread in and pushed down the lever. "Do you want jelly or just butter?"

"Just butter, thanks, Mom."

"Oh, jelly? What kind?" Cara asked as she lifted the jar.

"Strawberry. There's juice in the fridge, and the coffee is ready." Kelleigh spread a thin layer of butter on both slices of toast and set the plate down.

"I don't think I can handle any caffeine right now. My stomach is already jittery." Ava retrieved the apple juice from the fridge and poured herself a glass. "Want some?" she asked Cara.

"Nope, I'm going for caffeine."

Kelleigh passed her the toast. "Cara, I hope you don't mind that I took over the kitchen this morning."

"Not at all. It's been ages since someone cooked me breakfast."

The second set of toast popped, and Kelleigh repeated the process. "You didn't sleep very well last night, did you?"

Nibbling toast, Ava shook her head. "Not really. I'm just so pumped to start, and then last night with Owen..." Her voice trailed off as she remembered how they had locked eyes at the end of the song. How the light had hit his eyes—how devastatingly blue they were.

"He is dreamy. And that voice..." Cara murmured.

Kelleigh looked from Cara to Ava knowingly, reached out a hand, and gently laid it on her daughter's arm. "He is pretty special. I like him a lot. Just don't get too ahead of yourself."

"I know." Ava propped her arm on the counter and rested her chin in her hand. She let out a deep sigh and pictured his face. A warmth spread through her as she remembered how he held the door open for her and spoke so gently to the homeless woman, his kindness unmistakable as he brought her a meal. There was the way his eyes softened when they sang together—how their voices blended perfectly. But nothing could top the moment his hand reached for hers.

"Oh, boy." Cara giggled.

"My thoughts precisely," Kelleigh said as she spread jelly over her toast.

"What?" Ava asked, trying to refocus on her mother and sparing a glance at Cara.

"Nothing," Kelleigh said with a smile. "Finish your toast. You need to stop daydreaming and go."

Before she could answer, her phone chimed. Unable to contain a smile, she said, "It's Owen." Ava read the text to herself.

Kelleigh reached for the bread bag, squeezed out the air, and wrapped a twisty tie around the open end. "What does the young troubadour have to say this morning?"

"He just wished me luck on my first day."

"That's so sweet," Cara sighed. "I'm envious. And I can't believe you didn't tell him you would be working at Cognac Creek. That's a little sneaky, isn't it?"

"More like coy," Ava corrected as she typed a quick response. "Can't show all my cards at once."

"That's smart," Cara agreed, checking her phone.

Ava slid off the stool and hurried into the bathroom to brush her teeth. In the bathroom, her cell chimed again as she applied toothpaste to her brush. She opened the message. This time, it was a video from Molly.

"Glad you're finally here!" she said, a curious gleam in her eye as she stared at the camera. The clip played, and Molly's face, a little too tired for comfort, filled the frame. Her voice rasped through the speaker as though it had been drug across sandpaper, and her eyes were glossy. "Let me know if you need anything... any help. See you." The clip ended abruptly.

Ava finished brushing. Dropping her toothbrush in the holder, she gave herself one last look in the mirror—fingers tugging at her hair, straightening her clothes—before pulling her phone back up. With a deep breath, she hit record.

"Good morning," she said, her voice slightly breathless from the excitement. "I'm so ready to get started. This place is epic. I can't wait to catch up on everything. We need to make a date and meet somewhere ASAP. Until then, wish me luck!" She hit send.

Back out in the kitchen, her mother and Cara waited for her.

"Are you going to take off soon?" Ava asked her mother.

"Yes, I'll pack up and head out shortly." Kelleigh looked around at the apartment, her eyes a little misty.

"What are you thinking?"

Kelleigh shrugged. "Just that my little girl is all grown up and all this," she lifted her arms to encompass everything around her.

"This apartment, Nashville—seems a little surreal."

Ava leaned in and gave her mother a big hug as tears threatened in her eyes. She squeezed even harder and then released her. Holding her mother at arm's length, she said, "We have to go, or we'll be late."

Her mother nodded. "Call me when you get home. I want to hear all about your day."

"I will. Do you remember the code for the door in case you get locked out packing the car?"

"Yes. But I have to say I miss just having a key in my hand."

"Yeah, I'm surprised too, but that's how they do it here, I guess."

"Do you have stamps in case you need them?"

Ava tapped the pad of paper that lay on the counter. "It's on my list of things to get and do. See?"

"Of course it is."

"I wish you could stay a few more days," Ava said, and she meant it. The irritation she had felt with her mother was already forgotten.

"Me too." A hint of a sad, watery smile played on Kelleigh's face. "Another Tennessee wish."

"I guess so." She gave her mother another hug, not wanting to let her go. This time, though, her mother broke the connection.

"Go. Have a great day. You too, Cara."

"It's not my first day, but I appreciate the sentiment. Thanks, Mrs. Morgahn." Cara's eyes sparkled with amusement as she bounced on her toes and ducked out the door.

Ava hesitated momentarily, pulling the door open wider, and turned back to her mother. "I love you," she said softly, her voice filled with an unexpected tenderness.

"I love you too," Kelleigh replied, her eyes glistening. She placed her hand over her heart, and Ava mirrored the gesture, a quiet connection passing between them.

   With a final, lingering glance, Ava stepped out, pulling the door gently shut behind her.

FIFTEEN

His fingers danced over the keyboard with the practiced precision of someone who'd long since lost any sense of guilt. The passwords came easy, with no resistance at all. Birthdates, Social Security numbers, bank account details—everything was at his fingertips, a well-oiled machine of exploitation. He withdrew just enough, meticulously calculating the amount to avoid suspicion, moving the stolen funds between accounts. Each transaction was seamless, a quiet victory, as the shadows of his mounting debts receded, replaced with a temporary calm.

But the calm was fragile. The loan sharks were always watching, always circling like hungry vultures. Even now, he could feel their presence, a gnawing, sinister undercurrent to his every action. They still hadn't identified the first two women, but it was only a matter of time. He leaned over and threaded their cards into the shredder. He needed to be careful, or the paper trail would catch up to him. It was time to move on before the police caught wind of him.

Would they soon? The thought made him fidget, but he quickly suppressed it, knowing he was always one step ahead. He pressed his lips together, forcing himself back into the cold efficiency of his work. His fingers moved faster now, slick with sweat, the weight of the sharks' unseen eyes making his pulse quicken.

He opened another purse, the familiar scrape of leather against his fingertips somehow more unnerving. The smell of perfume lingered in the air, the kind of scent that clung to his skin and made him feel exposed. The card slid into his hand like it belonged there, a quiet promise of easy money. He made the purchase, each keystroke a step deeper into the labyrinth of his own making. His plan was in full swing, and working beyond his expectations.

But there was no escaping the darkness that loomed around him. The loan sharks—men with eyes cold as glass, voices like gravel—were getting closer. He could almost hear their laughter, the way they'd look at him, knowing that every step he took was one closer to a reckoning. They didn't care about his debts, his plans, his survival, or his gambling problem. They only cared about the blood price they would extract when the time came.

For now, though, he pushed the thought away. He laid the card aside, watching it, hearing the untapped dollars call to him.

His plan was working, if only temporarily. But deep down, he could feel the crushing weight of inevitability. The sharks would come and bleed him dry. When they did, there would be no escape. He needed more and fast.

SIXTEEN

Detective Wyatt Lockhart

The scorching hot sun seared his skin, and ninety-degree temps intensified the fishy smell of the murky water. Wyatt peered down at another lifeless body. Her red hair was plastered to her face, her skin pruned, and there were rope burns around her wrists and ankles.

He shook his head in disgust as he straightened and glanced around. The tally was now up to five. As if he didn't already know, the jackass had marked another victim. A bold, black "5" marked the inside of her palm, scrawled in permanent marker. He hadn't needed to see it—he had known it would be there, but he had forced himself to check, praying it wasn't.

He spat on the ground. The numbers were rising quickly, and he wasn't any closer to solving the case. But the thing that disturbed him was that this time, there hadn't been three weeks between victims, only a couple of days. Was the killer getting impatient? Was he growing bored? More desperate? Or were the women that easy to obtain?

Wyatt walked a short distance from the scene and glanced at the pedestrians forming on the bank. "Crowd control," Wyatt muttered. The tourists needed to be pushed back further. The crowd was growing by the minute. "Ransick," he bellowed.

"Right here, Sergeant," he answered, subtly stepping away from the female officer he'd been speaking with.

"Get these people moved back. Widen the perimeter. Push back the barricade. Give us more room to work. We don't need all these gawkers. Half of them have their phones out, taking pictures or filming the scene. Get them out of here," he barked.

"Yes, sir," Ransick answered. He called out orders and gave directions, having officers move barriers and string more yellow caution tape.

Wyatt scanned the area for any sign of surveillance on the nearby buildings. He was drawn to a shadow creeping along the bank just beyond the yellow tape. The figure had large, sorrowful dark eyes, a slightly hunched posture, and a look of melancholy that seemed almost palpable. He registered a flash of military-green against a gray T-shirt with a spot of hot pink, swinging. Just as he was about to approach her, Ransick reappeared, interrupting his focus.

"Looks like the deceased has some of the same abrasions as the others," Officer Ransick stated, eager to report. "Around her wrists and ankles. Looks like the Cumberland Killer strikes again."

"You might be right," Wyatt said, his frustration evident. He didn't want to give the younger officer the satisfaction. "But I've told you before not to jump to conclusions."

"I'm not jumping to conclusions," Ransick replied. "It seems like a pretty straightforward case. Why do you always have to complicate things?"

Wyatt shook his head, clearly exasperated. "Because, Ransick, it's my job to dig deeper. It should be yours, too, if you're doing it properly." He peered at Ransick from behind his dark glasses. His patience with him was already spent. "Make sure you have the witness reports on my desk this afternoon. Call the morgue and tell them we're bringing them another body."

The words hung in the air, thick with the weight of the case. He didn't need to say more—his tone said it all. There was no room for hesitation, no time for small talk. Another victim. Another family would be shattered if and when they could identify the body. He rubbed his temples, the pressure of the investigation mounting.

Wyatt left the scene but wasn't ready to return to the office.

Ahead, he spotted a Dunkin' Donuts. *Coffee.* He needed it more than he cared to admit. He pulled into the parking lot, the familiar sight, the bright colors of the place offering a brief sense of comfort. This was life, he thought. A busy world where everything seemed normal. And right now, that's exactly what he needed— just a little normalcy.

He got out of the car and headed inside. There was a line that almost deterred him, but the smell of freshly brewed coffee and rising yeast called to him. His stomach rumbled. He stepped into line behind a woman, grumbling to himself.

She turned to look at him. "The line is moving pretty fast, but if you're in a hurry, you are welcome to go ahead of me."

"Sorry, did I say that out loud? I didn't mean to. Just been one of those days."

She nodded her pretty head knowingly. "I get that. Well, hopefully, the coffee will help."

"What about you?" he asked as they both stepped forward, moving up in line.

"Well, it started a little sad. But now it's getting better."

"Oh?" he assessed her with a practiced glance. Her brown hair framed her face with understated elegance. Hazel eyes held a warm, engaging depth and a subtle hint of a Midwestern accent that added a touch of familiarity. "Care to elaborate?"

She laughed softly. "Where do I begin?"

He looked beyond her to the front of the line that was moving. "Looks like maybe the abridged version might be best."

She gave a casual wave of her hand. "Absolutely. My daughter just settled into her new place. Today's her first day at a new job. I had planned to head home this morning, but she had this list, and

I thought…"

He detected a complex blend of pride and sadness, interwoven in a way that spoke volumes beyond her words. "And you thought?" he prompted.

"I don't know what I thought." She hesitated as if trying to justify why she was still here. "Maybe that I had one more day before I needed to go home and be back at work. I could tick off items on her list, stay and hear about her first day in person instead of on the phone." She shrugged and moved up in line.

"And how is the list coming?"

"I've managed to check off several things," she said proudly. "And without getting lost."

Wyatt chuckled softly and nodded. "Good for you." He pointed. "Looks like you're up."

She placed her order. Wyatt was surprised when she ordered a mango pineapple refresher with green tea instead of coffee, paid, and stepped aside for him. He ordered his usual and took his place next to her to wait for his coffee as if it were the most natural thing to do. He wasn't ready for the conversation to be over.

"I'm sensing a little more to the story."

She laughed. "What, are you a mind reader or something?"

"Not quite."

She shrugged and said, "I'm worried that if I handle everything for her, my daughter might feel like I don't believe she can manage on her own. It's not like a twenty-two-year-old needs her mother. I don't want to undermine her independence."

"Do you want to know what I think?"

"Certainly. We've come this far into the conversation."

"I completely understand your concern. Granted, I have never met your daughter and don't have any of my own, but after a long day, she'll be glad you took a few items off her list and stayed one more day."

Names were called.

"That's me."

"And me," Wyatt said as they both approached the counter. Drinks in hand, they both started for the door. He held it open, allowing her to step through first.

Once outside in the parking lot, she paused and turned to him. "Thanks for listening to a stranger ramble on."

With a genuine smile, Wyatt said, "The pleasure was all mine. I truly enjoyed our conversation." He lifted his cup and clinked it against hers. "Here's to a brighter day ahead. You've certainly brightened mine."

She returned his smile. "And mine as well."

SEVENTEEN

Ava Morgahn

Ava threaded through the tables and returned to the main bar. The place was hopping. She would swear it was nine at night if she didn't know the time. The lights inside were down, setting the mood perfectly for day drinking. People poured in by the dozens, wanting to cool down from the heat and get something refreshing to drink and hot and spicy to eat.

Ava thanked the bartender, loaded her drinks onto her tray, and set off across the wide expanse of the room through the strategically placed tables.

Stella, the manager, had anticipated Ava shadowing another waitress for most of the first day and the next until she grew comfortable. Unfortunately, they were down two servers, and with the number of people coming in, she had thrown Ava to the wolves, giving her a section and telling her to holler if she needed help.

It's not that she couldn't handle it. Ava had plenty of experience. She had waited tables all four years in college, and her experience ran the gamut from the hostess stand to working behind the bar.

It was a good rush as the crowd and the music increased. Waiting tables always had its moments. She had already had a drink spilled on her shoe, a dish break, and one guy had asked for her number. She had efficiently dealt with all of them.

On the brighter side, she had captured memories for families, joined in bachelorette party celebrations, and carried out shots for a twenty-first birthday. Her pockets were overflowing with tips.

The rewards far outweighed the challenges of working at an establishment like this. She delivered her drinks with practiced efficiency and stopped to check on a few others at the back of the room.

In addition, the staff was incredibly friendly and had a wealth of valuable information. She gained insights into how Stella selected and hired bands for her stages—knowledge that was nothing short of priceless for Ava's next step.

Amidst everything, Ava's mind kept drifting back to Owen and the unforgettable moment on stage. Every time the back door opened, she couldn't suppress the desperate urge to glance toward it, her heart racing with the faintest hope that he might walk through it despite knowing he usually had Mondays off.

The back door opened, and she held her breath. She released a small sigh and was torn between disappointment and relief. If he walked in now, she knew what he would see. Her hair was up in a messy bun, jeans and a black T-shirt with the Cognac Creek logo on her chest, and her short sleeves rolled up even further. Not the picture of perfection she wanted to portray, but then again, this was her. At least one side of her. The working side, determined to make it on her own side, and she was proud of that.

She shimmied sideways with her empty tray to get through a particularly tight spot and bumped into someone.

"Oh, I'm so sorry," Ava started.

"No worries, little lady," he said, steadying her.

He released her and tipped his hat. The brim was down low, and with the pulsating lights from the stage, she couldn't quite make out his features, only the glint of his eyes in the dimness.

"Can I buy you a drink?" he asked in a low southern drawl.

"I'm sorry, I'm working."

"What time do you get off?"

She gave a little laugh, trying to be polite. "I'm not sure. It's my first day."

"I can wait. Surely, they will give you a break at some point."

"Thank you, but I already had mine."

"Pretty little thing like you shouldn't have to serve or buy her own drinks in a place like this."

She forced a smile. "Again, thank you for the offer, but I am working and need to get back to my customers." She inched past him, but his hand shot out, fingers curling around her wrist with an unsettling pressure.

"You sure?" his voice dropped to a murmur, a subtle threat lingering in the air.

She flinched, her skin crawling under his touch, but forced herself to stay calm. "Positive. Thank you, though." With a quick tug, she pulled away, her movements stiff, like a spring wound too tight. She heard him mutter something low under his breath, the words too soft to understand. A shiver crept up her spine, but she shook it off, brushing the encounter aside.

EIGHTEEN

Kelleigh Morgahn

Kelleigh glanced at her watch in surprise. It was already past five. She hoped Ava and Cara would be home soon, but had no way of knowing when either of them would arrive. She dropped the shopping bags on the small kitchen island, turned on the evening news, and set to work to make Ava's favorite meal.

She found a large pot, filled it with water, and set it on the stove to boil. While waiting, she tidied the counters and pulled out a skillet for browning ground beef. She then turned her attention to the lasagna noodles, tossing them into the boiling water. Cans of tomato sauce and spices were selected from her bags, and the timer was set for the pasta.

Amidst this chaos, Kelleigh straightened the living room and set the table while the reporter droned on about the Cumberland Killer. Despite being safe in the cozy little apartment, she shivered at the newsanchors' broadcast.

The timer went off, indicating that the pasta was done. She quickly drained the boiling water, rinsed the noodles, and set them aside. When the ground beef was browned and seasoned, she began layering it with the noodles, sauce, and cheeses into a glass Pyrex baking dish, covered it with tin foil to keep it from drying out, and placed it in the oven.

As the lasagna baked, she decided to wait to pop in the French bread and get out the salad. The smell of the baking lasagna filled the apartment, promising a well-deserved reward for her efforts and the anticipation of Ava's arrival.

Kelleigh was exhausted. The day had passed quickly with all the errands and the anticipation of being here when Ava got home, but now, with nothing else to do, she sank onto the couch, a mix of trepidation and fatigue washing over her.

"Perhaps I'll just rest my eyes for a few minutes until they get home," Kelleigh mused. Then, reconsidering, she quickly texted Ava to let her know she'd stayed another day. She didn't want her daughter to walk into a surprise, feeling like her space had been taken over and her needy mother had intruded on her new life.

The text sent, Kelleigh leaned back on the sofa, turned off the TV, and closed her eyes forcing what she'd heard on the news out of her mind.

NINETEEN

Owen Layne

Owen sat on the back patio, his guitar slung across his shoulders, fingers idly plucking the strings with a kink forming in his neck. Between trying to craft a melody and scribbling down half-formed notes and lyrics, he'd managed only a few bars and a chorus that seemed to flow pretty well.

As he gazed across the tiny porch, he noticed the German Shepherd lying in the corner. Gunner looked forlorn. Owen sighed, realizing it was time for a walk. Owen knew the dog deserved more —a sprawling yard to run and play in, not this postage stamp or this concrete porch, and someone who loved him. Really loved him. Not that he didn't. It was just that every time he looked at the dog, he was reminded of the loss.

He unstrapped the guitar and gently placed it back in its case. With a whistle, he signaled to Gunner, who perked up instantly. "Ready for a walk?" Owen asked, watching the dog's soulful eyes. They didn't hold adoration, but Owen wasn't looking at Gunner with such affection either. Ava, on the other hand, was an entirely different story.

The mere thought of Ava brought a smile to Owen's face as he clipped the leash onto the dog's collar. "I bet Ava would enjoy walking you," he said, glancing down at Gunner. The German Shepherd tilted his head as if pondering the thought, too. "Let's go."

As Owen and Gunner strolled down the street, his thoughts

wandered again to Ava. He wondered how her day had unfolded, whether she was finished with work, what her first day might have been like, and where exactly she worked. "Why had she been so cryptic about where she worked? Maybe I should send her a text," he mused aloud, only to second-guess himself. "It might be too soon. I already reached out this morning. I don't want to come across as too eager." But she had answered almost instantly, so maybe it wasn't.

He caught himself talking to the dog about his love life— or lack of one. It felt odd, but at least he was considering the possibility of romance again. Ava had stirred feelings in him that had long been dormant. Though a bit lonely, talking to Gunner was better than silence. With Toby at work and Gunner once belonging to his brother, it almost felt like a small connection to him. Without human company, a dog's companionship wasn't the worst substitute. Gunner may not talk back, but his presence was still comforting.

They rounded the corner and were in the thick of things as the duo maneuvered through the crowd like a unit. Downtown Nashville was alive with energy in the middle of happy hour. The air buzzed with laughter, music pouring out from every honky-tonk and bar. Bright neon signs flickered overhead, casting colorful reflections on the bustling pavement.

His grip tightened on the leash as they navigated through the streets, the rhythm of their steps syncing like a well-rehearsed dance. They moved seamlessly, dodging tourists snapping photos, friends shouting to be heard over the lively tunes, and couples swaying to the beat of live bands spilling out onto the sidewalk. On any given day in the summer, the streets downtown teamed with people.

The scent of grilled food wafted through the air, tempting them. As they continued, the energy of Nashville wrapped around him, vibrant and infectious. In this moment, Owen felt like a part of something bigger, a tapestry of voices and sounds woven together in the heart of the city in a way that he hadn't felt in months.

He turned the corner again, away from downtown this time, back to his townhouse.

He cleared his mind from the crowd, and instantly, a couple of new lyrics popped into his head. There could be something to this. Regular exercise may be good for his writing. He knew that and did run regularly up until six months ago. He had just gotten out of the habit and was not able to find the desire or the energy to deal with the dog and exercise.

But now that the lyrics were rolling around in his head, he picked up the pace, jogging with Gunner by his side, eager to get back to the house and write them down.

The bad part about the lyrics was the reminders of why he had difficulty writing new songs. It was hard to remember what it had been like before…before the accident that had taken his brother and injured Gunner. Before he had nursed the German Shepherd back to health. Before Laura said she didn't love him. Before she left.

It wasn't that he wanted Laura back because he certainly didn't, but it had been a big adjustment not to have her constantly around. He knew he was better off without her. She was a liar, a manipulator at best.

His phone buzzed, a harsh reminder of the reality he couldn't escape—the bi-weekly alert he'd set to force himself to call the detective, as if he could forget the ongoing case—the one that had haunted him since that night.

He needed to call. His stomach tightened at the thought of hearing more details that could lead him down a road he didn't want to travel. But it had been weeks since he'd gotten an update, and it wasn't like the detectives were calling him.

He ran up the stairs, let Gunner off the leash, pulled his phone from his pocket, and dialed. It rang twice before the line clicked.

"Police Department. How can I help you?"

He paused, swallowing hard. "I'm calling about an ongoing case. Could I speak to Detective Lockhart?"

"He's unavailable at the moment. I can transfer you to Officer Ransick."

"Thank you." Owen made his way to the backyard, and Gunner followed him. He paced back and forth while the line rang again. With nothing else to do but survey the backyard, Owen was acutely aware that the grass needed to be mowed. It was high, and the weeds were taking over.

"Ransick speaking."

"Officer Ransick, this is Owen Layne. I'm calling regarding a case." Owen rattled off the case number. "The case... with my brother, Officer Dylan Layne...I was wondering if there's any new information."

"Owen, right. I'll check the file." There was a brief silence on the other end, and then the officer returned to the line. "It's still an ongoing investigation, and I don't have any new information to release to you. I will let Detective Lockhart know that you called."

Before Owen could say anything else, there was a dial tone in his ear. So much for that, he thought, exasperated. The ache in his chest resurfaced.

He spotted a dandelion, and Ava's face came to mind again. The pain eased slightly. Was she the answer? Maybe she was the one to make this pang in his chest disappear completely. He went back into the house and got a blue Solo cup and a spoon because he didn't have a hand shovel.

In the yard, he bent and dug up the entire weed, placing it and the dirt in the cup.

Dandelions were interesting, he mused. Most people hated them and spent thousands of dollars to eliminate them. Not Ava, he thought. She was different.

Dandelions started as small yellow blooms, and sometimes those blooms grew to the size of a silver dollar. Eventually they would turn white and fluffy, and their seeds would scatter in the wind. No wonder Ava liked them. She saw the beauty in its simplicity, and delighted in the magic of its transformation, and the tradition of wishing on the seeds. He grinned, lifting the blue cup to admire his work. He had a little dot of sunshine in a plastic cup. Somehow, it made him feel slightly better.

He carried the cup in and placed it in the window. Now every time he saw it he would think of Ava.

Ava... Even her name made him happy—just the simple thought of her.

If she were interested, he would have her sing again at their set on Thursday night. Her voice was incredible, and he knew a rehearsal beforehand would make it even better. It was the perfect plan.

He would have loved someone giving him this chance a few years ago. It would have made the whole process easier. Not that he was anybody—yet. But if he could help another wannabe country singer, why not? It was just plain good karma to at least give it a shot. There was only one way to find out if she was interested. With a deep breath, he fired off a text to her.

TWENTY

Ava Morgahn

Ava stood on the corner of Broadway and Second Avenue, thrilled that Owen had texted. Ole Red's windows were open to let in the night air, and the music poured out.

When she received the text, she had made a quick change in the bathroom. She swapped her jeans and black Cognac T-shirt for a sage-green maxi sundress. The soft, flowy fabric was ideal for packing in her backpack—wrinkle-resistant and effortlessly chic, it exuded a quiet elegance while remaining incredibly comfortable. It looked like she'd put in a lot of effort when, in reality, she had literally just thrown it on.

She hadn't had time to do much with her hair, so she left it in a messy bun and reapplied a light touch of eyeliner and lip gloss.

She felt a strange sensation in the pit of her stomach as she waited all alone for him. Not truly alone, of course—there were hundreds of people around her, strolling down Broadway headed out for the night, chatting in clusters, laughing, and a few hurrying on their way to meet someone. But despite the crowd, the world around her seemed to blur into a soft hum, leaving only the anticipation of his presence in sharp focus.

Her eyes scanned the faces, a silent ache building with every passing second. Maybe he wouldn't show. The fear of it built inside her, it was all so new...

She pushed the thought aside and focused on her surroundings. She wasn't quite used to how the city moved, the ebb and flow of life that never seemed to stop, but she liked the rhythm and steady tempo.

As the sun started to sink behind the cityscape, the buildings casting long shadows across the busy street, everything felt suspended, as if time held its breath.

She should text her mother back. The thought flitted across her mind.

She felt him before she saw him. Her mother forgotten, knowing he was near. It was a feeling she couldn't explain—something magnetic that tugged at the center of her being.

And then, as if on cue, their gazes locked. He crossed the street, his focus solely on her. The chaos of the world didn't matter anymore. The noise, the bustle, and the colors of the city faded as her heart recognized the one thing it had been waiting for. In that instant, she felt a wave of warmth and belonging wash over her. It wasn't just the sight of him—it was the way he made her feel seen, the way his eyes spoke to her soul without a single word.

The world shifted and came into focus, becoming just a little more precise, a little more precious.

He stopped three feet from her, barely off the street, put his hand to his heart, and took her in despite the people pushing past him. "Wow. You look incredible."

"You're not so bad yourself." That was an understatement. Her heart tumbled at the sight of him. Tall, dark, and handsome was such a cliché, but she couldn't help it. He was. "You're going to get yourself run over."

"That's fine." He stood where he was. "I'll die happy, simply standing here looking at you."

A car laid on its horn as it tried to turn, the corner overflowing with people.

She tugged him forward, further onto the sidewalk. He moved without any resistance straight toward her as pedestrians pushed past, shuffling along the crowded street.

"What do you say we get away from this crowd? Go somewhere where we can sit and talk."

"Sounds perfect," she answered.

"There's this little dive bar on First Avenue with the best smothered nachos and spicy margaritas I'd like to take you to."

"I could go for a margarita."

He linked his fingers with hers. "I don't want to lose you in this crowd. I'll never find you again."

"And I don't want to be lost," she said, squeezing his hand. They threaded their way down Broadway toward Riverfront Station, where there were fewer people, and the music was not as loud—then turned onto First Avenue. It wasn't long before he opened a door and ushered her in.

It would be an exaggeration even to call it a dive bar. It was more like a forgotten hole in the wall. The building was clinging to its last breath. The ceiling, exposed with bare rafters, loomed above, while the floor, worn and slightly sloped, seemed to tilt with every step. The booths, high-backed and shrouded in shadows, promised privacy and escape. Yet, despite its rough edges and faded charm, the air was thick with the mouthwatering scent of chili and lime that lingered as a server carried piping hot plates across the room.

He indicated a booth in the corner, the barkeep nodded his approval, and they slid in.

"How did you ever find this place?" Ava asked.

"When you have lived here all your life, you tend to find places and things that you can enjoy off the beaten path, away from the crowds. And this is one of them. The building may be a two or three at best, but the atmosphere and margaritas here are five-star."

The server came, and they ordered. The margaritas were delivered quickly. Ava took a salty sip and savored the tangy, liquid gold drink as it slipped down her throat.

"Mmmm, I swear I can taste every ingredient: the smooth tequila, the freshly squeezed tart lime, the Triple Sec with its subtle sweet orange flavor. And… what's that spice?"

"Jalapeno. That's the secret ingredient."

He reached over with his hand, and with his thumb, he brushed off a crystal of salt from her bottom lip. She tried not to tremble from his touch, but just that brief contact shot a warm, delicious feeling through her.

She eased back in the booth, needing some distance from him to protect her heart because it was tumbling toward him way too fast. "So," she drew out the word, long and slow. "All your life, huh?"

"Yes."

"Except for four years in Kansas?"

"Yes."

"What made you decide on Kansas, when there are excellent schools here?"

"Basketball, which you knew." He shrugged and took a gulp of his margarita, watching her over the top of the wide rim. "They gave me a full ride. And even though I love it here, sometimes you have to see what's out there to appreciate what you have here."

"I would agree with that." She liked his answer. Understood it. Wasn't that what she was doing? She loved Iowa, her home, her family, and her friends. She could have played it safe and stayed in Des Moines, taking the teaching job in the fall. And maybe she still would. But for now, she was here… for the experience, for the adventure, and to see what might be. To see if making wishes on dandelions and sending out all her dreams into the universe was all talk or if her heart, her mind, and her soul were really and truly behind every wish, every breath of air that sent those tiny seeds drifting out, up, and away… To see if her prayers would be answered.

Their nachos arrived, and both their hands reached simultaneously, brushing. He smiled slightly, as if it could be or should be an apology made purely out of manners, but didn't retract his. "Ladies first."

She didn't move her hand either. "I think the dish is big enough for both of us." She pulled a few chips from the plate as the sauce dripped onto her own. Melted cheese strung out, connecting her plate with the serving dish. Meanwhile, he popped his directly into his mouth, making it look easy.

"What?" She laughed as she tried to pile the string of warm cheese onto her plate.

"There are so many questions I want to ask you," Owen said as he watched her navigate the unruly nachos.

"Like what?" she asked, finally able to separate a chip to put in her mouth.

"Like... What made you come to Nashville? How long do you plan on staying? Where are you working? Why won't you tell me? But most importantly... Do you have a boyfriend back home, drowning himself in alcohol because you left him to come to Nashville?"

"Wow." She propped her elbow on the table and placed her chin in her hand, her eyes wide. "That was a lot of questions all at once."

"Oh, Miss Ava, that was just the tip of the iceberg."

"I think I can answer those one at a time. Five questions. Five answers." She held up her hand and ticked off answers on her fingers. "One, Nashville has always been a dream. Two, I don't know. Three, you'll find out soon enough. Four, I like to make sure I'm in control of certain things, and revealing where I work is one of them. And five," she paused, pulled in a small breath on her last finger. "No."

He leaned in closer with his cocky grin. His dimples etched

deeply into his cheeks. He was so close she could make out the details in his eyes: the tiny flecks of midnight in a sea of cornflower blue, mischief, and a wanting engraved so deeply it left her reeling.

"Next time, I'll be sure to ask one question at a time. But I appreciate your efficiency and attention to every inquiry."

"I'm nothing if not efficient," Ava answered matter-of-factly as she reached for her drink and her hands trembled. She clasped the glass tightly, trying to still her hands so he wouldn't notice how deeply he affected her.

"Even though your answer to number five was the briefest answer, I liked that one best."

She pressed her lips together, then forced herself to ask, "Why is that?"

He slid closer on the cushion and slipped his hand around the small of her back. "Because if the answer had been yes, then I wouldn't be able to do this." His other hand brushed her cheek and waited for a reaction, a hesitation from her. When none came, he lowered his hand and pressed his lips to hers.

She could taste the flavor of salt and lime on his lips, his tongue, and feel the heat from his palm as it lightly caressed her back through the thin material of her dress. The noise of the bar fell away as his mouth explored hers, deepening the kiss. He was tempting her and pulling her in, drowning her in a flurry of wants and desires. Her hand slipped between them and gently pressed against his sturdy chest, feeling the steady beat of his heart beneath her palm.

The server came over to check on them. Clearing her throat she placed a hand on her hip, and cocked her head. "I didn't know that was on our menu tonight."

And then it was over. He eased back and grinned, lifting an eyebrow. Caught, Owen laughed. "I don't believe it was."

"Well, it certainly should be on the dessert menu."

Ava felt her face flush as she turned, as much from embarrassment as the passion surging within her.

"How would you describe it, if she wanted to add it to the menu?" Owen asked coyly.

Ava bit her bottom lip lightly, still able to feel Owen's mouth on hers. She batted her dark lashes at him and answered, "Decadently sinful."

"Now, honey, that's my kind of dessert." The server winked at Ava. "I'm afraid I'm gonna hafta charge extra for that."

TWENTY-ONE

Kelleigh Morgahn

She dreamt of tangy sauce, bubbling cheese, and the intoxicating blend of oregano, basil, and... smoke.

The dream was abruptly shattered by a relentless beeping that jolted her awake. Her eyes flew open to find the room permeated with the acrid smell of burnt food and a dense, suffocating fog creeping from the kitchen.

"Oh, no!" Kelleigh cried as she leaped off the couch with a frantic urgency. She punched the button of the exhaust fan above the stove and twisted the knob to shut off the oven. Smoke rolled out in a dark wave as she opened the oven door.

"Oh, my heavens!" she exclaimed, pulling out the charred remains of the casserole and setting it on the stove. "I've ruined dinner."

Coughing violently, she fanned the smoke with a kitchen towel and made her way across the room, turning on lights and opening windows. "Why on earth is it so dark in here?" Kelleigh squinted at the digital clock on the microwave glowing through the haze. The shrill beeping persisted. "I can't think with that noise," she muttered.

Desperately, Kelleigh fanned the smoke detector, trying to clear the air. Her arms began to ache, straining under the effort, and gradually, the room started to clear. The relentless beeping ceased. "Finally!"

Cara's door flung open, and she stumbled out. "What the heck is going on?"

"Cara!" Kelleigh exclaimed, startled by her appearance. "I'm so sorry to wake you, but I burnt dinner."

"Oh, that's too bad. I smelled it earlier when I came home, and it smelled delicious."

"Why didn't you wake me?"

Cara ran a hand through her messy blonde hair. "It didn't occur to me that I should. Sorry."

Silence settled around them.

"What time is it?"

"It's almost midnight." Cara rubbed her eyes. "Is there anything salvageable?" she asked, peering at the casserole. "I'm kind of hungry."

"I'm afraid not." Kelleigh peeled back the layer of scorched tinfoil, or what little was left of it that wasn't stuck to the charred remains. Disappointed with herself, she dug through drawers, looking for a spatula to scrape the burnt lasagna into the trash. Finding one, she glanced at Ava's bedroom door. "I can't believe all this commotion didn't bring Ava out. She's usually such a light sleeper."

"Maybe she just had a long day, and she's drained." Cara went to the fridge, pulled out a water bottle, twisted the top, and looked at Kelleigh. "I'm surprised to see you here. I thought you were leaving this morning."

"I was. Sorry. I hope you don't mind, but I decided to stay one more day."

"No worries." Cara glanced around the messy kitchen and then back at Kelleigh. "You got this?"

She waved her off dismissively. "Go back to bed. I'll check on Ava, and then I'll clean up. It's not like her to sleep this heavily."

A tinge of worry rose beneath her calm exterior, but Kelleigh quickly pushed it down.

Taking a deep breath, she grounded herself. "One step at a time," she murmured, trying to regain control. With her nerves steeled, she crossed the small apartment, her footsteps quiet on the worn floor. But when she opened the door—it was empty.

TWENTY-TWO

Kelleigh Morgahn

"9-1-1 What's your emergency?"

"I need to report my daughter missing."

"How old is your daughter?"

"She's twenty-two."

"When was the last time you saw her?

"This morning around seven."

"Ma'am, what is your name and address?"

"My address or where I'm currently at?" Kelleigh asked in a shaky voice. She couldn't think straight.

"Your first and last name and where you are located right now."

Cara placed a hand on Kelleigh's arm and gave the address.

"Thank you," she mouthed to Cara.

"And this is the last place you saw your daughter?"

"Yes."

"Are you currently in any danger?"

"No."

"What's your daughter's name?"

"Ava Lynn Morgahn." Kelleigh bit her bottom lip to keep it from trembling.

"Have you tried her on her cell phone?" the operator asked.

"Yes. Several times. It goes straight to voicemail."

"Is it possible she's asleep?"

"No, I'm currently at the apartment. I have been all night. She never came home from work," Kelleigh said with a hitch to her voice. She paced back and forth across the tiny apartment, feeling restless and confined, much like she assumed a caged animal would.

"Okay, Kelleigh. Stay with me, alright?"

"Yes," she nodded even though she knew the operator couldn't see her.

"I'm going to dispatch an officer to your location. He can talk to you directly and take down the pertinent information. I have one in your area. He should be there shortly. If you could turn on any outside lights for him, that would be appreciated."

"Yes, we can turn on the lights."

Cara got up and flipped them on without any fanfare, illuminating the top flight of stairs.

"We're on the second floor of the building. The lights are on."

"Officer Ransick will be the responding officer."

"I see the police car pulling in now," Cara told Kelleigh, peering out the window. She went out the door, stood at the top of the stairs, and flagged him down.

"The officer is here," Kelleigh told the operator, then thanked her and disconnected.

"Ma'am," the officer said as he ascended the stairs. "Are you Ms. Kelleigh Morgahn?"

Cara opened the door wide. "She's inside. Please," she indicated the open door. "Come in."

The officer dipped his head and entered the apartment.

"Please, have a seat." Kelleigh indicated the sofa, and she took the straight-back chair, perching on its edge.

"I understand you think your daughter is missing?" Officer Ransick asked.

"Yes, that's right."

"And you are?" he questioned, looking at Cara.

"I'm her roommate."

He nodded and turned back to Kelleigh.

"What makes you think she's missing?" He scanned the room.

"She didn't come home from work. I've tried calling her multiple times. The calls go straight to voicemail, and she hasn't responded to my texts."

"And you've been here all night?"

"Yes.

"What time does she normally come home?"

Kelleigh hesitated. "Well, I don't exactly know. This was her first day."

"Your daughter's first day?" he questioned.

"Yes, my daughter just started a new job." Kelleigh quickly discussed the move, the apartment, and her intention to return to Iowa today.

"I see." He glanced around the room. "Is it possible that she went out after work?"

"It is, but why wouldn't she have called?"

"You said she wasn't expecting you to be here, that she thought you were leaving today and would be in Iowa. If that was the case, why would she hurry home? Most likely she turned off her phone at work or maybe had to put it in a locker. It's possible she went out with someone from work, maybe had too much to drink, and stayed the night somewhere so she didn't have to drive."

"I see your point," Kelleigh said, her voice trembling, the weight of the officer's words sinking in, but it just didn't seem right, not something Ava would do. *But she packed a bag.* With a cold, unrelenting dread, the possibility was there, and it plagued her, but it was the gnawing sense of something truly awful that had happened that was nearly unbearable. "Is it possible to check with the hospitals to see if anyone matches her description?"

"Ma'am. It hasn't even been twenty-four hours since you spoke to her."

"I know. I know." Kelleigh wrung her hands. "It's just that we had discussed her calling me after she got off work and...and she didn't."

"Where does she work?"

"Cognac Creek. She's a server."

He glanced at his watch. "Technically, they aren't even closed yet. Is it possible she had to work late or stayed for last call?"

"I guess she could have."

"I'm sure she'll be in touch soon. In the meantime, is there anyone you can contact? A friend, coworker, or perhaps her boss?"

Kelleigh's heart pounded furiously from fear and embarrassment. Had she jumped the gun and overreacted because of a serial killer on the loose? She should never have watched the news. "I don't really know anyone in Nashville except my daughter and one of her close friends."

"Do you have a number for this friend?" he asked.

"I'm not sure." Desperately, she swiped through her contacts, fingers shaking uncontrollably as she searched for Molly's name. Her mind raced through the terrifying possibilities: Ava's car could have broken down in the middle of nowhere, or she could have been assaulted, lying on the sidewalk somewhere. And what about the Cumberland Killer... her mind stopped working the minute that name entered her thoughts again. *Stop!* She scolded herself. *Don't go there.*

Each scenario was darker than the last, spiraling into a

nightmarish abyss of what-ifs. The room felt suffocating, the walls closing in as her fear took on a tangible, almost physical form.

Kelleigh scrolled through the list, looking for the contact, but she already knew she didn't have it. Why on earth had she not insisted that Ava give it to her? Who else could she call? *Owen.* She racked her brain for his last name and couldn't come up with it.

Cara sat silently on the other end of the sofa, but quickly offered, "Let me see if I can search for Cognac Creek's number. She tapped lightly on her phone. "Here it is."

"Do you want to call?" the officer asked.

Reality rushed in, and Kelleigh hesitated, second guessing herself. The officer's explanation made sense. Now she was afraid if she did call, and Ava was there, she would be embarrassed her mother was checking up on her. Maybe she was overreacting. Stilling her nerves, she said, "I think I'll wait a little longer."

"Very good."

Officer Ransick stayed only long enough to assure Kelleigh he would be in contact if he heard anything.

As he got up to leave, he offered a reassuring smile. "Rest easy, Ms. Morgahn," he drawled. "I'm confident there's nothin' to be worried about. She'll turn up. They usually do. I'll keep you updated if I receive any information." He eased out the door, closing it firmly behind him.

TWENTY-THREE

Owen Layne

Owen wasn't ready for the night to slip away. As his fingers curled around hers, the warmth of her hand surged through him, anchoring him to the moment. The bustling street was alive with energy, late but never empty. They navigated the crowds, their steps slowing, stretching the distance between now and goodbye. A silent understanding passed between them—neither one willing to let the night go. Neon lights flickered above, casting electric blue, red, and yellow hues across her face. He stopped in the middle of the street as the concrete parking garage loomed large. He pulled her close, and for a heartbeat, time seemed to pause. He lowered his lips to hers. The kiss was brief but electric, its intensity sparking as a man abruptly collided with them.

Her smile broke the kiss, her eyes twinkling with mischief. "First, the waitress, and now some random stranger ruining our moment."

He grinned, pulling her closer, feeling the heat of her body. "Guess we're just too irresistible," he teased, his lips brushing against hers again. "You certainly are."

She laughed softly, the sound warm and carefree. "Maybe," she said, "or we might need to start picking better spots."

He raised an eyebrow, his hands finding their way to her waist. "What, like a hidden rooftop or a private island?"

"Exactly," she smirked, "somewhere the only interruptions are us." She let out a deep, contented sigh. "As much as I don't want the night to end, it is getting late, and I have to work tomorrow."

"Still not going to tell me where?" he asked curiously.

"Not yet."

"Afraid I'll stop in and check on you?"

"Something like that."

"Come on," he grinned and tugged her forward.

They walked into the dimly lit structure, the echo of their footsteps bouncing off the concrete walls. The sound was oddly comforting in the building's silence. The hum of distant cars, the lull of conversations, and music drifted through the open space, creating a magical backdrop.

Her fingers brushed against his as they made their way up toward the far corner, where her car sat. The flickering fluorescent lights above glowed softly on the space, making it feel like their own little world.

"Well," she said, looking up at him with a playful glint, "looks like we've found the perfect spot."

He chuckled, his hand finding hers again, pulling her closer. "It's like you read my mind."

She laughed, the sound ringing out in the vast space.

They stopped in front of her car, and she leaned against the door, glancing around the deserted garage as if making sure no one was watching.

He moved in, his lips curving into a mischievous smile. "No one's here but us, right?"

She raised an eyebrow, his body inching closer to hers. He grinned, watching, waiting for her reaction, playfully challenging her to stop him. The look in her eyes made his heart race.

"No interruptions here, Ava Lynn."

"Seems that way."

Without another word, one hand slipped behind her waist and nestled against the small of her back, the other gently held the side of her face. His thumb traced lightly over her full lips. His eyes flicked up to hers and back down to her mouth. Then he leaned in and kissed her, this time with a sense of urgency, as though the world outside the garage was insignificant, disappearing until nothing else mattered but them.

TWENTY-FOUR

Detective Wyatt Lockhart

Detective Lockhart stormed into the morgue on a mission, but the quiet of the room rushed at him, slowing his progress.

"Yikes, it's frigid in here. It's like walking into an ice box," Wyatt stated.

"I feel like you say that every time you enter, which lately seems to be almost every week," Emmett Denlinger, the medical examiner, said dryly, pushing up his glasses. "And yet you always manage to seem surprised."

"It's a shock to the system, that's all. Especially when I'm coming in from 95-degree weather."

"Let's dispense with the pleasantries," Emmett said, his tone crisp and focused. "I take it you're here regarding my report?"

"Precisely," came Wyatt's reply. "I'm curious what other similarities there could be between the five drowning victims other than the obvious."

"It's not just about the similarities of the cause of death but the other facts that are akin to each victim," Emmett said flatly.

"Like what?" Wyatt bristled and asked in disgust, "Surely you have some reason for dragging me down here into the land of sterilization, where Hell freezes over to keep the bodies from rotting."

Emmett stood at his full height of five feet seven and looked undeterred at Wyatt. "Of course I do."

"Damn it, man, spill it," Wyatt pressed.

Emmett replied steadily, "In layman's terms, her death was attributed to an excessive amount of benzodiazepine in her system and fluid in her lungs due to submergence, which both exacerbated drowning. The second unidentified woman ..."

"Drowned with the aid of a large dose of benzodiazepine," Wyatt finished for him. "Tell me something I don't already know."

"If you kindly let me finish," Emmett said, peering over his glasses at him.

Wyatt sensed the irritation in the older man and apologized. "Sorry. Please," Wyatt gestured. "Continue."

"There are similarities, making the deaths almost identical. All of the deceased have dermatoglyphic loss."

"Fingertips?" Wyatt questioned as if he hadn't heard the medical examiner correctly.

Emmett nodded and methodically opened several folders laid out before him. "Their fingertips are badly distorted from prolonged or frequent exposure to friction, injury, or skin irritation, which has made it extremely difficult to get a good print. Thus delaying the process of identification."

Wyatt pressed, "What could be the cause of this?"

"I am still in the process of determining the precise etiology," Emmett responded. "However, based on the samples and preliminary evidence, it appears that the dermatoglyphic loss may be attributed to prolonged exposure to concrete or excessive abrasions."

"Concrete?" Wyatt questioned. "Abrasions?"

"Yes."

Wyatt had to stop and think. "Could abrasions be due to trying to work the rope off their wrists?"

"Yes. All the women had profound tissue damage around their wrists and concrete residue under their nails."

"Three people, drowning within weeks of each other, with the same fingertip damage. Couldn't this just be a coincidence?"

"It is a possibility," Emmett concurred. "However, if you take into account the additional cases..."

"The additional cases?" Wyatt inquired, already fearing where this was going.

Emmett adjusted his glasses and continued, "The two new homicides." He slid two additional folders toward the detective. "Exhibited the same deterioration and were found to have elevated levels of benzodiazepine in their systems. Their recorded cause of death was drowning."

"The previous drowning victims had concrete under their nails, and now the fourth and fifth do as well," Wyatt stated. "Where is it coming from?"

"That's the million-dollar question, isn't it? My guess, and it's just an educated guess thus far since I am still running tests, is that it's environmental."

Environmental. Wyatt's mind was running in a hundred different directions. Were the victims trying to claw their way out of a damp, dark basement? Or were they being held captive at a construction site? Or were they locked in an empty warehouse surrounded by chemicals and other imposing materials? Hell, concrete wasn't just a material—it was everywhere. Landscapers, carpenters, masons, engineers... all of them used it in their work. His mind worked out possibilities.

He needed to pinpoint the location. If he had that...

He paced back and forth across the cold, sterile room.

He stopped short when an idea struck him...One possibility was the old abandoned concrete plant on the city's east side. It had been shut down for years. His thoughts collided with the haunting possibility that it might be perilously close to where the women had allegedly fallen into the river. He'd have to check the map.

"Get me copies of these files. ASAP," Wyatt demanded.

The question nagged at him. His next course of action was predetermined. He knew what he needed to do next: head downtown and investigate the concrete plant.

He had sent Ransick downtown multiple times, but each time the officer returned empty-handed. Frustration etched across his face.

Wyatt couldn't shake the feeling that something crucial was being overlooked. The streets buzzed with life—people, stories, connections. He was determined to dig deeper. Maybe a fresh perspective would yield answers where Ransick had failed.

With a sense of urgency driving him, he gathered his thoughts, the weight of the unresolved cases heavy on his shoulders. He would find the truth, one way or another.

"Now that we have the first two women's names, I'll try to run them through the system and see how they are connected. This seems like random victims caught unaware or easy targets getting picked up in a bar."

"I would say so," Emmett agreed, but there was something in his tone—something hesitant. He paused, eyes narrowing as though a thought was just out of reach. "But if they're not random... then what are we dealing with here?"

"There's something more to this," Wyatt muttered under his breath, almost to himself. "Something we're not seeing yet."

TWENTY-FIVE

Kelleigh Morgahn

Kelleigh drove aimlessly through the streets, a sense of confusion washing over her. She scanned the surroundings for any familiar places, signs, or landmarks—anything that could help her regain her bearings. But as she peered out the window, her heart sank when another of her calls went straight to voicemail.

The landscape was a blur of unfamiliarity. Each building, corner, and street blended into the next. And so did the people. She knew it was a long shot that she could hope to find Ava aimlessly walking along the street, but she couldn't stop scanning their faces.

With Cara off to work this morning, Kelleigh gripped the steering wheel and felt desperation creep in as the hours passed with no word from Ava, leaving her feeling adrift and utterly lost.

She had spent most of the morning driving around, searching for Ava, unsure of what else to do. Returning to Iowa without knowing her daughter was safe was not an option. She remembered the officer's words about calling with any updates, but he hadn't yet.

He also said it was probably nothing serious—these things happened constantly and offered a perfectly logical explanation. Ava might have just spent the night somewhere else with the intention of going straight to work, perhaps embarrassed about not coming home. After all, young women often found themselves in these situations, or so Officer Ransick said.

She could almost hear Officer Ransick's thoughts—an overprotective mother clinging too tightly to her daughter. He probably saw her as a typical 'Karen,' flapping around like a mother hen, worried about her little chick leaving the nest. But it wasn't like that. Ava had already been living on her own at college.

She felt a wave of self-doubt wash over her. Was she just another stereotype? Maybe she *was* overreacting, letting her fears cloud her judgment. Maybe Ava really did do this kind of thing on a regular basis. After all, Kelleigh didn't keep track of her twenty-four hours a day. Perhaps this was just what young women did sometimes, and she was being too dramatic. But deep down, she couldn't shake the feeling that something was off.

Ava wasn't like that, Kelleigh insisted. Her mind sent out a little prickle of doubt, or was she? She shook her head with disgust that the thought would even enter her mind. No—she knew her daughter better than anyone. Ava simply would not do that.

But as Kelleigh pulled up to the apartment, a sinking feeling gripped her gut, and the ground seemed to shift beneath her. An unmarked, white van with a small crew was hauling out trash, suitcases, and belongings like they were yesterday's garbage.

Panic surged as she jumped out of the car, recognizing her suitcase. "Hey! Stop! That's my stuff!" she shouted, her voice cracking with desperation.

One of the workers turned, a smirk playing on his lips. "We're here to clean a room."

"What do you mean?" Kelleigh asked, her confusion morphing into sheer panic. "This is my daughter's apartment!"

He laughed, a harsh sound, that cut through her. "That's rich. Why don't you try again."

"She just moved in on Saturday," Kelleigh said, confused.

"I was hired to come by and clean out this apartment at noon today, and that's what I'm doing."

Her heart raced, the world spinning as she struggled to process everything. "No, no, please! There must be some mistake! My daughter—she's supposed to come back here!" Each word tumbled out, more frantic than the last, as she reached for a teetering suitcase on the sidewalk's edge. Desperation clawed at her throat, and she felt tears prick her eyes. "Please, just give me a moment to figure this out!"

"We don't have a minute. We're on a tight schedule and need to stick to it."

"At least let me have my things and my daughters." Kelleigh looked around. "Don't throw it away." She lifted a bag still packed full of clothes.

"Lugging out all your shit has set us back."

The audacity! "I want to speak to your manager!" Kelleigh demanded.

He towered over Kelleigh. His hot breath, smelling of onions and garlic, turned her stomach.

"Sweet cheeks, I *am* the manager."

Kelleigh swallowed hard, forcing down the fear. "What about the owner?"

His lip turned up into a snarl. "I'm the manager, the owner, and the frickin' CEO. You wanna take it up with anybody, you take it up with me. You're damn lucky I'm letting you have the stuff back. Usually, I take it and sort through what's left."

"Stop right now!" She demanded. "Who hired you?"

He stomped to the front of the vehicle and yanked a clipboard off the seat.

"Call whoever hired you and verify that you have the right address."

"I have the right damn address and the code to the door. What do you take me for? Some idiot? How else would I have gotten in?" He riffled through the stack of papers looking for the name. "Cara

McCray." His lips curled as he drew out her name.

"That's my daughter's roommate. Don't touch anything else," her voice rippled with anger and frustration. "I'm calling Cara."

He looked at her, and she swallowed hard, afraid he'd shove her to the ground the way he had lurched at her, but instead, he crossed his arms and waited.

"You got sixty seconds."

She pulled out her phone, stepped away from him, and called.

Cara answered almost immediately. Kelleigh quickly explained the situation while keeping a trained eye on the man and his crew.

"Oh, bless your heart!" Cara exclaimed. "This is totally my fault. I originally had them scheduled for today to clean the spare room. But everything happened so quickly with Ava taking the room that I had to get another crew to clean before she arrived, and forgot to cancel this one."

Kelleigh let out a breath. "Oh, that makes sense. Can you tell him that? I don't think he'll believe me. He's hell-bent on doing his job."

"Of course."

Kelleigh handed the phone to the man.

He barked into her cell, "Got me an irate lady accusing me of being at the wrong place." He glared at Kelleigh as he listened for a split second. His expression remained set in a deep scowl. "I still want my money," he paused, then clicked off the call. "Grab your gear," he barked to his crew.

"My stuff?" Kelleigh inquired.

"Leave it," he growled at his crew, and they dropped everything. "Load up! We are outta here!"

She watched hesitantly as they all piled into the white van. When the vehicle backed out, she quickly began gathering their things.

TWENTY-SIX

Owen Layne

Out of habit, Owen tucked a small bottle opener in his left pocket and a wine key in the other. From the back, he pulled out his cell phone. He scrolled through his texts and scowled.

"Trouble in paradise?" Toby asked as he hefted in two buckets of ice, handing one off to Owen. "That's the fifth time you've checked your phone since we arrived."

Owen stuck his phone back in his pocket and dumped his pail in the bin. He didn't correct Toby, but it was more like the tenth since he'd gotten up this morning... and it was only ten-thirty.

"I just get antsy when my mom picks up the dog. He's usually very well-behaved for her, but I still worry." That was only partially true. Yes, he was concerned for his mother and how having Dylan's dog for the day would affect her. He was never sure how she would react. Some days, having him eased the loss of his brother, and other times it didn't. But today, his mom wasn't the only thing on his mind.

It was Ava—more so because he hadn't heard from her since he walked her to her car last night. He would have liked to say that wasn't like her, but really—how did he know? He had only just met her. He corrected the phrase—it didn't seem like something she would do.

"When are you going to start calling Gunner by his name?"

Owen lifted a shoulder to brush off the question and get

Toby to drop it. The dog was the least of his worries. Using his name meant an attachment, a commitment, a responsibility that Owen wasn't interested in having. He wasn't *his* dog. He was his brother's.

"He had a name before your brother died, and it's still the same. He's the same dog. That hasn't changed."

"No, his owner has," Owen said coldly.

"You liked him once upon a time. Why can't you like h m now? He's a good dog, for t1e most part," Toby added. "When he's not tearing apart our furniture. He's been through a terrible trauma, too, and barely survived."

"I think you just answered your question."

"I did?" Toby asked. He scratched his head, thinking. "I don't get it?"

"He survived. My brother didn't." Owen's tone dropoed low. "It should have been the other way around, don't you think?" He didn't wait for an answer, just turned his back on his friend and opened his drawer, determined to end the conversation.

Both men fell silent as they counted their bank. Making a note of the total, Owen pulled out his bar mop and wiped down his section of the bar. Next, he grabbed a stack of napkins from the supply closet, gave half to Toby without looking directly at him, and fanned out his own, placing them in front of the bar with the hard edge toward him and Cognac Creek's logo facing out. He knew he shouldn't be taking his foul mood out on Toby. Hell, he shouldn't even be in a foul mood after the night he had with Ava.

Ava—eyes like a dappled forest in the morning light, and a personality that drew him in from the first encounter, and left him in awe. Just the thought of her laugh sent a delicious spike through his body.

Forcing his mind to focus on work, he examined the bottles in his well and reviewed the mental list to ensure they were in order. "Vodka, gin, rum," he recited. "Triple sec, tequila, bourbon, scotch

—the gang's all here."

"Mine too," Toby commented cheerfully, clearly not letting Owen's gruffness get to him. "The rum is almost empty. Why is the rum gone?" Toby asked in his best pirate voice. "Mind handing me a fresh bottle from the stash?"

Without comment, Owen pulled a bottle and handed it to his friend. He dipped into the kitchen, brought out a fruit tray, grabbed a small cutting board and knife, and started preparing limes. He made a line down the middle, slicing it in half, then made a small slit on the inside and proceeded to cut the large lime into ten pieces. The steady rhythm of it allowed his mind to wander again.

Why did it bother him so much that he hadn't heard from Ava or that Toby was right about the dog? Both thoughts twisted and turned in his mind until they were wrapped up as one, almost interchangeable. But the image of Ava standing next to her car in that long green sundress after he'd kissed her goodnight shone through. There was no competition. That image of Ava was etched into his mind.

He had only known her for three days. Three days. They had no commitment to each other. But, like it or not, there had been an instant connection. Something so different and foreign to him that it kept him slightly off-kilter when she was around. She somehow managed to get under his skin and sink into his bones, his very being. He wasn't used to that. But he wanted it. All of it. All of her.

He was willing to take a chance at it—whatever *it* was—with her. To see where that feeling might lead. He had even let her come up on stage and sing with him and the band on day number two. He never did that. Especially when he wasn't sure of her level of talent, her capability, or if Stella was still in the building. He couldn't imagine what she would have done to him had the whole thing been a flop. He shuddered to think of it.

When he realized how talented Ava was—that voice like silk, sliding over the melody, intertwining with his like pure magic—he offered to let her come out and sing with them some other time. That wasn't like him either.

Even before Laura.

And now what? Was she ghosting him? He hadn't seen that coming. Last night had been... What was the word he was looking for? Special. No, that wasn't enough. Completely unexpected was more like it. And Ava... Ava had been captivating.

He hadn't expected to kiss her at the bar, but damn if it hadn't been a near-perfect kiss until the waitress had interrupted. Or again on the street outside Luke Bryan's under that neon sign. Even better. Then he had gone and done it a third time, pressing her against her car, making the kiss even deeper and more infectious than the two before. It was all he could do to force himself to ease back and walk away, leaving her in the pale fluorescent light, looking ethereal, his body humming.

He shook himself. Refocusing his attention, he concentrated on finishing the limes. Then he moved on to lemons and repeated the process on half the batch. The other half he turned, cutting off the ends and producing lemon wheels. He finished off his fruit prep by shaving off slices of oranges.

He filled his garnish tray, placing cherries, olives, limes, lemons, and orange slices in all the slots.

He felt his cell phone vibrate in his back pocket, and his pulse spiked. Maybe it was her. He washed and dried his hands before he pulled out his phone. It made no sense to seem too eager. He tapped the screen to light it up.

"Well?" Toby asked.

"Well, what?"

"Did she text?"

"Who?" Owen asked carefully.

"Miss Iowa State."

"What makes you think I'm checking to see if it's her?" Owen

127

asked, a little perturbed that his friend knew him so well.

"Before Saturday, you hardly ever checked your phone, not since..." Toby didn't finish the thought. Instead, he let the comment trail off. "And now you check it every ten minutes."

"That's not true." But he knew it was.

"Is it her?" Toby asked again, leaning over to take a look.

Owen shrugged him off. "Do you mind?" He stepped back, checked the new text, and outwardly deflated. "No, it's my mom. She's taking the dog for a walk."

Toby nodded knowingly. "Good. They will both enjoy that. Listen," he said, leaning against the bar. "I'm sure Ava will text or call. She didn't seem like the type of person who would just blow you off."

"That's the impression I had, but..."

"It's only been a few hours, and she's got a lot happening right now with just moving in, the new roommate, her mom leaving, and starting a new job. She's probably overwhelmed," Toby reasoned. "Did she say she was working today?"

"Yes, she did."

"See. She probably just woke up late, running behind, and unable to text you."

"I hadn't thought of it like that." Owen contemplated his friend for a moment. "Huh."

"What?" Toby asked.

"Who knew you could be the voice of reason?"

Toby tapped his head and smiled wide. "I'm not just about my rockin' good looks or getting girls. I have a pretty solid head on my shoulders. You should listen to me more often."

"Not sure I'm willing to take that risk."

"You don't realize how much wisdom you're missing out on." Toby clapped him on the back. "But seriously. Give her a couple of hours, maybe even the whole day. If you still haven't heard from her, then call her."

"You're probably right. I guess I just—" he stuffed his hands in his pockets as his voice trailed off, unsure how to finish without letting too much slip, trying to mask the uncertainty.

Toby raised an eyebrow, a knowing smirk on his face. "My guy's got it bad."

"Shut the hell up," Owen cursed good-naturedly, whipping the bar mop at him. "Don't you have anything else to do before we open?"

"Naw, annoying you is always my top priority." He started laughing then and couldn't stop.

Owen flipped on the playlist, and a wailing guitar filled the room, the music drowning out his so-called friend and his laughter.

TWENTY-SEVEN

Owen Layne

The lunch crowd had been steady since the doors opened, and Owen found himself in a rhythm, unable to think about much else but the task at hand. But now the afternoon slump hit, and he tried to busy himself with mundane tasks like cleaning the beverage gun, washing an extra rack of glasses, and wiping down the back bar bottles. He concentrated hard on an extra sticky smudge, but Ava Morgahn continued to pop into his thoughts despite that.

Wiping the bar, he noticed Stella approaching at a fast clip, her cowboy boots tapping an angry cadence across the wooden floor.

"Hey, Owen. Got a minute?" There was a slight edge to her voice.

"For you?" He questioned Stella, noticing how her head tilted and her brow furrowed. Her telltale signs when something was up. It felt like a loaded question, much like the day six months ago she'd asked him if he had a minute and told him in no uncertain terms that he was needed at home. So he went, and then the bottom dropped out from under him.

The police were at his parent's home to deliver the news that his brother was dead. Surely, it couldn't be that bad. He hesitated for a split second, then decided to take the bait. Would he regret it? Probably. "Always."

"Smooth, aren't ya?"

"He likes to think he is," Toby said, emptying the trash. "But we all know I'm the one that's smooth as Tennessee Whiskey 'round here."

"Keep telling yourself that, buddy," Owen grinned despite himself, unable to shake a feeling of dread. "Why do you ask?"

Stella propped herself against the bar. "Got someone downstairs here to see ya."

"Oh?" He cocked an eyebrow, his pulse spiked, the dread turning into a little tickle of hope, thinking of Ava. "What does she look like?"

"She's pretty."

"How old?" Toby leaned in, curious. "Are we talkin' cougar or barely legal?"

Stella ignored the comment. "Rope off the second floor after you take the trash out. It's slow. We will keep everyone downstairs until the evening rush. No use stretching ourselves thin," she said, directing the comment to Toby. Tossing her silky black ponytail over her shoulder, she answered the question. "I would guess my age."

Toby snickered and mouthed cougar as he hefted the trash bag, backing into the kitchen. If looks could kill, Stella was throwing daggers. The swinging door cut off his laugh in mid-howl.

"Really?" Owen asked, surprised and disappointed. "Are you sure she's asking for me?"

"Yes. She knows your full name. Come to find out, she's the mother of the new server I hired."

"Really?" Owen asked, intrigued.

"Yeah. She started yesterday. Was good too, but didn't show today. Who does that?" Stella didn't wait for his reply. "Damn hard to hire good help that sticks." She rolled her shoulders as if to ward off the negative vibes. "Anyway, I told her I would see if you were available. I can shoo her off if you don't want to talk."

The staff consistently looked out for each other when someone asked for a specific person. It always seemed innocent enough, a friend stopping by or a regular wanting to chat. But they couldn't be too sure with everything happening in Nashville.

"How did she seem?"

"Normal enough, but a little nervous, and… desperate, if you ask me. Or maybe embarrassed. I would be if my daughter didn't show up for work," Stella said with a flash of temper in her eyes and a jerk of her thumb toward the balcony. "See for yourself. She's sitting at the bar, waitin'. She said it was *very* important. Whatever *it* is."

He came out from behind the second-floor bar, and they walked to the railing together.

"Third one from the end. You tell me. Do you want me to say you just left? Or do you want to go down and see what she wants?"

His heart lurched. "Be right back."

"I guess that means you'll talk to her," Stella called after him when he didn't look back. "See if you can find out why her daughter didn't show."

Owen descended the stairs quickly, skirted the outside of the room, then cut diagonally to the bar, stopping short. "Mrs. Morgahn?" he questioned.

She spun on her stool, her eyes wide with desperation, and looked up at him, a surge of relief visibly flooding her.

"Oh, thank heavens it's you," she breathed, practically throwing herself at him, wrapping her arms around him in a tight, frantic hug.

"What are you doing here? I thought you were leaving yesterday." He eased her off. Holding her in place, he lifted his brow with concern. "Is everything alright?"

"I was, but then I didn't. And no." She glanced around. "Is there somewhere we could talk privately for a few minutes?"

Thinking quickly, he gestured toward the stairs from which he had just come. "This way."

Upstairs, he tucked her neatly in a booth. The question of why Ava wasn't with her lay on the tip of his tongue. "Can I get you anything? A glass of water, soda, or something stronger? Are you hungry? When's the last time you ate?" She looked pale, and he couldn't decide if it was from lack of sleep or food.

She folded her hands, rested them on the table, and he noticed them tremble. "Water—water would be fine. Thank you."

"I'll be right back." He skirted the bar, and Stella, as she stood with her arms crossed and eyed the other woman. He poked his head into the small kitchenette, called the central kitchen, and ordered a quesadilla and some fries. Then, he filled a glass with ice and water.

Stella murmured as she breezed past, "Find out why her daughter didn't come to work. If it's not a damn good reason, she can tell her to consider her fired and to not even think about performing on one of my stages."

"Calm down, Stella," he said, his voice tight. His mind raced—did Ava have a job here? Was that why she'd been so secretive? A dozen unanswered questions tumbled through his mind. His jaw clenched. "I'll find out."

He slid into the booth and handed Kelleigh the glass. He waited for her to take a sip, watching her silently, trying to judge her frame of mind. What on earth could have brought her here—alone? His stomach twisted. *Nothing good.*

"Where do I start?" she asked with a weary smile.

"How about from the beginning?" Owen offered. "I'm assuming this has something to do with Ava since she's not here with you." *And didn't come to work.*

"It does." She shifted on the bench. "I think Ava is missing."

He lifted his eyebrows. "Why would you think that?"

"She didn't come home from work last night."

Owen sat back against the booth, surprised. "When was the last time you heard from her?"

"Monday morning, before she went to work."

"Really?" Owen asked, taken aback, unsure if he should reveal that he had been with her part of the night.

Kelleigh nodded. "She never came home last night." She reached for the glass and ran a shaky finger around the outside, wiping off condensation. "Something awful has happened. I just know it."

"How do you know she didn't come home? I thought you were leaving right after she went to work."

"That was the plan, but then there was this list..." Kelleigh's voice caught for a moment. She sucked in a deep breath and proceeded to tell him everything.

When the quesadilla and fries arrived, Kelleigh fell silent. He thanked the server as she placed the food on the table between them.

"Please," Owen indicated. "Help yourself. You look like you're starving." When she didn't move, he separated the appetizer plates the waitress had left and put a triangle of quesadilla on each, sliding one plate in front of her.

"I don't think I can eat anything," she said.

"I get that, but at least try." He knew exactly how she felt—sick to her stomach because he was too. He scolded himself for thinking poorly of Ava when she could be missing, hurt, or worse. He wouldn't go there yet. He had to believe there was a logical explanation for where she was. But first things first, Mrs. Morgahn needed to eat. She looked like she was about ready to collapse.

Owen pushed the fry basket toward her. "Let's call Officer Ransick and see if we can get an update on the situation. Do you still have his card?"

Kelleigh nodded.

He watched her. The anxiety that surrounded her was almost palpable. He could feel the dread creeping in like an unwelcome guest.

"Good. You call him." He picked up a fry and bit into it, the crunch a contrast to the growing unease gnawing at him. "So Ava's job, where she works," he confirmed, trying to wrap his head around what was happening, "Is here at Cognac Creek?"

"Yes, and I confirmed with the manager that she didn't show up this morning. She didn't seem very happy about it. I'm afraid Ava might lose her job."

"Let me handle Stella. First things first." He could see the worry in her eyes as she nodded. He pulled out his phone. "What about social media?"

Confused, Kelleigh asked, "What about it?"

"Have you checked it? Maybe Ava posted something about where she is or might be."

"No, I haven't. I didn't think of that."

"Mind if I do?"

"Of course not."

Owen pulled up his social media and then searched for Ava. Once he located her profile, he started scrolling. At first, it was just casual, but the more he looked, the more his unease grew. Her pictures were smiling, carefree, and surrounded by friends. He registered that she posted regularly—two to three times a day, every day, religiously. She always posted first thing in the morning. There's nothing yet today. That was his first real clue that something was wrong.

He clicked on her most recent post yesterday evening. She was on Broadway, grinning at the camera, her eyes bright. Then it hit him. She's standing at the corner of Broadway and Second, waiting...for him. His stomach tightened. His thumb moved faster, scrolling through her feed with a growing dread that he couldn't shake. Why hadn't she posted anything today? Maybe Kelleigh was right.

A wave of panic surged through him as the silence in her feed screamed out at him—no posts, check-ins, or updates. Owen stopped scrolling and stared at the screen. His hands suddenly became clammy, the weight of the situation settling over him like a thick fog. He requested to follow and sent her a quick text, hoping there'd been some mistake and that she'd answer.

While he did that, Kelleigh tried to call Officer Ransick. She waited patiently while she was connected, but the call went straight to voicemail. He could see the tension ripple through her as she left a message, her voice shaking slightly.

He looked up Ava's friend Molly on social media to stay on task. "The name of Ava's close friend here in Nashville is Molly Calhoun, right?" He held out his phone so she could see a photo of the woman.

"Yes! That's her," Kelleigh said with relief evident in her voice.

"We can call Ava's friend through the account." He tapped the phone icon, but it went straight to voicemail. The pit in his stomach deepened. He handed his cell to Kelleigh, urgency coiling in his gut. "Here, leave her a message."

When she finished, she returned the phone to him.

"Any other ideas?" The question lingered in the air between them like a storm cloud.

"I don't know," he answered truthfully.

"I refuse just to sit and wait around," she stated, her eyes filled with fear but fueled by the determination of a mother who wouldn't give up hope.

TWENTY-EIGHT

Ava Morgahn

Slowly, ever so slowly, she came into consciousness. Her head throbbed. Her mouth was a desert, her tongue like sandpaper. Her eyes felt gritty and dry, as if filled with dust. She rolled her eyeballs under closed lids, desperate to moisten them before prying them open. Taking a breath, she blinked and little by little opened her eyes. But whether open or closed, the darkness enveloped her like a suffocating shroud, a sense of dread creeping in.

Where was she? The thought nagged at her, but she couldn't focus. Images formed but didn't solidify. She couldn't remember. Her thoughts were scattered, her brain foggy. Ava struggled to raise her head, and a wave of nausea swamped her. It hurt too much to think, to lift her entire frame. So she wouldn't.

Are you sleeping? The voice crept into her subconscious.

A dark image wavered in front of her, humming an eerie tune. A firm hand held her face, fingers pressed hard, squeezing at her cheeks, forcing her lips apart. A liquid was poured into her mouth, causing her to cough and sputter. Despite everything, she choked down most of it.

"Good girl," the voice murmured, sending a chill down her back.

Water dripped from her chin as her head fell forward, her shoulders slumped, and her eyelids shuttered closed, pulled down by the heavy weight of sleep. The sound of a distant whimper and a haunting melody drifted through her head: *Are you sleeping? Ava Lynn, Ava Lynn. The river is cunning. You should be running.*

TWENTY-NINE

Detective Wyatt Lockhart

Wyatt sat at his desk, sifting through the victims' files, searching for any connections. It had taken weeks to identify the first two victims. Each woman was in her early twenties, single, and attractive, but beyond that, the parallels faded, seeming to have no link to Nashville and very little to no family.

Despite coming from different states, how they ended up in the Cumberland River was a complete mystery to him. Had they been in town for business or pleasure? Were they visiting, or had they moved here like so many others, hoping to find a job in the booming music industry?

In a way, he saw that as a possible link—a tentative one, at best. They seemed to fit a pattern—single, with no strong family ties. This eerie connection only deepened the mystery of their deaths, suggesting their paths had somehow converged in Nashville, possibly at the hands of the Cumberland Killer. But once in Nashville, the trail grew cold. It was as if, once here, they had simply disappeared—only to resurface later in the Cumberland.

The more he read, the more it became clear that this couldn't be a coincidence. These deaths were deliberate, each woman seemingly chosen on purpose. Selected. Hand-picked. The link —not just between the two women he was investigating, but between all five victims was just beyond his grasp.

He leaned forward, his mind racing. What was he missing?

The pattern was deliberate, chosen for... he wasn't sure yet. There had to be something deeper... something darker at play than just their looks because other than their bindings around their appendages, there was no sign of sexual assault or physical abuse.

Had they been friends lured here by something or someone? Social media offered very few clues as if a dark shadow had fallen over their lives the minute they decided to come to Nashville. It was as though they had been erased, vanishing for the last weeks, only to reappear when pulled from the river. What chilling secrets lay hidden in those days? What unspeakable experiences haunted their final hours?

His mind was on an endless loop.

Wyatt tossed the latest folder onto his desk and rubbed his tired eyes, feeling the weight of the day pressing down on him. It was time for a break. He leaned back, stretching his tired muscles, and glanced at the clock. It was past ten, and the department was vacant except for a few people. He knew he should go home, but nothing of importance was there, just a messy townhouse and an empty bed. Not very tempting.

He glanced at the folders, decided to give it another hour, and then call it quits for the night. He grabbed his empty coffee cup and headed out for a fresh cup.

As he passed through the lobby, voices snagged his attention from the reception area.

"My daughter is missing. Surely someone else in this precinct knows something or can help me besides him."

"Ma'am, I'm sorry. No one else is aware of the situation."

Something about the urgency in the woman's tone pulled him in. He hesitated, instinctively drawn to the scene unfolding just beyond the corner. He paused, hoping he wouldn't regret getting involved.

"Excuse me, Officer Dour. Is there something I can help you with?" he asked, keeping himself partially hidden behind the wall, reluctant to engage with the situation fully. The files on his desk were calling his name.

The young rookie turned to him with a frazzled smile. "Yes, sir." Her voice lowered as she stepped away from the counter. "They insist on speaking to Officer Ransick, but he's gone home for the day."

Wyatt inhaled deeply, then let it out in a huff. *Always Ransick.* "Give me the short version of their situation."

"The woman's daughter never came home from work Monday night. She called 9-1-1, and Ransick was the responding officer, but hasn't followed up with her."

"Has her daughter returned home?"

"No, she hasn't," Officer Dour said reluctantly.

Wyatt furrowed his brow. "Did you check the dispatcher's reports?"

"No, sir. I haven't had a chance to yet."

He nodded, knowing full well that the rookie was in over her head. "Let me see if I can get to the bottom of this."

He rounded the corner and took in the man quickly with his well-trained eye. Late twenties. Cognac Creek logo on his black polo. He looked familiar, but couldn't place him just yet. His eyes flicked to the woman, and he had an instant recognition. The woman from the Dunkin' Donuts—mango pineapple refresher with green tea—her drink coming to him quickly.

"Hello again," he said as a way of greeting. "I'm surprised to see you."

A ghost of a smile played across her lips as she recognized him. "I could say the same thing. I didn't realize you were a police officer."

"Detective," Wyatt corrected. Making a split-second decision, he said, "Why don't you come back and tell me what's happening." He held her gaze, feeling that unexpected connection. Without taking his eyes off her, he addressed the rookie. "Dour, if you could please buzz them through."

"Yes, sir."

They were let in, and Wyatt waited for them in the hallway. "I'm sorry we haven't officially met. I'm Detective Lockhart."

"Kelleigh Morgahn. And this," Kelleigh indicated the man beside her, "is Owen Layne."

They shook hands.

"Layne?" Wyatt questioned. "You're Officer Dylan Layne's brother."

Owen held his gaze. "Yes, sir."

Wyatt could see the resemblance, remembered a brief encounter with him at the funeral and had spoken to him several times on the phone. "Again, I'm sorry for your loss. I can't say it enough, your brother was a good man and an excellent cop. I want you to know that the investigation is still ongoing. I won't rest until we have found the culprit."

"Thank you, sir. I appreciate that."

"Such a damn shame." Wyatt's comment hung between them as if lost in the moment, caught between what was and what is. The haunting details of that tragic morning replayed relentlessly in his mind. It had been an early December day, crisp and quiet, when Officer Layne and his loyal K9 set out for their routine morning run. The early hour was still dark, and fate took a cruel turn. In a split second, a vehicle sped by. A hit-and-run. The driver was indifferent to the devastation left in their wake. Officer Layne lay lifeless at the scene, his dreams and duties extinguished in an instant.

The injured, heartbroken, and fiercely loyal German Shepherd had fought against the attempts to separate him from his fallen partner, a desperate struggle that echoed their bond. Despite his injuries, the dog's instincts to protect had surged.

"How's Gunner?" Wyatt asked quietly.

"Physically, he is recovered."

Wyatt gave Owen a solemn nod and cleared his throat. "I was just about to get some coffee. Would either of you like a cup or a bottle of water?"

"No, thank you," Kelleigh said.

"I'm good," Owen offered.

Wyatt escorted them down the hall. "Let's go to the conference room." He indicated the large table and chairs. "Make yourself comfortable."

They sat together at the far end of the expansive table, the tension in the room palpable. He placed his empty cup on the table and then settled into the chair opposite, his curiosity piqued about the matter they had come in for.

"Why don't you tell me what's going on? Last time we spoke, you were busy checking off items on your daughter's to-do list. What's changed since then?" Wyatt asked.

Kelleigh leaned forward, gripping the edge of the table like a lifeline. Her eyes reflected a mixture of determination and vulnerability. She took a deep breath, the weight of what she was about to say pressed down on her, and began to unravel the details that had brought them there.

"Why don't you go and get some rest," Wyatt offered, taking in Kelleigh. "You look exhausted."

"I am, but I don't really want to go back to the apartment alone."

"I understand, but you need some sleep," Wyatt said. "You'll feel better and think clearer. Maybe remember something Ava said before this all happened."

She folded her hands and dropped them in her lap. "I guess you're right. I just feel so helpless. Right now everything seems like a horrible dream. I'm afraid if I go to sleep and wake back up to this nightmare…"

He placed his hand on top of hers and let the warmth spread between them. "Believe me, I understand." Before she sucked him completely in and let his heart cross a line that he had spent years behind, Wyatt removed his hand. He always hated this part. When the victims' families felt disoriented and defeated, mirroring his uncertainties, he couldn't say anything to improve the empty void or the waiting.

Now, the work shifted to him and his department. Even that didn't make him feel any better. Usually, he liked having control and wanted to put the puzzle pieces of each case together. But the department's number of unsolved cases had been slowly creeping up over the past year, a constant reminder of the pressure weighing on his shoulders. And, like it or not, this was another young woman who fit the profile of his drowning victims. He couldn't shake the feeling that if he didn't locate Ava soon, he might find her face down in Cumberland.

Wyatt needed to dig deeper into how a killer would know these women were all relatively new to the city? What type of access to them did he have?

He shook himself mentally. He needed to get Kelleigh out of here, away from the police department, for a few hours so he could work and concentrate. With her here, he would never be able to focus.

"How about I let you go for now?" He rose from the table and hoped they would do the same. When they did, he continued. "I'll keep in touch."

Kelleigh reached out and took his hand. "Thank you. I can't tell you how much I appreciate everything."

"I'm just doing my job, ma'am." But with her, he wasn't so sure that's all it was. The warmth of her hand against his sent a rush of something deeper through him. He didn't want to let go. He was acutely aware of how soft her hand was in his, and a longing flickered within him—an ache he hadn't expected. At that moment, with her gaze searching his, he felt a connection that transcended duty and pulled him in like a gentle tide.

He reluctantly released her hand. "You have my number if you need anything."

Wyatt noticed the brief hesitation in her gaze, the way her breath caught slightly as she held on just a moment longer than necessary. The connection was soothing and comforting, and for a heartbeat, everything else faded away. She seemed both grateful and surprised by the moment's intensity as he was, and he couldn't help but wonder if she felt the same longing that flickered to life within him.

"I do."

"I'll be in touch."

As he watched them walk away, that sense of longing tightened in his chest. He prayed he would be in touch soon—and with good news. The weight of their unspoken connection hung in the air, a silent promise that made the distance between them feel almost unbearable. He couldn't shake the feeling that this moment was just the beginning, a fragile thread weaving their lives together in ways he could hardly comprehend.

THIRTY

The conscience was tricky, like a tightrope stretched over an endless chasm.

On the one side, or in this case, hand, the conscience seemed simple—a steadfast compass pointing north toward right and away from wrong, directing a person toward good. But those who had spent long enough walking a thin line hovering between good and evil, chased by their own demons, knew that the voice of reason whispered quietly and was easily ignored, meaning everything could come crashing down with a single mistake.

A shaky hand lifted papers, bills, and overdrafts off a cluttered desk.

The numbers screamed out from the invoices like the flashing neon signs that hung in downtown Nashville, one amount larger than the next.

Yet, there was a smug satisfaction with the knowledge that an unknown padded account made the risks necessary and worthwhile.

The numbers weren't what kept sleep from coming. It was the faces that haunted—the secret those individuals covered.

The bottle was opened, and pills were dumped out into a damp palm. If sleep wouldn't come naturally, then it would be induced. Swallowing them in a gulp, a face surfaced in the mind's eye.

The first had been a friend that had turned into a foe. *Don't think about it.* It doesn't matter now. What was done was done. Resentment and jealousy surged. This was survival. Contaminated and convoluted as it was.

Each woman was lodged in a different corner of the mind. Friend or stranger, it didn't matter. They served a purpose, or at least that's what the mind repeated to the conscience to convince, to pacify the tip of guilt that tried to surge.

Five women were easily lured. Easily manipulated. Easily claimed to cover a secret—a means to an end.

But would it end?

On the other hand... an actual hand was held out, studied, and fingers were used to tick off names... Five fingers for five dead women, and they weren't enough. *It was never enough,* the conscience whispered. Greed and fear dominated this world. Add in jealousy... The good hand was now in play. Two more fingers ticked up. That trap had been sprung. The monster had been unleashed.

THIRTY-ONE

Detective Wyatt Lockhart

Donuts. Wyatt could smell them a mile away, so he could think of nothing else when the pink box passed his door. He sat back and stretched. He had been at it all night, and now it was morning, and he was starving. One donut wouldn't hurt him, he argued with himself.

He walked down the hall and snagged a pastry from the kitchen, choosing a chocolate-covered cream-filled confection. The more sugar, the better, he thought. If he was going to splurge, he would make it count.

He took a bite and sunk his teeth into the gooey goodness. Yeast and sugar attacked his senses. Almost immediately, he felt more alive than he had in hours. Instantly, his mood brightened.

Ransick met him in the hall, and his light dimmed a little.

"Here's the latest report on the third victim pulled from the Cumberland. Seems she is an only child. Parents have been deceased for the past five years due to a car accident—no other living relatives."

Wyatt took the folder, tucked it under his arm, and took another bite of his donut as he walked back to his office, cream oozing out the sides of his mouth, determined not to let the man ruin his sugar high.

He tossed the folder on the desk and reached for a pile

of leftover napkins from his midnight run to McDonald's. After shoveling the whole thing into his mouth, he wiped his mouth and sticky fingers with the napkins. He discarded them in the trash, pulled out his chair, and sat. Again.

If he didn't solve these cases soon, he would have to forgo the donuts and the late-night fast food runs. The stress, the junk food, and the lack of sleep were starting to catch up with his gut. He deliberately pushed the idea of a second donut out of his mind.

He flipped the folder open and scanned the records. It was just like Ransick said. Not that he didn't believe him, but he just had to see it for himself.

He was vaguely aware that Ransick hovered right inside his office door.

"What?" Wyatt growled.

Ransick shrugged. "I was just curious to see if you saw a pattern."

A pattern? Wyatt lifted a bushy eyebrow. He quickly scanned through the report, specifically targeting the identifying marks. It was blank.

He must be more tired than he thought. Was there something else he wasn't seeing? Or was the kid just being cocky? He'd play along.

"Do you mean the one where the women are all Caucasian? Or the one where they are all in their early twenties, college graduates, and not from Nashville. Or the pattern of them all ending up in the Cumberland, floating down the river until we drug them out? Which exactly are you referring to?" Wyatt grumbled.

Ransick held up his hands. "Okay, so you are aware. The guy has a type. I was just trying to help."

Wyatt sucked in a deep breath and relented. He knew there was no reason to be so irritated with Ransick. "I'm sorry. It's just been a long night. I need coffee."

"Did you want me to make a fresh pot?"

"No. I need to run out and get some. Get out of the office and take a short drive. Maybe then I can think a little clearer. "

"Sounds like a good idea to me. Let me know if you need anything—like help on the Cumberland Killer case."

"Right," Wyatt said, irritated, grabbing his keys off the desk and walking down the hall.

Once outside, the sunshine and the heat hit him. It was going to be another sultry day in Tennessee. He jumped in his car and went to the closest Dunkin. He was going in when he thought of Kelleigh Morgahn and his brief encounter with her just a few days ago. How quickly the tables had turned.

Wyatt had been instantly drawn to her, an undeniable magnetism that gripped him from the moment they met. Even now, as he delved into the case of her missing daughter, his thoughts kept spiraling back to her. Her delicate features and those haunting hazel eyes stirred something deep within him— a fierce desire to protect and comfort. It was a feeling he rarely experienced to such depth, a primal urge to wrap her in his arms and shield her from the pain. The intensity of his longing unsettled him, leaving him wrestling with emotions he hadn't expected to confront.

He couldn't imagine what Kelleigh was going through, especially since he had no children. It wasn't for lack of desire; his first marriage had shown him the strain his job as a police officer put on family life. His wife couldn't bear the thought of him getting hurt, and then it happened—her worst fear came true, he was shot.

After a week in the hospital and a month recovering at home, returning to work felt like one of his best and worst days. His colleagues welcomed him back with open arms, but while he was grateful, he was still sidelined, only able to push papers.

When he came home, expecting a comforting meal, a big hug,

a how was your first day back kind of conversation, he found a note instead—his wife had left and taken everything. She couldn't fathom how he could go back to work after nearly dying; the daily fear was too much for her. That was the end of their marriage.

Wyatt had dated on and off since, but none of those relationships lasted. He found women fascinating yet predictable, wanting security, a home, and children. He understood their desires but knew that his job would always come first for him.

Or at least he thought so until the other day in the coffee shop. Until those hazel eyes meet his. For the first time in over thirty years, he thought about something other than his job and what he would have for dinner.

How could a woman do that, he wondered. How could she flip a switch in him that had been dormant for decades and rip open a longing so deep he wanted to retire tomorrow?

He didn't know, but the moment he saw her standing in the precinct lobby, he knew he needed to find out. And then the inevitable happened: she was there for the disappearance of her daughter. The moment was fleeting, and he had to put his feelings on the back burner. He had to concentrate on the case and finding her daughter.

And that's what he vowed to do.

He approached the counter and ordered his usual, wishing Kelleigh had been in line in front of him. He stepped aside. He could get her a refresher and take it to her to see how she was doing this morning. He quickly squashed the idea, nipping the thought before it could fester and morph into something more. He couldn't face her—not yet, anyway. He needed something good to report. He needed to concentrate on the case, and when he had concrete evidence, he'd call her or stop by.

His name was called, and he retrieved his coffee from the counter, went back outside, and decided to swing by Cognac Creek. He had a series of crucial details to unravel, each one hopefully leading him closer to the truth. First, he needed to confirm whether she had shown up for work on Monday. Then, he'd have to trace the hours she spent at the restaurant, piecing together who she interacted with and how the day unfolded. He needed to pinpoint when she left. Knowing that would make it easier to follow her progression. He needed to track down anyone who might have seen her go, or perhaps even been with her when she walked out the door.

Once he had all the facts—confirming she had arrived, done her job, and left—he would need to answer one key question: Did she leave of her own free will? If so, perhaps there was a clue in how she departed. But if she hadn't gone willingly, that could suggest something darker. In either case, someone must have seen something—he just had to find out who.

With a plan and an address, he got into the vehicle and tucked Kelleigh's pretty face into the recess of his mind. As he pulled out of the lot, he indeed hoped she would stay there so he could do his job.

He parked the car in an alley behind the refurbished old brick building, slid his sunglasses into place as he got out, and closed the door of his unmarked SUV. The sound of the door clicking shut was lost in the din of the nearby street traffic. He adjusted his jacket, the weight of the task ahead pressing on him.

As he slowly turned in the back alley, his experienced eyes scanned the area. His gaze flicked to a corner near the loading dock —there, mounted high on the wall, was a security camera. Another one was positioned near the rear entrance. He made a mental note. He'd need to check the angle of the camera and the footage later, but for now, his focus shifted.

He moved, making his way toward the front of the building, his mind already piecing together the questions he needed to ask. Depending on what door Ava had used, the security cameras outside the building could offer valuable insights.

Wyatt walked into a bustling hive of activity, slipped off his shades, and let his eyes adjust to the dim interior as he scanned the restaurant.

A teenager stood behind the hostess stand, dressed in jeans and a black Cognac Creek T-shirt. Her blonde hair was pulled back in a sleek ponytail, and a wad of gum sat in her cheek. "Can I help you?" she asked as she peered up at him under thick lashes.

He smiled at her. "Yes, I'm looking for Stella Doyle. Would she be available?"

The hostess snapped her gum and raised her pierced eyebrow, "Le'me check."

She spoke into a headset. "Stella?" She paused, waiting for a response, watching him with curious blue eyes. "I got a silver fox at the hostess stand. Wants to talk to you." She formed a big pink bubble between her lips, stuck a finger in the middle before it could pop, and pulled the gum out into a long pink elastic string, wrapping it around her finger as she listened. She stuck the wad back in her mouth and smiled at him. "She'll be right down."

"Thank you," Wyatt said. Silver fox? He wondered what that was code for.

True to her word, Stella Doyle descended the sweeping staircase that pressed against the outside wall of the second floor. Stella's stride was purposeful, each step deliberate and powerful as her cowboy boots clicked steadily across the polished hardwood floor. Her gaze swept the room, and without a word, her servers parted for her. There was no mistaking it, Stella commanded the space, a force of nature who had earned every ounce of the respect she obtained.

Her outfit and hairstyle mirrored the teenager's, but that was where the similarities ended. There was a subtle maturity to her in the fine lines around her eyes and mouth, and the knowing look behind the sharp, dark eyes that deliberately took him in. She gave him a reserved smile, and those fine lines creased slightly. "I'm Stella Doyle." She stuck out her hand.

"Detective Lockhart. It's a pleasure to meet you," he said, accepting her hand. Wyatt pulled out his badge and a business card and handed the latter to her.

"I would like to say the pleasure is all mine." She glanced at the badge and then the card. "But the jury is still out," she said coolly.

He tucked his badge back in his jacket pocket. "Is there somewhere we could speak privately?"

She didn't hesitate. "Follow me."

They wove through patrons and tables, following the maze back to her office. She opened the door and ushered him in. "Please," she indicated a wooden chair that matched the others on the restaurant floor.

Wyatt sat, his practiced gaze sweeping over the small, meticulously arranged office. The space was tight, yet every detail seemed carefully considered, from the personal pictures on the wall to the ceramic boot with the Cognac Creek logo stamped on it holding her pens. The only furniture in the room consisted of the worn chair he occupied and a large, solid desk crafted from repurposed wood, its rustic charm complemented by the sleek, modern office chair that sat behind it. The space felt purposeful and unpretentious.

His attention shifted to her. She moved with an effortless grace, circumnavigating the desk with poise. With a fluid motion, she settled into the chair across from him, her presence adding an air of calm authority to the room.

"Now." She folded her hands and placed her elbows on the top of the desk. "Why don't you tell me what brings you in."

"I'm here about a new employee you just hired."

"You'll have to be more specific. I have recently hired several. It is the season for it, after all."

He lifted a brow in question.

"Tourist season," she explained.

"I understand." He leveled his gaze, wanting direct eye contact with her when he said Ava's name to judge her reaction. "I'm here about Ava Morgahn."

He saw the flicker of recognition at the name and then a smidgen of irritation as her forehead furrowed slightly between her eyes. She quickly smoothed out her features.

"What about her?"

"Did you hire her?"

"Yes."

"When did she start?"

"Monday." Stella leaned forward. "Listen Officer Lockhart."

"Detective," he corrected.

"Detective," she smiled, trying to cover the annoyance he could feel festering within her. "If there is something specific you want to know, just spit it out. I don't have time for your games." She pointed to the door. "As you can see, we are very busy."

When he didn't answer right away, she started to rise.

"You seem slightly annoyed at the mention of Miss Morgahn. Why?"

Stella straightened. "Because... I go through the process of fishing through resumes and applications, interviewing, hiring, and training a new staff member, only to have them work one day and not show the next. You have no idea how frustrating that can be. It's especially annoying when it happens more than once, and with someone like Ava—it's a big loss."

"Care to explain?"

"Ava had extensive experience and blended seamlessly with the other staff members. She was a good fit from the minute she walked through my door. A fast learner, polite, and capable of working independently with minimal instruction," Stella ticked off Ava's attributes. "Not to mention, she had a natural talent for singing and the patience to wait tables—willing to pay her dues for the chance to perform on one of my stages. Or so she said."

Wyatt could tell Stella was gearing up with plenty more to say, anger mounting.

"I stuck my neck out for her. Even passed up a couple of other locals to wait for her after I received her job application. And then she works one day." Stella threw up her arms. "Who does that?"

"Why do you think she didn't come back?"

"The hell if I know," Stella said, clearly frustrated. "Probably found what she thought was a better gig."

"Did you try to contact her when she didn't show up on Tuesday?"

"You're damn right I did." Stella shifted in her chair. "Listen, I'm as human as the next person. I know things happen. People get sick, oversleep, cars break down, and maybe she bit off more than she could chew being far from home, but damn it, call and let me know. I'll work with anybody. I just need to be kept in the loop. That's all I ask."

"So she didn't say anything when she left for the night on Monday, indicating that she wouldn't be back?"

"No. I was under the impression, and I think everyone else was too, that she had a good day. She was a great asset to the team. No one was more shocked than I was when she didn't show up Tuesday. I called and got voicemail. I also texted her twice. That's my limit. I'll be damned if I have the time to call around to all her contact numbers and track her down." She shifted her mouse and tapped the key on her computer, ready to dismiss him. "I'm their boss, the bar manager, not their mother."

It was time to level with Stella Doyle, Wyatt thought. She seemed genuine. "What if I told you I think she is missing?"

Stella leaned back in her chair, the anger visibly deflating. She tapped her fingers on the arm of her chair, thinking. "That I would believe and it makes more sense. Her not showing for any other reason just doesn't fly with me. She was too invested, even after one day, too excited to be here to blow me off without a word."

Wyatt leaned slightly closer, his tone shifting to reflect the seriousness of the matter. "I am currently investigating the disappearance of Ava Morgahn. This is quite a serious situation, Ms. Doyle. You or someone on your staff may have been the last person to speak to Ava." Wyatt let the gravity of the situation settle over the compact space. "Do you know if she had words with anyone on staff?"

Stella shook her head. "Like I said, she meshed well with the others. And believe me when I tell you I have a pretty good pulse on my staff."

"What about an irate customer?"

"Not that I'm aware of."

Wyatt believed it. He ran through the other questions he had to cover his bases, then shifted gears. "I'm assuming you have security cameras."

"We do," she replied.

"I'll need to review your surveillance camera footage."

The bar manager looked down at her computer, her expression shifting from routine focus to attentive engagement. A mix of concern and professionalism washed over her features. Her fingers danced over the keyboard, pulling up the relevant tab.

"I understand the gravity of this situation. Let me ensure you can have access to the footage you need." She paused, considering the logistics.

"Do you know what door Ava would have left from when she went home for the evening?"

Stella tapped away. "We have cameras at the front door, on every floor, and in the back alley. Most of our employees come and go through the back door. It's easy access to their lockers and to clock in and out."

She tapped the keys again and then turned her monitor to angle it so he could see. "But I know Ava came through the front door in the morning since she was new. All new employees co." She touched the screen with her index finger, pointing. "Here. That's her arriving on Monday."

Scooting forward to get a better look, he said, "Let it advance."

Stella moved her mouse and clicked play. Wyatt watched Ava come through the front door, smiling and clearly happy to be there.

"This is exactly what I need."

There was a tentative knock at the office door simultaneously as Wyatt's phone chimed.

Stella paused the video. "Come in."

The blonde from the hostess stand poked her head in. "Sorry, Stella." She cracked her gum, and her eyes drifted to Wyatt. "Didn't mean to interrupt, but we have a sitch," she hooked her thumb over her shoulder. "Out front."

"I'll be right there." She stood. "I'm sorry, Detective Lockhart. I'm going to have to excuse myself. Apparently, there's a situation."

"I understand." He glanced at his phone. "Looks like I have one as well. Would it be possible for you to forward that video and a couple of other angles to my email and the videos from the alley so I can go through it at my convenience?"

"Of course."

"Thank you. My email is on my business card."

Stella extended her hand. "Consider it done, Detective."

"I appreciate it."

"And please keep me in the loop. I did like Ava Morgahn and would love to have her back. I sincerely hope everything is alright."

"Me too."

THIRTY-TWO

Kelleigh Morgahn

Kelleigh turned over, squinting from the sun that shone through the blinds. Where was she? Then it hit her like a wave crashing down. The apartment. Nashville. It all came flooding back.

Ava was missing. She sat up and listened—the room was quiet. She glanced at her phone. It was well past noon. How in the world had she slept so long?

She hadn't slept much the last few days, and the stress of missing Ava and not knowing if she was alright was taking its toll.

She threw back the covers and tiptoed to the bedroom door, peering into the living room. She wasn't sure what she had expected or hoped for, but it certainly wasn't this emptiness.

She looked around and took in the small apartment. The soft blues of the couch, rug, and drapes made the room peaceful and relaxing. The sunny and modern space, the soothing decor juxtaposing the storm of emotions inside her.

She grabbed a mug from the small counter and placed it under the coffee maker. After inserting a K-cup, she waited patiently for the cup to fill.

She wasn't sure what to do, where to go, or how to continue helping search for Ava. She felt useless, lost, and like a stranger in someone else's home. And that's truly what she was. Ava hadn't been here long enough to make the shared space hers.

Kelleigh removed the steaming cup, took a tentative sip, and looked out the window, trying to decide her next move.

The sun's warmth felt comforting as Kelleigh took a moment to breathe, trying to shake off the heaviness in her chest. One step at a time. First, she needed a shower. She set the coffee cup down and went to the bathroom, mentally preparing herself for the day ahead.

As the water cascaded over her, she let her thoughts drift. Images of Ava flooded her mind—laughter, shared secrets, and late-night talks that felt like a lifeline to the daughter she longed for. She scrubbed her hair, trying to focus, but the worry returned. Ava was missing, and every minute felt like a lifetime.

Once dressed and feeling somewhat human, Kelleigh returned to the kitchen and made another cup, savoring the moment of normalcy amidst the chaos. As the second cup did its magic, she flipped through her phone, scrolling through messages, praying for a text from Ava. She searched the news articles, but there was nothing about her disappearance or the Cumberland Killer.

The thought of contacting Detective Lockhart again crossed her mind, but she hesitated. He was doing his best, but Kelleigh felt a nagging sense that she needed to take matters into her own hands. Maybe she could retrace Ava's steps. There had to be someone who might know something or have seen something.

Kelleigh finished her coffee and grabbed her phone, deciding to text a few of Ava's friends from home. She needed leads, any hint of where Ava could be. After a few minutes, she received several responses, but nothing concrete. Frustrated, she tossed her phone onto the bed and took a deep breath.

"Okay," she whispered to herself. "Think."

Determined, she picked up her phone again and searched for information on Cognac Creek. This wasn't just about finding Ava anymore; it was about piecing together what was happening, and the bar was a crucial part of that puzzle. After all, this was possibly the last place she had been seen. She searched for

Cognac Creek on social media and discovered it ranked among the top destinations, with the best spots for dining and live music in Nashville, receiving rave reviews. Not a single negative comment could be found about the establishment.

Kelleigh's stomach dropped. That was a dead end, but she didn't know where else to look or where to start. She certainly couldn't sit here all day. She would go crazy. She didn't want to be alone. Detective Lockhart came to mind. Being with him was the only place she felt comfort these past few days. She grabbed her bag and took a deep breath.

Right or wrong, she needed to see him and feel his presence— his warmth and steady reassurance, even if it was from across the room. The thought of being with him made everything else seem distant, less real. She headed out the door in hopes he had the answers she needed.

THIRTY-THREE

Detective Wyatt Lockhart

The car was found in the far corner of the parking garage, a block off Broadway. A lone security guard had stumbled upon it during his routine patrol, his eyes drawn to the missing license plates—a detail that seemed too deliberate to be overlooked. The front and back license plates had been hastily removed and discarded carelessly in a nearby trash bin, thrown away without a second thought. It wasn't much, but it was something—something that could be traced. The fact that someone had gone through the trouble of removing the plates, likely to prevent the car from being linked quickly to Ava, yet hadn't bothered to take them far raised more questions than it answered. Why go through the effort at all?

Wyatt felt a chill run through him despite the heat as his mind raced, the unsettling thought taking shape. Was it possible Ava had left on her own? The idea lingered, gnawing at him. Had she vanished willingly, driven by something he couldn't see, something she hadn't shared? The car, hidden away in a quiet corner, seemed to tell a story of someone trying to disappear—quietly, carefully.

But why? He had just seen a happy woman entering Cognac Creek on video. What would have pushed her to leave? He couldn't shake the feeling that something was off, that this wasn't just a case of someone walking away. Whatever the truth, the missing plates were just the beginning.

Had they been interrupted, on the verge of getting caught, forcing them to dispose of the plates in the first available spot?

Or was it a calculated move, a careless mistake, or perhaps a sign of desperation, something meant simply to slow them down while trying to find her? The thought gnawed at him.

Wyatt sat in the driver's seat and looked around. The glove compartment was open, and its contents had been meticulously removed—no papers, receipts, or hints of anything that might connect the vehicle to Ava.

Wyatt's fingers brushed over the smooth surface of the steering wheel, his mind racing. The car had been empty and wiped clean. Every inch of it had been scoured as though someone had been determined to erase all evidence of its owner—except the air inside. It smelled of sunshine and flowers, much like the image of Ava he had formed in his mind. However, anything of any substance tied to Ava was gone.

He ran a hand over his polished head and hit the visor. The car was small, and he was a big man, so there wasn't much headroom. Without thinking, he flipped down the visor and raised the lid on the mirror. Much to his surprise, a small photo was tucked into the corner of the mirror.

He felt like he had hit the jackpot when he saw Ava's face peering back at him from the center of the photo. Whoever had cleared out the car had no idea the photo was there or thought to look. A sense of protectiveness suddenly overtook him as the team worked around the outside of the vehicle.

Instinctively, he tucked the photo into his jacket, shielding it from prying eyes, and exited the car.

"Whoever wiped the car clean missed a spot," Ransick said, approaching Wyatt from behind. "The forensic team lifted several usable prints."

"Good." Wyatt did a slow one-eighty, letting his mind absorb his surroundings and the information.

"They were thorough in discarding things like receipts, wrappers, and personal items," Ransick said, thinking aloud. "But why leave the plates behind?"

Wyatt shrugged. "Maybe they thought the trash would come before the vehicle was found."

"That's possible. But why haven't we found anything else?"

"Maybe Ava Morgahn just kept her car clean, and there wasn't anything to dispose of. They've been combing through the trash, and the plates are the only solid evidence we have so far," Wyatt answered, thinking aloud.

There was a steady beep as the tow truck backed in.

"Looks like it's ready to be towed. I'm going to head back into the office. You comin'?" Ransick asked as he watched the tow truck driver get out to secure the car.

"I'll be a few more minutes. Want to check a couple of things before I head in."

"Suit yourself," Ransick said, going to his vehicle.

Wyatt walked away from the scene. With his back to the forensic team, he pulled out the photo again and scrutinized it. Two women posing for the photo, standing at the edge of a pristine, glassy body of water, smiling and carefree. He recognized Ava. She had her mother's eyes and wondered who the other young woman was.

His fingers tightened around the photo. He couldn't shake the thought of Ava near another far more dangerous body of water— the Cumberland River, where a killer used its depths to swallow his victims whole. A killer who might be watching, waiting for the next moment, the next victim to feel its murky bottom and lodge in its jagged banks.

Wyatt became increasingly disheartened at the office while scrolling through Ava Morgahn's social media account. Ava had posted almost religiously twice a day, sometimes more. With that track record, she was well overdue. She had over five thousand followers. Her posts ranged from inspiring quotes, clips of songs she was singing, foods she ate, recipes she tried, and failures and successes. She was funny, she was entertaining, and she was popular.

She was also easy to track.

One of the last things she posted was outside the apartment building. She was standing in front of her car with a huge smile.

He touched play to watch the video.

"Here I am," she said with a laugh. "Ready to start my new adventure in Nashville." She glanced over her shoulder, still holding the cell phone. "Cara!" she called. "Come get in my video."

The phone turned slightly to capture the other woman, who laughed and raised her hand to cover her face. "No paparazzi!" she giggled and ducked out of the frame.

"Well, that's Cara. My new roommate." Ava laughed. "She's a little camera shy, but I'll wear her down. I promise you'll see her again soon." Ava started walking backward closer to her car.

Wyatt paused the clip and took a screenshot of the image. Then continued.

Once again, Ava's bright, cheerful voice filled his office, instantly lifting the mood like a burst of sunshine. "Wish me luck!" she called out, her excitement practically bubbling over. "Today is the first day of the rest of my life—here's to all my dreams coming true!" Her energy was contagious, radiating through the screen.

"And my wish for you? May your day be absolutely amazing, and may you chase your dreams with all the passion in the world. Never let anyone dim your light!" she exclaimed, her enthusiasm practically glowing. As she signed off with a quick wave, her infectious smile was like a burst of fresh air, leaving him feeling lighter, brighter, and completely uplifted.

At the video's end, he lingered on the image of her waving goodbye. A pang went through him. He mentally shook himself and turned to the comments, scrolling through what had quickly amassed in the wake of her post.

There were well over five hundred comments, a testament to Ava's popularity and the genuine connection she had cultivated with her followers. Wyatt took his time, carefully reading through each one, a smile creeping onto his face as he absorbed the myriad responses.

"Good luck, Ava! You've got this!" cheered one follower.

Another chimed in with a playful, "Can't wait to see what you've got in store!" Each comment reflected the warmth and encouragement that Ava inspired, and Wyatt felt a swell of pride for this girl he didn't know, knowing she touched so many lives.

The comments vividly depicted her impact—a community built around shared experiences, encouragement, and mutual support. Each one reaffirmed the importance of her voice and her positivity. As Wyatt finished reading, he felt a renewed sense of urgency.

This was not a woman who would voluntarily disappear without so much as a word to her mother.

He watched the video again, noting that Ava had tagged her roommate. This time, he paused the video and screenshot the roommate's image. Following the tag led him to Cara's profile, which was almost nonexistent compared to Ava's.

Wyatt's phone rang. "Hello," he said distractedly, still studying Cara McCray's face.

"I have Mrs. Morgahn here to see you."

Wyatt sat up a little straighter. "I'll be right out."

In a matter of minutes, Wyatt had Kelleigh in the conference room. "Please," he indicated to a chair. "Have a seat."

"Thank you," Kelleigh said politely and perched on the edge of the chair. "I'm sorry," she said, looking around nervously. "I know you're busy."

"Nonsense, it's fine." Wyatt moved around the table and sat, his body instinctively putting some space between them. But it wasn't enough. Seeing her again—her quiet beauty, the raw, fragile emotions she wore so openly—shook him to his core. It stirred something deep inside him, a fierce, protective instinct he couldn't ignore. He wanted to shield her, keep her safe from whatever hurt she was carrying.

He cleared his throat, trying to steady himself. "Now, what can I do for you?" he asked, his voice softer than he intended, the weight of his feelings impossible to mask.

But if she noticed, she didn't respond. Instead, Kelleigh had her eyes downcast, studying her hands.

Wyatt got up from his chair, circled, and settled on the corner of the table. He couldn't stay away from her. "What is it? What's on your mind?"

"Do you think Ava's friend Molly Calhoun could know where she is?"

He didn't answer directly; it was a name he was unfamiliar with. "Care to explain?"

Kelleigh held his gaze. "She's one of the reasons Ava took the job at Cognac Creek and came here to Nashville."

"Are you asking me if I think Molly is involved?" He decided not to answer the question just yet. "I have a photo I'd like you to look at. I'll be right back."

He quickly went across the hall, retrieved what he needed, and was back.

He pulled out the 4x6 image he had found in Ava's car. "Do you recognize this woman?"

"Of course I do. This is Ava's friend Molly." Kelleigh tapped her index finger on the photo.

"Do you know when the photo was taken?"

"Just a few weeks ago. Where did you get that picture?" Kelleigh asked, breaking into Wyatt's thoughts.

He cleared his throat. "We found Ava's car today."

Kelleigh's breath caught. "Where?"

"In a parking garage a block off Broadway. We are now checking security footage to see when the vehicle entered the garage. The good news is we have a time frame to work with, and there wasn't any sign of foul play in or around her car. My team was also able to lift a few prints off the vehicle. It may take a few days, sometimes longer, to get the report back and know if any matches are found."

He pulled out five AI-generated photos created from the deceased's images, hoping to find a link, a match, to identify them.

"Do you know any of these women?" He spread the photos out on the table. "Take your time."

She scanned each one. "No. I'm sorry. I don't know any of them. Why does it matter?" Kelleigh asked.

The names of the victims hadn't been released to the press yet, as protocol dictated that the next of kin must be notified first. His role as an officer, governed by strict procedure, told him that divulging any information before the proper channels were followed could hinder the investigation. The need to respect the system and adhere to the rules that kept the process running smoothly pulled him in one direction.

But then, there was her face—pale, worried, her eyes pleading for anything that could comfort her. She needed answers. And his heart ached to see her so vulnerable, her every word steeped in fear and confusion. He knew she wasn't ready for the whole truth. Not yet. His instincts told him that breaking the news, or his fear, too soon would only cause more pain, more shock. He wanted to protect her from that, to shield her from the rawness of the situation, even though his duty was to give her the facts. His protective instincts—his desire to make her feel safe, even for a moment—pulled him in the other direction.

He inhaled deeply, weighing the consequences. Honesty. He could tell her enough to let her know the situation was serious, but not enough to crush her spirit. Or, he could be strict, play it by the book, and risk alienating her, leaving her in the dark longer than necessary. The rules said to wait. The procedures were clear. But his heart told him that sometimes, there were moments when rules should bend.

He got up, closed the door, and came back and sat beside her.

"What I'm about to tell you can't leave this room."

Kelleigh sat a little straighter. "I'm listening."

He hesitated, weighing his words carefully, the gravity of the situation pressing on him. "These women," he indicated, "the photos are connected to another case I'm investigating, and I was looking for a possible link to Ava's disappearance."

Her breath caught in her throat. "How?"

He leaned forward, eyes intense, filled with urgency. His gut said that Ava was another victim of the Cumberland Killer, and his gut was seldom wrong. He just didn't know how or when he would prove it right.

"I can't give you all the details yet, but I have every reason to believe Ava is in grave danger. And time is running out."

THIRTY-FOUR

Owen Layne

Owen and Toby walked the streets of downtown Nashville, weaving their way through pedestrians toward Cognac Creek with Gunner at their heels. Gunner was accustomed to the city's sights, smells, and sounds, so he trotted beside Owen with little fanfare.

But the usual trek that excited Owen felt mundane. Any other day, any other time, he would be thrilled he was headed into Cognac Creek, not to bartend but to perform. And not on the regular stage but at the top-paying level. But tonight, knowing that Ava was out somewhere lost, missing, possibly hurt, or maybe... no, he couldn't complete that thought. He wouldn't survive if he thought *that* was true. He wouldn't even allow his mind to go there. Those thoughts caught him without the usual enthusiasm he typically had or needed for a performance.

"How you feelin'?" Toby asked as they paused at a red light.

Owen didn't answer, instead waited for the light to turn green. Stepping off the curb, he said, "I don't know, man."

"Talk to me."

Owen sidestepped a chalkboard sign depicting the buy-one-get-one sale at the Boot Barn. "Do you remember the week leading up to Dylan's death? How I couldn't shake this terrible feeling deep in my gut?"

Toby nodded as they stopped short of the back entrance to the bar. "I do."

"Well, I have it again, and it won't go away."

"Did you sleep at all last night? I heard you prowling around at all hours."

Owen visibly sagged against the back door, his hand on the knob. "Not much. I kept replaying the walk to the car. How excited Ava was, enthusiastic, and happy." He left out that they kissed. That part was way too special. It was a moment between the two of them, and he wouldn't kiss and tell.

"I didn't speak with her for long, but had that same impression."

"Someone that excited wouldn't just walk away without a reason." Owen shook his head in frustration. Because if she did have a reason—did that mean he had meant nothing to her? Those intimate moments they shared snuggled in the booth or pressed against her car meant nothing?

He replayed their conversations in his mind, the laughter and connection that felt both exhilarating and terrifying. It was as if he had known Ava all his life, not just a few days. She consumed his thoughts—her smile was the first thing that greeted him in the morning and the last thing that lingered in his mind as he drifted off to sleep. How could someone he had just met leave such a profound mark on him?

She was a force of nature, unlike anything or anyone he'd ever encountered. Every little glance, every laugh pulled at his heartstrings with an intensity that left him both intrigued and slightly off balance. No one had ever touched him so deeply, unraveling him in ways he had never thought possible. He was falling, tumbling headfirst into an abyss of feelings, and he was terrified—yet utterly captivated. And now she was missing.

He felt helpless because there was nothing he could do for Ava. Disheartened, he realized he was right back to where he'd been a week ago, before her.

Visibly shaking himself, he turned the knob. "Guess we'd better go in."

"We'll figure it out, man. Give yourself a break. Let's go do what we love."

They walked through the door and straight to the elevators, which led to the rooftop with Gunner leading the way.

The German Shepherd took his place at the edge of the stage, the lights dimming slightly around Owen and the others as the atmosphere buzzed with anticipation. He nodded to the band members, their camaraderie evident in the easy banter exchanged as they moved about the stage.

Each member had their routine—some adjusted their instruments, while others chatted animatedly about the last gig or the latest song they'd been working on.

The sound engineer, perched at the back, signaled for a moment of silence, and the band stowed their gear with practiced efficiency, laying out cables and checking their setups. The faint hum of the crowd settled over them.

After a few warm-up notes filled the air—a blend of chords and rhythms that melded into a cohesive sound—they exchanged glances of approval. Owen strummed a few riffs, testing the resonance of his guitar, while Toby tapped out a steady beat on the snare, ensuring the tempo felt right.

As the final adjustments were made, the band members gathered for a quick huddle, sharing a laugh and a last-minute pep talk.

"Decent crowd tonight," Toby said, his eyes scanning the room. He twirled a drumstick between his fingers. "Maybe we can double it if you yahoos can keep up with me."

"We can keep the beat. It's you who has a hard time finding it," the bass player said, razing Toby back. "You're so busy checking out the girls that walk by, you can't keep the beat or the girl."

"Wait. I got a joke. What do you call a drummer who doesn't

have a girlfriend?" the keyboard player asked.

"Toby," the bass player answered with a widespread grin.

"Screw you," Toby retorted. "Everyone knows that drummers get all the hot chicks."

"Yeah? Where's yours?"

"I can't be tied down to just one," Toby replied with a flip of his stick.

"You'd be lucky to get a cold one, let alone a hot one."

"Alright, alright," Owen said, trying to rein them in. "If you old biddies are done, let's blow the roof off this joint."

With a collective nod, they signaled to the sound engineer to begin. The lights came up slightly brighter, and the first notes echoed through the venue, marking the transition from preparation to performance.

Owen could feel the backbeat of the drums vibrate in his chest, a steady rhythm that resonated deep within. Each thump that reverberated through the wooden stage beneath his feet was like a heartbeat, grounding him in the moment and syncing him with the band's energy. He took a deep breath, inhaling the familiar scent of fermented beer, burgers, and warm electronics, a mixture that always filled him with a sense of belonging.

As he lifted his steel guitar, the cool metal felt reassuring against his fingertips. He plucked the strings, and the wail of his guitar sliced through the air, a melody that lifted his spirit with every chord. The sound swirled around him, a powerful reminder of why he loved to perform, why he was here.

He turned and saw the band was locked into the moment. Owen closed his eyes, letting the music wash over him. He could picture the crowd, faces turned toward him and the band. He opened his eyes, feeling the instant connection with the audience, an invisible thread that tied them together.

Then, he started to sing. His voice was rich and full of emotion as Ava's pretty face filled his thoughts. In the recesses, she wouldn't stay. But he decided that it was okay if she surfaced. She made him feel. He poured out that feeling through every note, every word, intertwining with the melody.

Each note felt like a story unfolding, a piece of his heart laid bare. The lyrics flowed easily. As he sang, he could see the audience leaning in, caught in the spell of the music.

Toby hammered away on the drums behind him, driving the rhythm forward, while the bass provided a solid foundation, allowing him to soar on his guitar. In that moment, surrounded by the vibrant sounds of the band and the energy of the crowd, Owen felt truly alive and inwardly prayed that Ava was too.

THIRTY-FIVE

Ava Morgahn

Ava woke disoriented and trembling, her heart pounding, her head spinning. The darkness slowly shifted around her. Sensations returned, slow at first. The air felt thick and suffocating as she leaned forward. A thin layer of white dust covered her skin, making her itch and hard to breathe.

Panic clawed at her throat when she realized she could only move so far. Her hands were bound behind her back, the cool metal of a pole between her shoulder blades.

Her entire body tingled. She shifted to regain feeling in her legs and arms, her eyes trying to adjust.

The remnants of words echoed in her mind, and she wasn't sure if it was reality associated with this nightmare or her mind playing tricks on her, but the voice was etched into her subconscious.

The sing-song rhythm ran through her head.

Are you sinking? Are you sinking?

Where did that come from? She shook her head to help clear the fog and rid her mind of the words. But the haunting melody wouldn't stop.

She shifted when she heard voices. She called out into the eerie darkness, her words echoing throughout the dark space, the sound playing tricks on her. She'd have to be louder if she wanted to be heard.

The thought crept through her mind like a rat scurrying in the dark. Did she want to be heard? What if who was out there was worse than being in here alone? What would they do to her if they heard her calling for help? What would become of her if no one came? Both thoughts twisted and turned in her mind, leaving her reeling and feeling desperate—the need to be found outweighed her desire not to.

Without warning, a blood-curdling scream tore from her throat.

The automated voice droned on in a monotone, buzzing in his ear as he punched in the digits. His ears perked. He stopped what he was doing, stood still, and listened. A sly grin etched his face, creasing lines so deep his face could pass as a mask at Halloween. Number seven was awake.

It was like music to his ears, her screams ringing out into the building's vast blackness and dying out into the ebony void.

He could go to her, shake her senseless until she shut up... tell her screaming was futile, but he didn't. Instead, he let her cry out like his mama used to let him. She never told him to shush. She let him scream until he was spent, humming the old nursery rhyme. But he liked his version better.

The melody was already forming in his mind, the lyrics transforming into the following lines: "Are you screaming? Are you screaming?" he hummed. "Ava Lynn, Ava Lynn. I am cunning. Your time is coming. Splish, splash, splosh."

THIRTY-SIX

Detective Wyatt Lockhart

Wyatt tucked Kelleigh away in the conference room with a sandwich and a Coke and promised to return for her shortly.

The air in his office was tense as he reviewed the footage from the Monday morning security cameras sent by the parking garage off Broadway and Stella Doyle from Cognac Creek.

He decided to start with the parking garage and follow what he could of Ava's day.

The Chevy Malibu came into view right at eight, its familiar shape gliding down the street and turning into the parking lot. A lone individual could be seen in the car entering the garage. When the car stopped for the ticket in order to proceed up the ramp, it was evident Ava was the driver. Once she turned the corner, she drove out of range of the camera. He switched to another feed to follow her further up the ramp.

It didn't take long before the car disappeared around yet another corner. He assumed it had parked in a dead zone of the garage, a spot out of camera range.

On purpose or by chance, he wasn't sure.

He watched for a while longer, but Ava did not appear back in the frame. He could only assume she didn't come out of the front entrance but used the exit toward Broadway.

He then switched to the footage that Stella Doyle had sent.

Wyatt leaned in close, anticipating Ava's arrival outside the bar, waiting to be let in. He pulled up multiple angles and let it play. Taking a bite of his sandwich, he watched Ava's movements, following her throughout the space, which were normal and unremarkable as the day unfolded. When she interacted with someone new, he paused the video and zoomed in.

He made a list of other employees and noted their names when he could read their name tags. Customers were usually in groups and a lot less easy to identify, so he simply looked for anything out of the ordinary.

Late in the day, a specific customer caught his eye.

He wore a black Stetson pulled low over his head, shielding most of his face. He had on jeans and a black nondescript T-shirt. Nothing about his appearance raised any alarms. Or not exactly. There was just something in how he moved, something too deliberate and smooth.

As Wyatt sifted through the footage, a creeping sense of unease began to settle in. An hour passed on the film, but the man never approached Ava, just continued to nurse a beer. But every time she came into the frame his head turned slightly. To most it would seem natural if they weren't paying attention, but Wyatt was. His senses were on high alert.

Two hours after his arrival, the man slipped out of the booth and casually zigzagged across the room. At the same time Ava appeared on the other side of the frame, as if a magnet pulling them, an unseen force dragging them toward one another. As if an author had written the perfect interaction, the ideal meet-cute they bumped into each other right on cue.

Wyatt's heart raced as he watched the scene unfold. At first, on the surface it looked like friendly banter, an unavoidable accident. But the minute the man's hand snaked out, Wyatt saw Ava's expression shift. The tide had turned. It was no longer friendly or coincidental.

Wyatt glanced out the door across the hall at Kelleigh. She was still in the same spot he'd left her, sandwich untouched.

"Something isn't right from the moment he walks into the bar," Wyatt muttered, scanning the footage again, his instincts prickling. Ava made the incident inconsequential, but the damage was done. Whatever the man said seemed to make Ava pause. The unease settled deeper as Wyatt considered the implications.

He watched the rest of the evening play out on the screen. It was like watching an old-fashioned movie, silent and grainy as the lights dimmed.

Amid the chaos, Wyatt eventually lost sight of the man in the cowboy hat. He rewound the video again and again, but each time, he hit a dead end. It was as if the man had simply evaporated into thin air.

The rest of her shift had been uneventful, but Wyatt couldn't shake the nagging feeling that something was off. He noticed she spent an unusually long time in the back, where the employee lockers were—something that didn't sit right with him.

He almost missed her when she reappeared some twenty minutes later in a long green sundress.

His gaze snapped up, locking onto her with a force that stole the breath from his lungs. Was she meeting someone? The question lingered in the air, heavy and charged, as he watched her cross the expanse of the restaurant, leaving through the same door she had entered some ten hours earlier.

Once back out on the street, the teeming crowd swallowed her whole, Cognac Creek, her last known place.

Wyatt took a deep breath, trying to steady his racing thoughts. He needed more footage from the parking garage. He had a time frame now. Maybe the main camera had caught her ducking into the garage for a minute or two to put her backpack in the car.

He made the call and the request. Once that was done, he knew he should speak with Kelleigh.

He had to be direct with Kelleigh to prepare her for the harsh reality without letting despair overwhelm her. But how could he frame it? He could picture her eyes widening in disbelief, the way her brows would knit together as she processed the information. He didn't want to see the spark of determination fade from her expression.

He glanced at the footage on the screen, which showed the empty parking garage and the entrance to Cognac Creek mocking him.

Wyatt's mind raced through the implications. If this man had been Ava's undoing, what exactly had happened? Where could she be? And how did Molly Calhoun play into all this? If she did. There was still no proof that Molly had anything to do with it, only Kelleigh's unanswered question.

The thoughts tumbling through his mind were disheartening as the Cumberland River rushed into his thoughts. The image of the past five women being dragged out dead and bloated. He vowed he wouldn't let that happen.

He got up, crossed the room and put one yellow pushpin with the initials AM on the map.

With a resolute nod, he decided he would be honest yet compassionate with Kelleigh. He would explain the situation clearly, ensuring she understood the gravity of their next steps. They couldn't afford to lose momentum now. They had to regroup and figure out where to go from here. But first, he had to find the right words to break the news. It was going to be a hard conversation.

Stalling, he decided to use the restroom first.

THIRTY-SEVEN

Kelleigh Morgahn

Kelleigh walked down the quiet corridor, her steps slow and heavy, her mind a haze of jumbled thoughts. It was late, and the night shift was primarily out of the building on patrol.

She pushed open the door to the women's restroom, the quiet click of the latch almost too loud in the otherwise empty hallway. Inside, the fluorescent lights buzzed overhead as she stepped up to the sink. Without thinking, she splashed cold water onto her face, the shock of the chill cutting through the fog of exhaustion. She stared at her reflection in the mirror, trying to shake off the grogginess.

The woman staring back at her wasn't someone she recognized. Dark circles hung under her eyes like bruises, and her hair, usually so neat, was slightly mussed. She dug through her purse, fingers trembling slightly, and pulled out a compact mirror. With practiced hands, she refreshed her makeup—a touch of blush, a thin line of eyeliner—anything to hide the weariness. Then she ran her fingers through her hair, trying to smooth it. Finished, she studied herself again. Not perfect, but better.

A hint of energy returned as she straightened her shoulders. She wasn't about to let exhaustion take over and wasn't here to win a beauty contest. She was here for a reason. To find Ava.

She pushed open the restroom door and went down the hall to Detective Lockhart's office.

His door was ajar, just enough for her to peek inside. She

knocked softly, then pushed the door open further, her breath catching when she saw the scene before her.

"Detective Lockhart?" Her voice came out softer than she intended, shaky even. She stepped inside, her eyes immediately drawn to the wall. A large map of Nashville covered most of it, pink pins scattered in two concentrated locations, lines connecting them like a web of some dark, unsettling puzzle. At the center, written in bold red marker, was a phrase that made her blood run cold: *Cumberland Killer.*

Her heart stopped when she noticed the yellow one with the initials AM.

"You shouldn't be in here." His voice cut through the silence like a whip, low and sharp, making Kelleigh feel like a child caught doing something wrong. She turned slowly, her pulse racing as she faced Detective Lockhart. He stood in the doorway, his posture rigid, arms crossed over his chest. His eyes, dark and unreadable, were fixed on her with a kind of intensity that made her stomach tighten.

"I—I'm sorry," she stammered, stepping back toward the desk, creating space between them. "I was just looking for you. The door was open, and I…"

Lockhart didn't let her finish. His gaze flicked over her, then back to the map on the wall, his expression hardening. "You shouldn't be in here," he reiterated. His voice held a quiet warning, suggesting he wasn't just talking about a simple breach of privacy.

Kelleigh swallowed, trying to steady her breathing. "I didn't mean to intrude. I… I thought you were in your office." She gestured vaguely, hoping to diffuse the tension, but her mind was reeling. *Cumberland Killer.* The words alone felt like a weight pressing against her chest. She hadn't dared to think it before, but clearly, he did.

Lockhart stepped further into the room, his presence filling the space. He didn't look at her directly but at the map, his gaze lingering on it with a strange intensity that made Kelleigh's unease grow. *He did.*

"You don't know what you're looking at." His voice softened, but the sharpness was still there, like a dagger to her heart.

She opened her mouth to protest, but the words died on her lips. She did know what she was looking at. She wasn't blind. She recognized some of the places marked on the map. What she believed was the location of the bodies, where they may have gone into the river, and where they were pulled from it. The paths that connected them—each one a grim reminder of the case that had haunted Nashville for weeks now.

The "Cumberland Killer" was real, and he was leaving a trail that no one could seem to track. And now Ava was missing... It didn't take a detective to guess what was happening here.

"Wyatt." She thought better of using his first name. "Detective Lockhart, I—" Kelleigh hesitated, the words heavy in her throat. She had never been good at hiding her thoughts, but now, with the weight of Ava missing pressing down on her, it felt impossible to speak freely. Still, she had to try. She had to know. "I came to tell you..." Her thoughts shifted, but she needed to hear him say it. "Is this... Do you think this is connected to Ava's disappearance?"

Her voice barely rose above a whisper, but Wyatt heard it.

He tensed, his jaw tightening as he glanced at her, the briefest flicker of regret flashing in his eyes.

For a moment, Wyatt just stood there, staring at her, his gaze piercing and full of something she couldn't quite identify. Then, without warning, he turned toward the map, running his fingers over the pins and string with a calmness that contrasted sharply with the tension in the room.

"You're right. I believe Ava's disappearance is connected. We would be naive to think that it wasn't. She fits the profile. The only difference is that you reported her missing. These other women —" he shook his head. "Haven't been. The best I can figure is they don't have much of a family to miss them, or they aren't close to the ones they have." His voice was colder now, distant.

Kelleigh's breath hitched—the Cumberland Killer. Just reading the words chilled her to the bone.

Before she could react, Wyatt's eyes flicked back to her, sharp as knives. "I need you to stay out of this, Kelleigh. It's not a game."

"How dare you! My daughter is missing. Believe me, I know it's not a game."

She turned on her heel and pushed past him, needing to escape. She took a few steps and realized she was headed in the wrong direction. She stopped abruptly and changed direction. Now, she was going to have to pass him. Again.

Wyatt stood in the middle of the hall, filling it with his body.

He held out his hand to slow her down. "Kelleigh, wait." Wyatt spoke, his voice calmer and more comforting. "I'm sorry. That was completely out of line. I was completely out of line. And it was highly insensitive. Please, I want to hear what you have to say."

Kelleigh's mind raced. Should she accept his apology? She had invaded his office unannounced and uninvited. It was her fault as much as his. She had breached his privacy. But the only thing she could think of was the chilling words written in red. *Cumberland Killer*. The unease clung to her like a second skin.

She wasn't going to walk away. Not now. Her daughter needed her. She relented. "I'm sorry, too. I should have never stepped inside your office when it was clear you weren't there. Please forgive me."

"Only if you forgive me."

"Apology accepted."

He looked back at his office. "Let's go back to the conference room."

She followed him down the hall. He pulled out a chair for her, and she sat, her half-eaten sandwich still on the table.

"Now, what did you want to tell me? Was it something you remembered?"

She pulled out her phone, her fingers brushing lightly against the screen as she navigated to the photo. "I took a picture the other day. It's the most recent photo of Ava I have." She shrugged. "I wasn't sure if you needed it for anything."

"That's good." His voice was low and warm, and she felt the subtle shift in the air as he leaned in just a little closer. Their shoulders brushed lightly, a casual touch, but the closeness felt intimate in a way she couldn't quite explain. He glanced at the photo, his breath close against her ear. "Can you send it to me?"

Something in the moment, something in their shared space, made her heart beat a little faster. "Of course."

"Detective Lockhart?" The voice cut through the quiet, and both of them turned at the same time.

The shift in his posture was almost imperceptible but enough for Kelleigh to feel the sudden distance between them.

A head poked through the door. Wyatt straightened up immediately, his expression neutral as he turned toward the interruption. Kelleigh felt an inexplicable mix of relief and disappointment, the moment slipping away as quickly as it had come.

"Sorry to interrupt," the young officer said.

"You're not. What is it?"

"A call came in for you from the parking garage off Broadway. They were able to retrieve some additional footage from Monday evening." She held out the message.

Detective Lockhart stood quickly. "Excuse me. I need to take this call."

THIRTY-EIGHT

Owen Layne

Owen drug himself out of bed and stumbled to the dresser, grabbing clean underwear and a T-shirt. He made his way into the bathroom and turned on the shower. He had tossed and turned all night again, his brain trying to decipher where Ava could be and how he could find her.

Stepping into the shower, he replayed how Stella had clapped him on the shoulder, her eyes sparkling enthusiastically. The conversation came back to him.

"I think those are the best sets you've ever had. You're coming into your own." Her words had felt like a warm embrace, filling him with needed validation.

"Thanks," he had replied, but he couldn't take all the credit. The band was on fire. The energy they had created together had been electric, each member feeding off the others' passion. But beneath that, he couldn't ignore the relentless images of Ava that danced in his mind. She had been his inspiration that had ignited a fire within him throughout the night.

Toby had stood there with a satisfied grin plastered across his face. He acknowledged the compliment with a confident head bob. "We were good, weren't we?" His voice held a mix of pride.

"Good? More like phenomenal!" Stella had laughed, her excitement infectious. "I mean, the crowd was into it. I could feel the energy in the air." She gestured animatedly as if trying to capture the atmosphere of the night with her hands. "You could see everyone hanging on every note, every word, completely lost in the music. That's what it's all about!"

Owen's heart had swelled at her compliment. He knew she didn't hand them out readily, but a twinge of anxiety had lingered beneath the surface. The applause had been thunderous, but amidst the celebration, he couldn't shake the feeling that something was missing, something was wrong.

"You think we've improved?" he had asked, seeking reassurance. Her encouraging smile was enough to dissolve some of his doubts.

"Absolutely," she replied earnestly. "You've got something special, Owen. Just keep channeling it—whatever *it* is." Her words had hung in the air, stirring a mix of hope and uncertainty within him.

He knew what *it* was. It was Ava.

Owen stepped out of the shower, dried off, and slipped into clean clothes. He made his way to the kitchen and noticed the German Shepherd waiting patiently by the back door, ready to go out. He let the dog out and proceeded to make coffee. The coffee trickled into the pot as he let the dog back in.

Gunner, he thought his name but couldn't make himself say it out loud. Owen watched the dog as he walked around the kitchen, ignored his food bowl, took a few laps of water, and searched for his favorite toy.

Owen always buried the toy in the house when the German Shepherd wasn't looking. For two reasons: the vet had said it was good for him to keep up his skills even just a little bit if there was ever any hope for him to heal and return to normal. And two, he couldn't stand the sight of the stuffed bear because it was a toy that his brother Dylan had given the dog when he had first brought him home from the academy.

Without fail, he religiously hid the stuffed bear all over the townhouse. Once found, the dog would curl up with the plush animal, its worn faux fur offering comfort.

The little toy, now faded and frayed, still had a blue Kansas wristband wrapped around its arms, matching the headband his brother wore.

The bear seemed to absorb the quiet sadness in the room, its once-vibrant brown now dulled by time. As the dog nestled closer, there was a gentle, almost mournful warmth—a reminder of something lost, yet still held close.

Owen couldn't take his eyes off the pitiful dog. "If only it were that easy for you to bring back a person."

"Are you talking to yourself again or the dog?" Toby asked, coming in from outside, sweat dripping off of him. He stepped into the mudroom and grabbed a towel to dry his moist face.

"The dog."

"Did he answer you?"

"No."

"What did you ask him this time?"

Owen shrugged and slumped back into his chair. "I just commented."

"Which was?" Toby asked, gesturing to pull it out of his friend.

Owen was irritated. "I just said if only he could bring back a person as easily as he finds that damn bear."

"I'm afraid, however well-trained that dog may or may not be, he'd never be able to bring Dylan back."

"You think I don't know that?" Owen replied gruffly. Then he straightened. "But what if he could bring back Ava?"

Toby raked the sweat-soaked towel over his damp head and tossed it in the hamper. "Now that would be something."

Suddenly fully awake, Owen asked, "Do you think it's possible?"

"I don't know. He's trained to sniff out drugs and shit, so

maybe."

"Narcotics."

"That's what I said, drugs and shit." Toby grinned at him. "Wasn't your brother trying to cross-train him just before he died?"

Owen tilted his head in thought. "He was. I don't know how far he got with it, though." He stood wishing he had paid better attention and looked at the dog. He picked up his cell and searched for the number. "There's only one way to find out."

Owen pulled into the gravel parking lot of the K9 training facility. The place was tucked away on the outskirts of town, a sprawling expanse of open fields and obstacle courses surrounded by woods, purposely built for training working dogs like Gunner. The facility was well-maintained and had a sense of organic organization. Different sections were set up for agility drills, scent detection exercises, and tactical scenarios—each designed to push the dogs to their limits.

Gunner, sitting upright in the passenger seat, was calm but alert. His eyes darted between Owen and the approaching entrance, his powerful frame vibrating with pent-up energy. It had been a while since he'd been here, and Owen could feel the dog's sense of familiarity set in—this was where Gunner had first proven himself and met Dylan.

The moment the truck rolled to a stop, Owen turned to Gunner, offering a rare but knowing smile. "Ready?"

The dog didn't need words. His tail thumped twice against the seat in answer.

Owen exited the truck, tossing the leash over the German Shepherd's head and clipped it to his collar. The dog was ready for something. Owen just hoped he was prepared enough himself, but in the same breath, he didn't want to be disappointed.

He had called his brother's buddy, Tharron, a seasoned K9

handler who ran the training facility. Owen had known Tharron for years, and Tharron was always happy to help. He'd been there after Dylan died, and Gunner needed rehabilitation from his injuries, guiding both of them through the healing process.

"Hey, Tharron." Owen stuck out his hand as the man came toward him. "I appreciate you seeing us today."

Tharron was friendly. "Yeah, of course. I've already got a few runs setup. You want to see him on agility first, or do you want to test him on a scent trail?"

Owen ran a hand through his hair, glancing at Gunner as the dog sat quietly beside him. His body humming with anticipation, he watched every move the men made.

"Let's start with agility. Then, depending on how he does, we can run him through scent tracking. It's been a while. I don't want to overstimulate him with something new just yet when I'm not sure how he will do with the basics."

Tharron nodded. "Sounds good."

They made their way toward the far side of the facility, where the agility course stood—an array of jumps, tunnels, and weave poles designed to test speed, coordination, and focus.

"I pulled his file before you arrived." He flipped open the manilla folder. "Looks like the vet gave him a clean bill of health the last time you were here."

"That he did." Owen unclipped the leash, a small pit in his stomach, and led Gunner onto the starting line.

Tharron waited by the start with the folder tucked under his arm. "Alright, Gunner. Let's see if you've still got it."

Owen gave a final look at Gunner, not sure what to expect. The dog was still, eyes locked on Owen's, as his hind legs quivered with anticipation. Owen gave the command, and Gunner shot off the line, sprinting toward the first obstacle.

Owen watched, a little apprehensive, as the German Shepherd

navigated the course, his movements smooth yet practiced. He cleared the jumps effortlessly, powered through the tunnels, and weaved through the poles with precision. The bond between handler and dog was undeniable—Gunner was in his element, and Owen wasn't far behind, moving at the same rhythm, giving quiet commands with every turn. Gunner leaped over the final hurdle, skidding slightly in the dirt before stopping at Owen's side.

Tharron clapped his hands, impressed. "Damn, Owen. He's got speed. Let's see how he handles something more challenging."

They tried another course, both dog and man, and found the trust and mutual respect they had lacked these past few months. Before, Owen had been just going through the motions, doing only what needed to be done to rehabilitate the dog. He was surprised at himself for how much he had retained and how much he enjoyed watching Gunner go through the course. Owen gave Gunner a good rub and a much-deserved treat when they were finished.

Tharron grinned at the two of them. "Wanna give him a shot on tracking?"

Owen nodded, letting Gunner catch his breath. "Let's do it."

Tharron set up a new challenge—a scent trail that would lead the dog through the woods. The area was designed to simulate real-world conditions, where the dog must track a suspect or locate a missing person. But since Gunner hadn't been at the facility in a while, Tharron kept it simple yet strategic.

"This'll be a good test of his focus and scent recognition," Tharron said as he dropped a glove along the trail and waved Owen over. Dylan was making good progress with him, but it's been a while. It will be a learning curve for both of you."

"That's an understatement. Can you remind me of some additional signals Dylan was working on with him?"

Tharron scanned the chart and filled Owen in on the commands.

"You ready?"

Owen patted Gunner's side, and the dog stood tall, sniffing the air. "Let's do it. What's the worst that could happen?"

Tharron gave the command and showed him the first item with the scent. Gunner immediately dropped his nose to the ground, his ears flicking as he began to search. Owen watched intently, his pulse steady but quickening with the anticipation of seeing Gunner's skills tested.

It was a moment of complete focus. Gunner's body was low to the ground, each step deliberate, his nose working in precise motions as he tracked the scent through the thick underbrush.

Tharron followed closely behind, watching Gunner's every move with a critical eye. "He's got a solid nose. Looks like he's found something."

Gunner suddenly stopped, losing the scent. He circled, the trees swayed, and the wind changed direction. His body tensed, and his gaze locked ahead. He let out a low bark and moved toward a tree where Tharron had hidden another item. Pleased, Owen was beginning to think this might work.

He made the call and prayed she'd pick up.

THIRTY-NINE

Owen Layne

Owen met Kelleigh in the parking garage where Ava's car had been located and where Ava was last seen.

She handed Owen the T-shirt without any fanfare.

"Please don't get your hopes up," he warned her. "Gunner is rusty, and this isn't usually the type of thing he tracks. He's been trained in narcotics, but my brother worked with him to start cross-training for missing people. Gunner is exceptionally talented."

Kelleigh nodded. "It's worth a shot, right?" she asked, her voice hopeful.

"It is." He took the shirt from her. "Although it's been a few days, the area is protected from the weather, so that should play in our favor." He took a deep breath. "Here goes nothin'."

Owen presented the T-shirt to the German Shepherd. His keen nose twitched as he took in the scent, and the canine's nostrils flared as he processed the information. Owen gave the command "track," and quickly, the dog began to circle. Gunner stiffened, and without command, he turned to the left, his nose lowered to the ground. While anticipating the dog's next move, Owen unclipped the leash and allowed him to take the lead.

The German Shepherd was off like a bullet, his nose to the ground, following the invisible line of scent that only he could perceive. Owen moved quickly, staying several paces behind as they began working across the concrete structure.

Owen had only been trailing Gunner for a few minutes, weaving in and out of parked cars, slowly descending the car ramp, when the dog suddenly slowed and veered toward the corner of the parking garage.

The German Shepherd's movements were precise and methodical as he worked around a Suburban. His nose hovered just above the ground, skimming the cracks and creases in the concrete. He stopped momentarily, ears flicking back. Something was there.

"Find it, Gunner," Owen urged.

He rooted through a pile of trash accumulated in the corner with renewed focus. Owen moved closer, scanning the area for security cameras. He could see a small one at the far end of the landing, where the ramp turned and declined. A few discarded plastic bottles and fast-food wrappers lay in disarray. It wasn't much—just the litter that accumulated in abandoned parking lots. But then, something caught his eye—a flash of black, half-covered by trash, its edges sharp against the fluorescent light.

Gunner was on it in an instant. His paws brushed against something, and he nudged it with his nose, letting out a sharp bark.

"Good boy," Owen whispered, kneeling beside the dog.

He reached into the pile of trash. Wedged between the concrete wall and a parking block, Owen could see a cell phone. Carefully pulling the phone free, he noted it was a smartphone. It was scuffed, and the screen was cracked, but hopeful that it was still functional. Owen's pulse quickened as he prayed it was Ava's. He checked the back for any identifying marks, stepped back around the large vehicle, and had Kelleigh take a look.

Tears welled as she nodded, confirming it was Ava's cell phone.

Owen tapped the phone's screen. It was dead. He left Kelleigh with the phone and returned to where Gunner was still working, his paws skimming through the trash. Gunner turned a slow circle and moved up and back. Owen was sure the trail stopped there since the dog couldn't seem to go any further.

He let the dog release and relax. The tracking was over.

"Let's go back to my vehicle and see if we can get this phone working."

"The sooner, the better," Kelleigh agreed.

They crawled into Owen's truck, and he plugged the phone in. The device flickered to life with a faint buzz, the crack in the glass distorting the display.

"It needs a password," Owen said.

"Try her birthday." Kelleigh gave him the numbers, and he punched them in. "That was it. I'm in." He hesitated. "Do you want me to look, or do you want to?"

"Go ahead," Kelleigh said softly.

He scrolled through the phone, feeling an increasing discomfort with each swipe. The process felt invasive—wrong even. What would Ava think if she knew a man she barely knew was rifling through her private messages? His stomach twisted at the thought, but he quickly shoved the feeling down. *She's missing, maybe hurt or worse,* he told himself, trying to rationalize the invasion of her privacy.

"See if you can find VIDCOMM. It's a messaging and video-sharing platform that Ava often uses with her friends," Kelleigh informed him. "Ava is always on it, sending short video messages, voice notes, and texts. That's how Molly contacted her about this opportunity."

Owen found the messaging video app that Kelleigh had mentioned. He tapped the icon. The first screen that greeted him was a wall of recent contacts and threads, each featuring a small thumbnail of videos. His eyes skimmed over the names.

His thumb hovered over the last thread. It was marked as "Read," and the contact name was Molly Calhoun. The timestamp showed that the previous message had been recorded days before it was sent. "Should we try this one?" he asked.

Kelleigh peered down at the screen as he hesitated over it.

"That's probably the one Ava watched on the way here or at the apartment before she left for work."

"Do you want to watch it?" Owen asked Kelleigh.

She nodded hesitantly. "I think we have to."

Molly's face appeared on the screen, and they watched the short clip.

"She looks different," Kelleigh said quietly. "There's something in her eyes."

"Like what?" Owen asked, curious.

Kelleigh shook her head. "I'm not sure. Maybe I'm imagining it, but there seems to be an urgency that doesn't fit Molly's carefree personality."

"Maybe we should watch another one and compare."

"Good idea. Go back a couple of weeks before Molly came to Nashville."

"Here's one from a month ago." Owen touched the thumbnail, and the video started. They watched in silence as Molly's voice filled the vehicle. "Hey, everyone! I just want to share my news! I got the invite! I'm going to Nashville! I found this cute place to live, and I'll be waitressing at Cognac Creek. The place is hoppin' and has such an authentic country atmosphere. I'm ecstatic to be working there and hope to get on stage sooner or later!"

"What do you think?" Kelleigh asked Owen.

Owen was silent for a moment. "I don't remember ever seeing her at the restaurant."

"I meant about the tone in which she's talking. The difference in her expression. That sort of thing."

"It's a different vibe than the last message, for sure. Let's show

Detective Lockhart."

"I agree."

"I'll give him a call."

She looked out the window, her eyes scanning the parking lot. He couldn't tell if she was lost in thought or just waiting for anything that might make this nightmare end.

"We won't stop. Not until we find her."

To his surprise, she asked, "Can I ask about your brother?"

He swallowed hard. "Of course. What do you want to know?"

Kelleigh looked at him with a sadness he only imagined a mother could have. "What happened?"

Owen pulled in a long breath to settle his nerves. "Dylan was the victim of a hit-and-run. Gunner, too." The dog lifted his head at the mention of his name. "Dylan was pronounced dead at the scene."

"I'm so sorry."

Owen accepted this with a slight nod.

"Do they have any leads?"

"Not many. It was very early in the morning, still dark. They were out for their routine run. Dylan kept odd hours but was religious about keeping Gunner on a tight schedule. So, it wasn't unusual for him to be out at that time. Dylan always joked that the only other people out at that hour were drunks and criminals." Owen shifted in his seat. "There was no traffic, no witnesses. The only thing they have to go on are some skid marks and tiny flecks of white paint embedded in Dylan's skin where the vehicle connected."

"How long has it been?"

"Six months."

"It's still fresh and new, then. I can't tell you how sorry I am that this happened to you and your family," she said, putting her hand on his arm.

"I appreciate it."

"Is there anything I can do for you or your family?"

He was surprised. Here was this woman he had only known for a few days, offering to do something for him and his family while her daughter was missing. A whisper of a smile played on his lips.

"No, ma'am. We're managing. Thank you, though." He started the SUV. "Let's get this over to Detective Lockhart."

FORTY

Detective Wyatt Lockhart

It was an understatement to say Wyatt wasn't happy with the two of them. He turned Ava Morgahn's cell phone over in his hand, frustration simmering beneath the surface. But, like it or not, they had made progress where he hadn't—and that stung. He didn't like it, not one bit.

To make matters worse, they had carelessly handled the device, oblivious to the potential consequences. In their haste to obtain the phone, they hadn't considered that it could contain crucial evidence or fingerprints—information that might play a pivotal role in the investigation.

It wasn't an excuse, but he was only one person, buried under a heavy caseload with an unreliable second in command. Ransick was either taking a day off or flirting with the women rookies.

Wyatt's blood boiled. He tried to push the man out of his thoughts as he swiped through Ava's cell phone and started the first video message.

Molly Calhoun's face filled the screen, and her voice, his office.

"Glad you're finally here!" she said, a curious gleam in her eye as she stared at the camera. The clip played, and Molly's face, a little too tired for comfort, filled the frame. Her voice came through the speaker a bit too enthusiastically and rasped like it had been raked with sandpaper. The background behind her was completely dark. She leaned closer to the camera, her eyes intense, but something in her smile didn't quite match the excitement in her voice. "Let me know if you need anything…" There was an exaggerated pause. "Any help. See you." The clip ended abruptly.

She seemed to be speaking quickly. Her words could be perceived as a nervous excitement. But he didn't think so. Her words were clipped, more anxious, like she was trying to get it all out before something happened. And if he wasn't mistaken, the word help seemed overly stated, as if she were asking for it.

He replayed the video, but this time, his eyes were focused on the background—dim lights, shadows on the edges of the frame. The location felt generic. What could be seen of it felt staged, and there wasn't enough of it to pinpoint the location.

Wyatt noted that Ava had opened it only a few hours before she went missing. This wasn't a normal conversation. It was possibly a warning or a cry for help. The timestamp showed it was recorded a few days before it was sent. The message was simple. Why not send it right away?

Owen asked it before he could. "Is there anyone that would wish Ava harm?"

"Not that I know of." Kelleigh must have sensed something in Wyatt's demeanor. "I don't understand." Kelleigh was still for a moment. "I need you to tell me."

"I'm afraid I can't share all the details right now since the case is still ongoing. However, since both families were notified earlier today, I can at least give you their names." He spoke the names aloud, watching Kelleigh's eyes well up with tears. "Do those names mean anything to you?"

She shook her head, unable to answer at first. "Should they?"

"No. I was just looking for a connection," he said softly, gently reaching for her hand. "Please believe me when I tell you, I'm desperately trying to keep Ava from being another victim. Another tally in the rising count of women the Cumberland Killer has taken." The words carried a weight that hung in the room like a cloud, laden with the fear of what might happen next. "We're getting closer. I can feel it. I just need more time."

Kelleigh's eyes flickered with fear. "What if we don't have time?"

Her question was a desperate admission that he didn't want to admit. They most certainly could be out of time. He was out of his depth in knowing or guessing how much time they had before another body surfaced. The Cumberland Killer was anything but predictable. The stakes had escalated beyond the usual boundaries of simple concern, and now it was clear. Wyatt wasn't just helping to find a missing woman—he was racing against time to save Kelleigh's daughter.

FORTY-ONE

Kelleigh Morgahn

The side of the bedroom was still piled high with bags, clothes, and toiletries, a mix of hers and Ava's that had been crammed haphazardly back into the room after she had rescued them from the clutches of the cleaning crew.

It had been long enough, she decided—too long. She couldn't keep walking around the clothes, this disorganized pile of belongings, an awkward reminder of a life she was trying to hold onto and make sense of. It was time to face it, to confront the reality of what had happened. Plus, she needed a distraction—anything to keep what Detective Lockhart had said and what he didn't out of her mind.

The closet doors slid open, and she maneuvered around the heap and started to sort. With a sigh, she stacked everything onto the bed.

The pile looked like a jumble of their lives—clothes she'd worn on the trip, toiletries scattered among jackets and shoes, but most of all, Ava's things. A T-shirt Ava had worn on her drive to Nashville, a pair of worn sneakers with the laces untied. and the blue hairband that Ava always wore. She could still see Ava in them and feel the weight of her presence.

Kelleigh set to work, dividing the items into two piles—hers and Ava's, and then a third for what was worn and dirty. It felt almost mechanical, but she couldn't stop now. The weight of the clothes and the mess of everything were too much. She had to do something with it, make it neat and hers again.

Her hand brushed against Ava's favorite Iowa State hoodie, which Ava had worn more times than she could count. Kelleigh's breath caught as she picked it up, her fingers brushing the soft fabric. She brought it to her face, inhaling deeply. The familiar scent of her daughter—the sweetness of shampoo mixed with the faint trace of laundry detergent—flooded her senses. For a moment, it was as if Ava were right beside her, laughing, teasing, maybe even rolling her eyes at her mother's need to organize.

But the moment didn't last. Instead, a wave of grief hit Kelleigh, raw and unrelenting, and her tears came hot and fast. She buried her face in the hoodie as if the fabric could absorb all the aching that had built up inside her.

She clutched it to her chest, trying to steady her breathing, but the emptiness felt too vast, too deep. She wished for a moment —just a moment—when things had been normal, when the mess on the bed had just been a part of the trip instead of a painful reminder of what had been lost.

She couldn't bring herself to put Ava's things in her suitcase to take home. It felt too much like defeat, like giving up, and Ava was gone and never returning. It was like giving up hope; she just couldn't bring herself to do that. At least not yet. So, instead, she opened drawers and placed Ava's things in the dresser.

Once the room was back together, she lay on the bed, buried her head in the pillow, and cried herself to sleep.

FORTY-TWO

Owen Layne

Owen strummed the guitar, letting the final chord resonate in the air before the last of its vibrations faded and the applause of the crowd erupted. His fingers rested on the strings, and for a moment, his gaze drifted down to Gunner, sprawled on the floor beside him. The dog's big brown eyes met his, and Owen couldn't help but feel a flicker of pride.

Gunner had come through today. It wasn't just that he'd found Ava's cell phone, though that was impressive enough. It was how the dog had figured it out—working with almost no training, no actual preparation, just pure instinct. Owen had half-expected him to get distracted by something shiny or run off while chasing a proverbial squirrel, but instead, Gunner had been diligent, took his time, and tracked the faint scent. Ava's phone lay hidden, unseen to the naked eye. Without him, they would have had to have a metal detector or something to find it. Finding the phone had been like hitting the lottery. It was a lucky break in a mess of dead ends and confusion.

He glanced down at Gunner again, a small smile tugging at his lips. The dog had stepped up in ways Owen hadn't expected. When he first took him in, broken and confused after the accident, Owen never thought the dog would heal properly. It had been difficult, to say the least, but looking back, Owen wasn't sure he would have survived the last six months without him.

And if there were any chance that the phone would hold a clue that could lead them to Ava... well, Gunner would officially be a hero. Owen wasn't sure how to express his pride, but it didn't matter at that moment. He was sure Gunner knew.

The buzz of the crowd in the bar seemed distant as Owen's mind drifted back to the problem at hand. Finding Ava was still the top priority. Every minute counted. He hoped Detective Lockhart found something on the cell to further the investigation.

The fading applause was soon overtaken by the faint tap of Toby adjusting his snare, the rhythmic click of his drumsticks against the drumhead filling the brief silence. Owen caught Toby's eye from across the stage and gave a subtle nod. Without a word, the band shifted gears. The transition was seamless.

Owen leaned into the next song, his fingers moving automatically over the strings. His mind, though, kept drifting back to the phone. He couldn't stop thinking about it or about Ava— where she might be and if she was safe.

The crowd's energy pulsed around him as the bass kicked in and the song picked up its pace. Owen had done this a thousand times before, performing in front of strangers, playing for the crowd, lost in the music. But tonight, it felt different. There was an edge to it. A desperation that he couldn't shake.

He strummed the opening chords of the next song, locking eyes with the rest of the band. It was time to let the music take over. For the next few minutes, he focused on nothing but the performance —lost himself in the rhythm and the sound. But inevitably, the thought of Ava worked its way back in.

Owen had an overwhelming feeling of being observed as the song rolled on. Not in the usual sense of a musician being watched by a crowd or even a loyal fan, but more of a scrutiny, a desire to be seen, to capture his attention.

It was as if the gaze was coming from somewhere more profound, more personal, and it settled over him like a weight. His fingers faltered slightly on the strings as the sensation grew, creeping under his skin and tightening his chest. It wasn't a feeling of admiration or even curiosity—it was something more invasive, like someone was sizing him up, measuring him for something unknown. It felt almost hostile.

He tried to shake it off, letting the beat carry him, but the feeling only intensified. He could almost feel it pressing in on him from every direction, like the eyes of a thousand strangers were digging into him, searching for something they could pull out— some weakness, some secret, something that would explain why, in that moment, he felt so exposed.

It wasn't the crowd. He knew several of the faces at the nearby tables. The regulars, who like clockwork, came out on a weeknight for dinner, a drink, and some live music. He could see them chatting, eating, and swaying, lost in the music.

No, this was something else, something deeper. It was a presence that felt just outside his line of sight.

His skin prickled. His eyes locked on the large space, watching everyone come and go.

The song was winding down, but he couldn't shake the feeling that he was being measured, as if the next step he took might be under the scrutiny of someone who knew far more than they let on.

Then, a movement caught his eye—faint, almost imperceptible —on the far side of the room. A figure standing just outside the shadows of the stage lights. Owen's stomach clenched.

The final chord of the song rang out, and as the last note echoed through the venue, Owen blinked, but the figure was gone. He couldn't even be sure if it had been real—if it had been someone in the crowd or if it had been his mind playing tricks on him. But as he settled into the quiet after the music ended, the unease didn't lift. Instead, it gnawed at him.

He shot a glance at Toby, adjusted his guitar, and took a step away from the mic. "Did you see that?"

"What?" Toby asked, flipping a drumstick.

"That guy," he said. "That person who just left on the edge of the room?"

"Naw, sorry, bro."

Owen gave a head bob, adjusted his guitar, fought the urge to run after whoever it was, and started on the next song—determined to keep a better eye on the crowd.

FORTY-THREE

Ava Morgahn

Ava sat in the dark. The fog in her brain had finally worn off, but her throat was raw from screaming. Even though her eyes had finally adjusted to her surroundings, she struggled to discern even the faintest details in the darkness: a bucket to her left, the faint glow of light around the edges of a door across the room, and the vague outline, a glint of metal what seemed to be a car in front of her.

The room was eerily quiet, but she could hear traffic and maybe what sounded like the chug of a ship in the distance. But that was a big maybe. The sound that bothered her the most was coming from inside the massive room. Every once in a while, she thought she heard an intake of breath or a soft moan.

The harder she focused, the harder it was to decipher. Was it her imagination, her desire not to be in here alone, or was there someone there?

Whatever the case, Ava was determined to find out. She had to start with what she knew was true and focus on that.

She had been abducted.

The word resonated within her. An unexpected panic erupted inside her at the mere thought of the word. She didn't dare speak it out loud for fear that it might swamp her, overwhelm her with a sheer wave of terror so strong that she might never resurface. So she wouldn't speak it aloud.

Abducted.

She tried to think of the definition just to give her mind something to do other than think about the ceaseless pain in her limbs.

To her, the word abducted meant—to be taken by force and deception. In her case, at least one was true. She'd been taken by force. She had a bump on the back of her head to prove it.

Admitting this didn't make her current situation more or less scary. It just made it true. It made it something tangible that her mind could focus on and try to correct.

She shifted and tried to stand. She needed to get feeling back in her legs. It was a struggle—beyond painful—but she managed to press back against the pole her hands were tied around. She succeeded in a kind of awkward shimmy up to a standing position. Once up, though, she was spent.

Instantly, the blood rushed to her feet, and she felt lightheaded. She swayed but kept her footing. Her arms ached with a passion, and the rope cut into her wrists as she twisted, but she forced herself to make a small circle around the pole to take in her immediate surroundings. What was once behind her was now in front of her. She could see a small slit of light coming from a crack in the wall. Light streamed through the minuscule opening, calling to her like a beacon. She took it as a sign and struggled to move toward it, but the pole and her bindings held her captive, cutting further into her wrists.

She let out a hiss, biting back the pain. An overwhelming sense of defeat swamped her. How was this her life right now? How had she gotten into this situation?

She racked her brain, trying to remember.

The last thing she remembered was standing in the parking garage near her car, fumbling in her purse for her keys. After that, there was nothing—nothing but the voice.

Her thoughts ricocheted around in her mind, leaving her dizzy with confusion and unable to focus. How had he known her name? The only people in Nashville who knew her middle name were her mother, Molly, and… Owen.

Her mother. Where was she? Had she gone home, assuming everything was fine? Or was she frantic, wondering where her daughter was? How long had it been? Hours or days? She wasn't sure. She had no sense of time in this ebony void.

If it were days, surely her mother would be worried. They spoke every day or at least texted. The thought that her mother had no idea where she was—that she could be searching, calling, desperate for any sign—sent a cold chill through her. What if her mother was already imagining the worst? Then again, it couldn't get much worse than this.

Ava's next thought was of Owen. She remembered the kiss in the parking garage. The feel of his lips on hers. The look in his eyes as he backed up, forcing himself to leave when she knew he wanted to stay. Did he realize she was missing, or did he think she was ghosting him? The idea that he might not even notice her absence stung more than the thought that he thought she was pushing him away. They had only just met, and maybe she was just a tiny blip on his radar, easily overlooked.

Had he moved on, busy with his life as if nothing had changed? The thought twisted her stomach, but she refused to believe he could be that indifferent. He cared, didn't he? They had a connection. She'd felt it, and Ava was sure he had too. It had been real. She had to believe it because, without that hope, she had nothing.

She braced herself against the pole and started to work at the ropes, giving herself as much slack as she could manage—the cold steel of the pole bit into her as she twisted. But after a few minutes, sweat beaded across her upper lip. Her wrists were raw, and her fingertips burned so much so that her pulse pounded at the tips. She slowly slid down the pole and sat, dejected, exhausted.

"Ouch," she muttered as something sharp jabbed into her when she sat down. Gritting her teeth, she inched away from the light, her hands fumbling to trace the object beneath her. Bolts—large metal protruding bolts—anchored the pole to the floor.

A thought flickered. If she could rub the rope against the protruding metal and wear through the cords, there was a chance. It seemed like a daunting task, but it was a start. She had to try. No matter how small the hope, the thought of escape made her heart beat faster.

She wasn't completely powerless, not as long as there was breath in her lungs.

FORTY-FOUR

Detective Wyatt Lockhart

Wyatt parked the unmarked car behind one of many unidentifiable warehouses. The abandoned concrete plant could be seen off in the distance. He exited and slid his sunglasses on to shield his eyes from the intense Tennessee sun. He knew from experience that many homeless people congregated and camped in the shadows of empty buildings, but today, the area seemed deserted.

Wyatt threaded through the maze of deserted warehouses, looking for signs of encampment or people nearby. The asphalt radiated heat, making the sweltering air even more unbearable, so he made it a point to stick to the shade near the walls.

Wyatt saw a few makeshift lean-tos, stranded shopping carts, and large barrels used on cold nights, but no people. He walked along, jiggled a few doors, and peered in dirty windows, but the closer he got to the plant, the more uninhabited the area felt.

The sound of shuffling feet drew Wyatt's attention, and he turned to see an elderly woman moving down the sidewalk with surprising speed.

"Hello," he called out.

She didn't acknowledge him. She didn't even slow.

"Shit," he muttered. "She's going to make me work for it." He jogged across the street. "Excuse me, ma'am. Can I have a word?"

She walked on as if she hadn't heard until approaching an

overhang that provided shade. She stopped abruptly.

"What?" she asked gruffly, glancing around to ensure no one was nearby. "I ain't done nothin' wrong."

"I didn't say you had, ma'am." Wyatt tried to soothe with his voice. "My name is Wyatt." He extended his hand, trying to project calm and friendly, though he felt the weight of her scrutiny. "What's yours?"

"Wyatt?" she questioned him warily. "That's it?" She studied him intently but left his hand hanging, a clear barrier between them. "You a copper?"

Wyatt tucked his hands into his front pockets, a gesture of both surrender and self-assurance. "I am."

Her eyes narrowed, suspicion hardening her features. "What do you want?"

Wyatt kept a few feet between them, keeping a professional distance. "Do you live around here?"

"No. Just passing through."

"Passing through to where?"

"Why's it matter?" she shot back, her voice rising defensively.

He shrugged, trying to keep his tone neutral. "Not sure that it does."

"Listen, copper..."

"My name is Detective Lockhart," he interjected, maintaining a steady gaze. "If you'd be so kind as to let me ask you a few questions."

Her expression softened momentarily, seemingly caught between her instinct to distrust and the faint glimmer to help, or at least that's what he hoped.

"What's in it for me?"

Wyatt pulled out his wallet and extracted a gift card from a local subway shop. He held it out to her. She hesitated for a moment, judging him. She plucked it neatly from his hand when he didn't retract it.

He took that as a sign that he could ask her a few questions. "I was wondering if you had seen anything unusual around here lately?"

She hesitated, seeing no other soul. She asked, "What do you consider unusual?"

"Vehicles or people coming and going that aren't usually here or aren't supposed to be."

"Maybe."

Wyatt narrowed his eyes, the memory of the shadowy figure who had slipped past the scene during the extraction of the last victim from the Cumberland flooded his mind. Two details hit him with pinpoint clarity, triggering an unmistakable recognition: a weathered gray T-shirt and a faded military-grade green backpack.

It had to be her. He was certain—the size, the shape, the way she moved—every aspect matched perfectly.

"You were there when we pulled the body from the river just a couple of blocks over."

"So what if I was? There ain't no crime in watching."

"No, ma'am, there's not."

"Oh, stop calling me that, for goodness sake. Name's Dorthea," she said tartly.

"Yes, ma'am. It is nice to meet you, but my mama didn't raise any fool. I was always taught to address a woman properly. If you'll forgive me, Miss Dorthea, I will keep addressing you as ma'am."

She smiled at him then for the first time. "Good 'ol southern boy to the core."

"Yes, ma'am." He congratulated himself. She sounded like she was warming up to him, so he plowed ahead. "About the woman we pulled from the river."

Dorthea rubbed the center of her chest unconsciously as if to scrub away the pain. She leaned back against the cool of the concrete wall. "I happened to be passing by." She looked over her shoulder. "She die before or after she went in the water?"

Wyatt shifted and leveled a gaze at the woman. "After."

She raised untamed eyebrows. "Well, you didn't come down here to tell me that. Just come out and ask me what you want to be askin'. I ain't got time for all this." She glanced around again.

"Do you stay down by the river?"

"Maybe." Dorthea cocked her head. "Why?"

"Have you seen anyone down by the river lately that may have looked suspicious?"

She was quiet for a moment. "Not see, but hear."

"What did you hear?"

"Don't know for sure." She wiped the sweat from her brow with the back of her hand.

"If you had to guess."

"The shuffle of feet. The dragging of something heavy, and the not-so-quiet way something is slipped into the water." She licked her cracked lips. "He thinks he's quiet or tries to be, but there is only so much you can mask by the darkness. No matter how slow you move, water makes sound, ripples, and laps at the banks. Most wouldn't notice, but me?" She shrugged. "I always got my ears trained for the unusual."

"You didn't happen to see anything when you heard these unusual sounds, did you?"

"Nope. I know when to keep my head down."

"I understand," Wyatt said, frustrated.

"I looked the first time, ain't no need to look any time after."

"The first time?" he questioned, praying she was about to reveal something significant.

"'Bout five or six months ago now, give or take."

Wyatt lifted his eyebrows slightly. Trying not to give away his surprise. That was the timeline for the first victim. "How many times have you seen him?"

"Only one. You ain't too sharp, are you?"

Wyatt amended the question. "How many times have you heard him?"

Her eyes sparkled knowingly as he played her game. "Altogether, five."

She glanced over her shoulder once more as if the buildings had eyes. "But you didn't hear that from me."

"Trust me, Miss Dorthea, I would never reveal you."

With a nod, she hobbled off before he could say or ask anything else, disappearing around the corner.

"Wait," he called after her, but she didn't slow.

He stepped forward but stopped when he heard a low and urgent whisper carry on the wind. "Don't follow me."

FORTY-FIVE

Dorthea

Dorthea hid in the shadow of the building, just out of sight of where she had left the detective. She watched him from her spot for what seemed like forever, trying to find a way into the plant. Eventually, he gave up and returned to his car. Without the proper tools or the know-how, he wasn't gettin' in. The fence was too high, too sturdy, and too secure. She smiled a smug, satisfied smile. She didn't need him nosin' about her territory. Too many people already doin' that.

Despite the sinking sun and the urge to hurry, she waited another half hour to make certain he wasn't coming back.

With one last glance in the direction the detective had gone, she eased out of the spot, finally alone.

The trash scattered on the dirty street just outside the concrete plant as the breeze toyed with it. She hustled toward her sanctuary by the river. The familiar path should have offered her solace, but the only way there was obstructed by the dreaded maze of the abandoned factory with its infinite complex building site.

Dorthea had traversed these haunting structures at least twice a day for the past two years, ever since she called the bridge home, yet the area seemed unsettling the last few months.

Slipping through the small opening in the fence, she scanned the area.

The deserted concrete plant stood like a ghost of industry, its hulking skeleton rusted and crumbling. The air smelled of dust and decay, mingling with the faint, acrid scent of old oil and forgotten machinery, with the occasional scent of river—earth and worms mingled in.

Concrete silos, once towering and pristine, stood tall and foreboding, like giants standing sentry between her and her home, daring her to cross their path. It was all in her imagination, she knew. They were nothing more than repositories streaked with grime, their exteriors cracked and weathered by years of neglect.

Graffiti, bold and raw, covered the walls of many buildings along the outskirts. The ground was littered with scraps of metal, crumbling bricks, and rusted pipes that snaked across the ground like discarded bones, twisted and corroded from exposure to the elements, some half-buried in weeds that had long since reclaimed the space, pushing up through the widening cracks.

There were tanks, equipment sheds, and a maintenance building. Then, the strange-looking hoppers, conveyor belts that ended abruptly, and an elevator that went nowhere.

The once-thrumming hum of industry was gone, replaced by an unsettling stillness, broken only by the creak of metal shifting in the wind or the distant echo of footsteps on cracked concrete. The place felt haunted, as though the ghosts of past employees still lingered, trapped in the ruins of what had once been an environment of purpose.

Particles and powder swirled in tiny motes caught on invisible updrafts, creating tiny dust storms that coated everything in a filmy, grayish-white substance.

Broken windows dotted the decaying buildings, some shattered entirely, leaving jagged shards of glass to catch the light in eerie glints. Their shattered windows, and even the boarded-up ones, resembled dark, watching eyes.

A chill ran down her spine, a feeling that she was not merely passing through but being scrutinized by something unseen. With every echoing footstep, the paranoia crept in, tightening its grip.

She quickened her pace. Shadows seemed to shift in her peripheral vision as the sun dipped lower, and the faintest rustle of wind felt like whispered threats. The air thickened with an uneasy silence, and Dorthea couldn't shake the sensation that the buildings were alive, their decaying walls harboring hidden secrets and watching her every move. Each time she crossed their threshold, she felt more like prey than a passerby, and the sanctuary she sought felt tantalizingly far away.

Headlights swept the area, and Dorthea took her five-foot-nine wiry frame and shrank, hunching her shoulders, lowering her head, and blending in with the shadows she had just been frightened of. She pressed against the wall, her dark skin and clothes her only camouflage.

The vehicle stopped, and Dorthea felt icy fingers snake down her spine as she heard the scrape and creak of a metal door rolling up, a sound that seemed to linger in the air. The vehicle drove forward and disappeared into the building, the door groaning ominously as it lowered behind it.

The screech of metal echoed through the stillness, twisting in her mind until it almost resembled a woman's scream. The haunting noise sent a ripple of dread through her, as if the very walls of the warehouse held onto forgotten cries, resonating something sinister.

Against her better judgment, Dorthea crept back, inching along the concrete wall, desperate to stay in the shadows. A sliver of light illuminated the corner of a blackened window. She crouched and put her eye to it, utterly unprepared for what she saw.

FORTY-SIX

Detective Wyatt Lockhart

"I've got this crazy idea," Owen told Detective Lockhart. "Hear me out."

A deep frown creased Wyatt's face. "That's not a good way to start. Without hearing what you have to say, I should nix the idea based solely on principle."

"Let me rephrase." Owen ran a hand through his dark brown hair. "I have this bold, unorthodox idea that could lead to the breakthrough we've been waiting for. It might just be the key to finding Ava. And that's the most important thing, right?"

"You're correct." Wyatt hesitated, not sure where this was going. "What's your crazy idea?"

"What if we use Gunner to find Ava?" Owen glanced down at the dog, who lay quietly at his feet. Suddenly, the dog's head popped up, and a low growl rumbled from his throat.

Before Detective Lockhart could answer, Ransick popped his head through the door. "Hey, Sarge... Sorry. Didn't realize you had company."

"Damn it, Ransick, if I've told you once, I've told you a hundred times. Knock!"

"Again—your door was open." Ransick looked at Owen. "You look familiar. Have we met?"

The low growl continued.

"Steady," Owen soothed Gunner and answered. "Don't think so,"

"This is Owen Layne," Wyatt offered.

"Right. Your Officer Dylan Layne's brother," Ransick said. "We've spoken a few times on the phone."

"Yes."

Ransick peered down at the dog. "And this must be his dog."

"It is," Owen acknowledged.

"Ransick, did you need something?" Wyatt asked, slightly perturbed by the officer's appearance.

"Huh?" Ransick pulled his eyes off the animal. "Umm, yeah. Some of us in the bullpen were going to get pizza. You want in on it? I'm buying."

What in the hell? Was he interrupting to ask about pizza? "Lost another bet, I presume. I'll pass. But thanks," he managed.

"Suit yourself." He turned to Owen. "Are you on your way out?"

"Just about. I have a gig I gotta get to."

"I can walk you out," Ransick offered.

"Um, sure," Owen replied. "I'll just be another minute."

"I'll meet you at the end of the hall when you're done." Without any fanfare, Ransick left.

Wyatt observed Gunner, noting the dog stopped growling when Ransick was gone.

"Sorry, Gunner doesn't usually growl at people unless he gets a wild hair up his ass. Not sure what got into him. Anyway, what do you think? Are you willing to try to use him to locate Ava?"

"I like your idea, kid. But I don't think the dog has what it takes."

"What do you mean?" Owen questioned, his tone edged toward frustration. "He located Ava's phone. I'm sure he could find her, too, if given a chance."

"The phone may or may not have been a fluke. After all, you had a good idea of where to start looking. Didn't you?"

Undeterred, Owen agreed. "You're right. I did. But..."

"How did you know where to look?"

"You told us where the car was found."

"I did, didn't I?" Wyatt nodded but anticipated how Owen would react when he told him he'd seen him on camera entering the parking garage with Ava.

"Why didn't you tell me you walked Ava to her car Monday night?" He saw the nervous flick of Owen's eyes.

"How did you know?"

"It's on camera. You and Ava... walking hand in hand into the parking garage." He watched the kid with a practiced eye. "Looks like you were the last to see her Monday night before she disappeared. Would you care to explain?"

Owen stiffened, clenching his jaw. "I texted Ava earlier in the day and asked if she would like to go for dinner and a drink after work." He put up his hands as if to ward off an attack. "Lock, I know what you're thinking, but don't. It was all completely innocent. I like Ava and would never do anything to hurt her."

"Then why didn't you come clean?" Wyatt asked, making direct eye contact with Owen.

"Because I know how the police work. My brother was one, or have you forgotten?"

"I haven't." Wyatt knew it was a dig on the investigation, but he wouldn't let it deter him from his line of questioning. "I'm waiting for an answer."

"I didn't want to get caught in the crossfire," Owen answered angrily. Then he drew a sharp breath, held it, and exhaled. "But I can see now, by not admitting it, how it must look."

"Like you're guilty of something."

"Well, I'm not. What would be my angle?"

"Mind you, I'm just spit-balling here, but my first thought would be..." Wyatt leaned back in his chair, threaded his fingers together, and laid them in his lap. "Maybe you're looking for some attention. Your brother is gone. You're stuck with his dog. Could be as simple as take the girl, use the dog to find her, and make a name for yourself."

"What the hell? You've got to be kidding!" Owen spat, fury written all over his face.

"It's just a theory." His voice low but unwavering.

"A *hell* of a theory if you ask me." Owen's fists clenched at his sides.

Wyatt shifted in his chair, leaning forward with a predatory calm. "It's my job to look at every angle. I'm sorry, Mr. Layne, if it makes you uncomfortable."

Owen's eyes narrowed, rage seeping into every word. "I *would* never lay a hand on Ava, or any woman. Don't you dare suggest it."

Wyatt's gaze hardened, icy and unyielding. "Remember this feeling the next time you even think about keeping things from me."

There was a long, charged silence as both men stared at the other unwilling to yield. Wyatt saw Owen's jaw clench, his fingers flex, but he held his ground. The silence stretched on.

Finally, Owen's eyes flicked downward, the hard edge in his posture softening just enough. He exhaled slowly, his voice low but steady. "I apologize," he said, the words reluctant but undeniable. "I was wrong to keep that from you. It won't happen again."

"See that it doesn't." Wyatt sat straighter. "Now tell me everything that happened from the moment you met her Monday night until you walked her to her car."

"Alright." Owen gave him the details.

Wyatt listened without interrupting and knew he could go back and watch the cameras to verify what Owen was saying was true.

When Owen was finished relaying his story, he asked, "Satisfied?"

"For now."

"Now, about Gunner..."

"Look, I'm not saying it's off the table," Wyatt began, his voice trailing off as he rubbed the back of his neck, stalling. "But without a place to start, and with a dog that's less than..." He cleared his throat, obviously hesitant to continue.

Owen quickly finished the thought for him, his voice dry—filled in the blank, "Discharged, injured, or broken. Take your pick."

Wyatt contemplated the animal but didn't disagree. "Right, well... let's say not adequately trained for this situation. It's more of a shot in the dark than anything else. It's not exactly the ideal scenario, and I wouldn't bet much on it."

"Okay, I hear what you're saying. What if I knew where to start?"

"Do you?" Wyatt asked, narrowing his eyes and sitting a little straighter.

"No," Owen visibly deflated. "But if I did, or if you had a good lead, would you consider it then?"

"If I had a solid lead, I might consider it. But that's a big if." He shifted uncomfortably, not wanting to admit how slim the chances were. "But I suppose if we're desperate enough, it's better than nothing."

"Right. That's all I'm asking." Owen stood and signaled for Gunner. Both man and dog stood just inside the door. "Can I ask one more thing?"

Already suspecting what he might ask, he said yes anyway. "Certainly."

"Any leads on my brother's case?"

It was a shot, and Wyatt knew it—one last-ditch effort for the guy to narrow the playing field. Disheartened by the answer he needed to give, he said, "I'm sorry. No. I truly wish there was. And I am still working on it. When one of our own falls, believe me when I say I won't rest until I have answers." He felt the shift in the air between them.

Owen bobbed his head slightly but didn't say anything. He didn't need to. Wyatt could see disappointment written all over his face. He felt the gravity of that himself, as if he had let Owen, Dylan, and now Ava down. He had to give the man credit, though he didn't say anything. Instead, Owen simply turned and walked out.

Wyatt flopped back in his chair, disheartened, and tapped his pencil on the desk, thinking.

It wasn't a bad idea to use the dog. It just wasn't the best. They had nowhere to start, and he didn't want to waste precious time or resources chasing after a dog that may or may not be any good at his job.

Ransick popped back into his office.

"Son of a bitch! Ransick, I swear!"

"Couldn't help but overhear your conversation with Owen Layne." Ransick dropped a file on Wyatt's desk.

"What's this?"

"The report on the dog. Just in case you're considering using him for anything."

Wyatt took a pen and lifted the top tentatively. "I assume you know what's in here."

"I do."

"Well?"

"The dog's spent. Broken. He may be physically rehabilitated, but... well, you heard him growl at me. He's not fit. Not mentally, not emotionally. Whatever's left of him, it's not enough for what we need. He's a liability at best." Ransick let out a long breath, the weight of the words hanging heavy between them. "He's not the same dog anymore." He backed out of the office. "Just thought you should know."

FORTY-SEVEN

Owen Layne

The last set ended, and the band gathered their gear. Owen signaled for Gunner, and the German Shepherd popped up from his place by the stage. He gave the command, and they headed for the elevator. On the first floor, the band split and went their separate ways. He, Toby, and the dog went out the back toward the alley, and the others went out the main entrance.

They paused in the alley so Gunner could get some relief.

Toby leaned against the wall, his back pressing into it as he laughed. "Can you believe that compliment from Stella? That's two in a row. It felt like we just won the lottery, didn't it?"

"It did," Owen admitted. "Compliments are hard to come by from her. But recently, she's been handing them out like candy."

There was a low growl from Gunner as someone lurked in the shadows at the edge of the alley. "He will attack if threatened," Owen warned the shifting figure.

"I-I don't want no trouble. Just come to deliver a message," the voice stammered.

"Dorthea?" Owen questioned. "Is that you?"

"It's me."

"Gunner," Owen gave the command, and the dog released, trotting back toward him. "Come on out, Dot. He won't hurt you." But Owen grabbed the German Shepherd's leash for good measure. There was no sense in tempting fate.

"You sure?" she asked, hesitating on the fringes of the street light.

"I am."

The homeless woman shuffled closer.

"What can I do for you?" Owen asked, looking her over. She looked tired, but then she usually did, he reasoned. Her lifestyle and living conditions accentuated her age. There was something else, though. Agitated was the word he was looking for. Her eyes were darting back and forth, anywhere and everywhere but directly at him. "Dorthea? Are you alright?"

"I will be."

"Let's go," Toby warned in a low voice that was barely audible, taking hold of Owen's arm. "She probably wants to sell you drugs, bum a cigarette, or get a handout."

"Hang on just a moment," Owen said.

Dorthea balled her hands together.

"You said you had a message?" Owen asked, taking a step closer to her.

"Not a message," she corrected. "More like somethin' you might want to know." She licked her lips and shifted unsteadily.

"Are you going to give it to him then?" Toby asked, getting impatient.

"Maybe." She glanced over her shoulder, shuffling closer. "What's in it for me?"

"See?" Toby shook his head. "I told you. She wants money."

"Not sure I should get involved, is all. Could be dangerous for someone like me." Her eyes flitted around nervously.

Owen wasn't sure what to think. He had no idea what information Dorthea might have. Toby was probably right. She just wanted money. He felt a pang in his chest. He only had a ten in his wallet, but he pulled it out anyway. She needed it more than he did. "Here," he said, handing it to her.

She eyed the bill but didn't take it. "I don't need your money," she said defiantly.

He put the bill back in his wallet. "If you are in danger, Dorthea, I can try to help."

"I ain't in no danger yet. She is."

Owen stopped in his tracks. "Who?"

"Your pretty friend."

Fear gripped him. "Ava?" he questioned. "Have you seen her?"

The woman nodded ever so slightly.

"Where? When?" Owen demanded, taking a step closer to her.

She backed up and hissed. "Keep ya voice down. Even the walls have ears."

Owen held out his hand as a sign of surrender. "I'm sorry. You're right. Dot, please. When did you see her?"

"Earlier tonight."

"Where?" Owen asked, moving closer to her.

"At the plant," her voice was so low it was barely audible. "Down by the river."

"The only plant that I'm aware of is the old concrete factory. It's been abandoned and closed for years," Toby said.

"That'd be the one," she responded.

"Isn't it securely locked and enclosed with fences?" Owen asked.

There was a small affirmative gesture from the woman.

"How did you get in?"

"I got my ways."

"Then that's where I should go."

"It's deadly if you don't know how to stay hidden. One wrong step, and you're exposed. And that place? It's like a maze. You'll get lost easy if you don't know what you're doing. End up trapped with no way out or wandering in circles trying to get your bearings." Dorthea licked her lips again. "Only I can get in."

"Can you take me?"

The back door opened to the bar, swinging between them, momentarily blocking Owen's view of Dorthea.

Stella stopped in surprise. "What are you boys doing hanging out in the alley? Thought you had gone home?"

Owen ignored her, desperate to get past and pushing the door aside, but it was too late. Dorthea was gone.

"Dorthea," he called. His words rang out into the void of darkness, echoing off the walls around them and finally dying a slow death. He half expected Dot to reappear from the shadows.

"What's going on?" Stella asked, caught off guard.

His pulse quickened. "We need to find out where she went.'

"You're not buying what she said, are you?" Toby asked in disbelief.

Owen didn't answer. He and Gunner took off sprinting down the alley, hearing Toby shout his name, but he didn't stop.

Dorthea had vanished, desperation clawing at his throat as he called her name. Each echo of his voice felt more hopeless than the last, swallowed by the oppressive silence that surrounded him.

Reaching the end of the alley, he paused, breathless, scanning the empty streets. He looked right, then left, his heart sinking with every passing second. The once vibrant city felt like a ghost town, stripped of life, and the realization hit him like a punch to the gut. Dorthea could be anywhere, hiding in a city that conceivably swallowed her whole. Worse, though—so was Ava.

FORTY-EIGHT

Kelleigh Morgahn

Footsteps. She thought she heard them—soft, barely audible, like whispers against the floorboards, the kind that lingered in the corners of her mind. She was too tired to tell the difference between dreaming and waking.

Kelleigh lay still, her body tangled in sheets, her heart hammering away inside her chest. She wasn't sure if it was the remnants of a nightmare or something more. The quiet, undetectable sound of movement seemed to crawl beneath the surface of her awareness, just beyond her grasp.

She tried to mentally shake it off, to retreat into the false safety of slumber, but the sound persisted, growing more distinct now, more deliberate. The walls were too thin, and Kelleigh was acutely aware of every little sound. Soft but undeniable, someone was in the house. The thought should have snapped her awake but muddled her senses instead. Her eyelids fluttered, heavy with the weight of sleep, torn between reality and fantasy, the line between the two blurring.

Kelleigh heard a door whisper open. A floorboard groaned. The shuffle of—paper. The creak of the bed frame as someone sat on the corner of the mattress. *Cara.* Her name registered in Kelleigh's mind, keeping the panic at bay. She seemed always to be sneaking in and out of the apartment.

There was a scrape of metal against wood, sounding as if something had been shoved hastily into place—the click of a latch, the turn of a lock, the retreat of feet.

Kelleigh relaxed as she heard one more door open and close, and then the apartment fell into an uneasy silence.

A shrill ring cut through the quiet. Kelleigh sat bolt upright in bed and snatched her phone off the nightstand when it rang again. "Hello?"

"Kelleigh?" the woman's voice questioned.

"Yes. Who is this?"

"It's Lydia. Molly's mom. I got your call."

"Oh, Lydia! Thank goodness," Kelleigh breathed out, sinking back onto the bed in sheer relief. The tension in her chest seemed to lift slightly, her mind racing to catch up. Maybe now they could contact Molly in hopes Ava was with her, or she might know of her whereabouts. The thought of them being together, wherever they were, gave her a glimmer of hope.

With a sense of urgency, Kelleigh didn't waste time with pleasantries. "I'm so glad you called," she began. "I don't know how to say this, so I'm just going to say it: Ava is missing. The police and I are working through every possible lead, but other than Ava's roommate, Molly, is the only person I know in Nashville. The problem is that I don't have her number and cannot reach her. That's why I called you. I was hoping you could give me her contact information so I can contact Molly."

There was a long silence on the other end. "Lydia? Are you still there?" she asked, her voice tight with anxiety.

"I am," came Lydia's response, her voice thick with emotion.

Kelleigh could hear the faint sound of muffled sobs. "Is everything okay?" she asked, her concern growing.

"No," Lydia replied, her voice barely above a whisper.

Kelleigh's heart dropped. "What's wrong?"

"I think something has happened to Molly, too," Lydia said, her voice trembling. "I haven't heard from her in over a week."

Kelleigh's heart plunged inside her chest, the weight of the news crashed over her like a tidal wave. "I'm so sorry," she said softly, her mind racing. "Have you contacted the police?"

"I did... just a few hours ago," Lydia responded, her voice cracking.

"What did they say?" Kelleigh pressed, trying to focus on practical details.

Lydia was silent for a long moment before responding with bitterness. "What could they say?" she asked quietly. "They asked all the basic questions—her age, address, workplace, social media accounts, and if she had friends or a boyfriend, but I don't have much more information to give them. And now..." She let out a quiet sob. "What kind of mother am I? Why don't I know more about where she is or what's happening with her? I'm a terrible mother."

"No, you're not," Kelleigh interjected quickly, her heart aching for Lydia. She had felt the same overwhelming guilt and confusion herself. "You're doing everything you can. You're not a terrible mother."

Lydia sniffed. "I don't talk to Molly daily, so I'm not sure if she's been missing for three hours or a week. I just know she hasn't returned my calls since last week."

"Can you give me Molly's address?" Kelleigh asked, trying to keep her voice steady. "I can at least go by her apartment and see what I can find out. Ava's been missing for three days." She hesitated, then said, "Do you think there's any chance they're together?"

Lydia was silent momentarily, and Kelleigh could almost feel her thinking through the possibilities. Finally, she spoke, her voice tinged with doubt. "I don't know. It's possible. I know Molly was looking forward to Ava coming."

The thought of the two girls being together, possibly safe,

oblivious to the drama they were causing, gave Kelleigh hope. But then Lydia's voice broke through with fresh panic.

"Have you seen the news? The Cumberland Killer—there are five victims now, all the same age as our girls. They haven't released any names yet because they haven't been able to notify the next of kin. Do you think that's what's happened to our girls?" she asked, her voice trembling as the fear crept in.

Kelleigh's heart skipped a beat. The mention of the Cumberland Killer sent a wave of cold terror through her. She could feel her pulse pounding in her ears. "I-I hope not," she managed to say, her throat tight with fear and denial. The map in Detective Lockhart's office quickly came to mind, giving her a shudder.

The thought of their daughters caught in the same twisted fate made her stomach churn with dread. She had promised Wyatt —no, *swore*—that she wouldn't reveal anything, but the silence now felt like a betrayal. She stood frozen, the connection thick with unspoken truths, unable to offer her friend even an ounce of comfort.

FORTY-NINE

Ava Morgahn

Ava worked the rope steadily. Her skin rubbed raw, torn, cracked, and bleeding as she threaded it repeatedly over the bolts. She could feel the chords begin to fray. Glancing over her shoulder, she noticed that the fragile light that once lit the tiny crack in the window had grown dark.

It was nighttime.

She had spent the day trying to rub through the rope. Her mouth was dry, her throat was sore, and her arms felt like rubber bands. Her body and her emotions were on the verge of breaking.

Then she heard it—the steady tap of shoes on concrete. It was so soft at first that she thought she had only imagined it. Despite believing it was a figment of her imagination, she screamed, "Help! Is anyone there?" She paused and listened. The footsteps were getting closer. "Help! Please! Someone! Anyone! I'm here!" Her voice was hoarse and scratchy, but she yelled out again. "Help me, please!"

The door *screeched* open, a sound like nails on a chalkboard, and a spot of harsh, blinding light spilled into the room. She recoiled, her vision searing, her heart hammering.

"Well, well. Looky what we have here." His low, mocking voice echoed off the walls like it was coming from everywhere. She couldn't see his face—just a dark, looming silhouette behind the blinding glow, a monstrous shadow against the painful brightness.

He stepped forward, intentionally shifting so the light hit her directly in the eyes with a vicious force. She squinted and closed her eyes, her vision swimming.

"Please," she begged, sounding almost feral even to her own ears.

"Wasn't good enough for you at the bar, but it seems you want me now." The figure loomed more prominent, his presence suffocating, every movement deliberate, every word a slow, torturous pull on her sanity as he chuckled and came closer.

"Do I know you?" She didn't need him to answer. She already knew. He was the man from Cognac Creek who wanted to buy her a drink. She still couldn't see his face, but she recognized his voice.

"Thought you were too good for me, didn't you? But I bet now you wish you hadn't ignored me."

"It wasn't like that," she started to protest. "I was work—"

"Shut up, bitch." He backhanded her across the face. "I don't want to hear your lies."

Her face stung from the impact. She saw stars, and the copper-metallic taste of blood filled her mouth. She felt the rope give slightly as her body jerked to the side from the blow.

"What are you going to do with me?" she asked, biting back a sob.

He sat back on his haunches, keeping the beam of light even with her eyes.

"I haven't decided just yet. But I like that you want me, need me now." He rubbed a finger across her chin and let his hand linger there. "Can't wait to see what a few more days in the dark will do."

She could hear the smirk in his voice. The deliberate slow lengthening of the words, and knew he was enjoying every second of it. Begging would do no good with him, she decided. That's what he wanted. "I brought you water. Want some?"

"Yes, please." He held it to her lips, and she drank deep. The lukewarm liquid coated her parched throat as she swallowed. The taste on her tongue was slightly bitter. But too much had slid down her throat before it registered. Instantly, she pulled back. "Thank you."

There was a low moan across the room, and both heads turned.

"Ahh. Sleeping Beauty stirs at last." He laughed.

"Is there someone else in here?" Ava asked, water dripping down her chin. Every once in a while, she had heard sounds, but she had thought it was just her mind playing tricks on her.

She could see his head jerk behind the light toward the sound. "Yeah, I've been keeping a regular rotation the last few weeks. Don't you know you're in the presence of greatness?"

"Who?" she asked.

"Me, of course."

There was just something about the way he said it that made her skin crawl—a pride that simmered just below the calm facade. He leaned in, mere inches from her neck, and inhaled deeply, drawing in her scent. She scrunched her eyes closed feeling his hot breath on her neck, the slight tickle of his lips as they hovered possessively along her collarbone. She willed herself not to shrink back, not to shudder. It's what he wanted, what he craved. She could feel it pulsating out of him. If she could help it, she wouldn't give him the satisfaction.

"Who are you?" she whispered, barely able to speak. Fear coursed through her like a raging river.

"Haven't you figured it out yet, baby?

"The Cumberland Killer," she hissed, scarcely audible, terrified to be right.

She could feel his lips part and curve into a sneer. "Look at that. You're one step ahead of the police." She could feel his control slipping, hanging on by a mere thread. "I like your tattoo," he murmured in her ear. "That's right, I saw it. A cute little dandelion tucked right above your left hip."

She trembled uncontrollably and tried not to think about what else he had seen while she was out cold. She could sense his hold on control was faltering as his hands skimmed down her bare arms.

"You know, I could loosen those ropes on your ankles. Make you a little more comfortable." He ran his hand down her bare legs. "If you do something for me."

She swallowed hard, weighing her options. If he did loosen the ropes around her ankles, she'd be one step closer to being free, but she was afraid to ask what he wanted. She inhaled deeply and forced herself to ask anyway, thinking of only escaping, "What do you want?"

His hand lingered on the ropes. "Your password for your savings account."

That surprised her. It wasn't what she had suspected. What was he doing? Was he emptying her accounts? "Let me go, and I will give them to you."

"That's not the deal I'm offering."

He would withdraw money from her accounts if she gave him the password. But if he did that, surely the police would be watching for any fraudulent activity or credit card activity since she's been missing. If she let him have it, it could trigger a warning. This could be a way to…

"You have exactly ten seconds to respond, or the deal is off. One…"

"Okay, okay! I'll give it to you, but not until you start untying."

He set the harsh light down next to the half-empty water bottle, ensuring it stayed in her eyes.

"I start to untie, and you start talking."

She gave him the password as his fingers worked the rope, feeling a slight rush of blood.

She heard a cell phone vibrate.

With a quick jerk of his hands, he yanked the rope back tight, then deliberately moved away from her.

"No!" she shouted, her voice raw with the sting of betrayal that she knew deep down was inevitable. "We had a deal!"

"That was your mistake, Ava Lynn." Standing, he towered over her and checked the phone.

"You're not going to get away with this!"

He laughed wickedly. "Watch me. I'll be back, baby, after I make sure the password works. Then, we can pick up where we left off. Try not to miss me too much."

He hummed the haunting tune, and as he closed the door, she heard him utter the last words: *I am cunning. You should be running, Ava Lynn.*

FIFTY

Owen Layne

Owen stood for a moment to catch his breath. He was about to turn around and head back to Toby when Gunner let out a sharp bark.

"What's the matter, boy?" Owen asked.

The dog's deep brown eyes locked onto something in the darkness, his head cocked as he nudged an object on the asphalt with his nose, a soft yet determined push that made Owen pause.

Owen approached slowly, his boots crunching lightly on the gritty pavement as he knelt. The object Gunner had discovered was small and bright—almost out of place in the darkness of the alleyway.

It was a bright pink rabbit's foot. He frowned, recognizing it immediately. He'd seen it before hanging off of Dorthea's tattered backpack.

"It must have fallen off," Owen said to no one.

Gunner sat at attention, his posture tense. Owen's eyes flicked between the small charm and the direction Dorthea had gone.

Owen held the rabbit's foot in his palm, his mind running through the options. He could return to Toby and head home or finish what he started. He glanced down at Gunner. "What do you think, boy? You want to help me track her down?"

Gunner gave a low whine, his tail swishing in the faint light. His focus was clear—he was ready.

Owen thought of Detective Lockhart and what he would think if he knew what they were about to do. He probably wouldn't be happy, but did it matter? He was following Dorthea, not Ava.

If this worked, if they could successfully find Dorthea with this trinket, maybe Detective Lockhart would let Gunner try to find Ava.

Or... he could head straight to the concrete plant and search for Ava, take the risk, and try to find her before it's too late. But still, the thought made him hesitate. Dorthea's warning echoed in his mind—*only I can get in.*

The streets, the maze of alleyways around that place, it wasn't safe. What if he got spotted? She said that he would be easily exposed. What if he lost his way and got trapped in some dead-end corner with no one around to help? He'd be useless to Ava, completely exposed, or worse, he might put her in more danger. That was the last thing he wanted.

The task at hand seemed the best option at the moment. Find Dorthea and have her take him to Ava. After all, she knew her way around. Owen glanced at the rabbit's foot.

He could feel the pressure mounting on his decision. The weight of everything he held dear was right here in the palm of his hand. If it could lead to Ava, he had to try.

Bending down, he held the furry pink item out to Gunner, let him sniff it, and then gave the command.

There was no hesitation; Gunner was already on the trail, with quiet determination at every step. It was like the world itself had shifted into motion. The chase was on.

Owen followed the dog, his pulse pounding. There was no turning back now. Whatever this path led to, it would be the difference between everything he had feared—a dead end, a loss, or everything he could still hope for.

FIFTY-ONE

Ava Morgahn

He was gone.

Ava couldn't see, her eyes still reeling from the harsh light.

She fought to stay alert. There had to have been something in the water because she could barely stay awake despite the urgency to escape. It didn't help that the room was warm and dark and had grown eerily quiet after he left.

Time was an elusive thing in this vast blackness. It was fragile yet all-consuming as the minutes ticked by, seconds seeming like hours, hours feeling like days, and reality hopeless.

How long he would be gone, she didn't know, but the need to work fast consumed her as if she balanced a tightrope between sleep and awake, death and life.

She could tell the binding was getting thinner. She had felt it tear when he had hit her, jerking her entire body. She had remained calm and gave him no reason to check her wrists.

Her brain scrambled to hold onto a cognitive thought as sleep tried to overtake her.

Escape.

She mentally grabbed the thought like it was a beacon in the dark.

Her fingers, slick with sweat, fumbled with the knots, but she was determined. She had to get free before it was too late. Every moment felt like it was stretching longer than the last. The rope was getting weaker. She could sense it, feel it, even before the sharp snap of fibers started to give way.

"Hello?" she called out into the dark room as she worked. "Can you hear me?"

There was a sound from across the room, like fabric rustling or someone shifting position. She worked her wrists against the ropes again, testing the give in the strands. She was close. Another minute, maybe two—if she could only get this last chord to break, the rest would fall off easily. But time was something she couldn't afford. His footsteps echoed through her mind like a countdown. Each moment he remained gone, another chance slipped away, the closer to his return.

Once again, Ava's voice broke the silence. "Is someone there?"

The sound of it in the boundless quiet startled her initially, but she forced herself to sound confident and steady. She needed to know who else was in here. Was she alone? Had he been playing her? Was someone else trapped in the black with her?

Her heart rate picked up. There was a rustling sound—a soft shuffling, the kind of noise someone makes when trying to stay still but not quite succeeding.

It was across the room, too far for her to reach, but close enough to send a ripple of tension through her body. She held her breath, listening.

"Can you hear me?" she asked again, a little louder this time, trying to draw out a response. The voice inside her head screamed that she had to be ready for anything—anything at all. She strained against the ropes, her fingers twitching, working faster.

The rustling sound shifted again, followed by a low, almost imperceptible exhale. The hairs on the back of her neck stood up. Someone was there, and they were awake. The only question now —were they friend or foe?

She tensed, every muscle in her body coiled tight as she waited for the next sound, the next move. The silence between them stretched on, thick with uncertainty. "If you can hear me, please answer."

There was a soft moan.

"Good. That's good." Ava acknowledged. "I'm tied up. Are you?" She didn't expect an answer, but now that she had started talking, she couldn't stop. "Can you tell me your name? Are you hurt?"

"Yes."

The word was so soft. Barely a breath of air had escaped lips to create it. But Ava imagined it had cost the person on the other end of it everything they had to utter.

"Okay, if it hurts too much to talk, you don't have to right now." She wanted to tell the person she was almost free, but she feared that if she did and he came back, they would tell him she was loose to save themselves. She had to free herself first and then go from there, one step at a time.

She felt another strand break. The final string between her and freedom fell away. A wave of relief washed over her, making her almost giddy. She moved her aching arms and brought them around to hug herself, trying to get the feeling and circulation back into them as her entire body tingled with the new rush of blood. She untied her legs with shaky hands and staggered to her feet. Feeling like a newborn colt, she could not get her footing.

Her first instinct was to go for the door. She knew what direction to go from the pole but feared she might not find it f she ventured into the dark odyssey around her.

She took a step toward the door, but her conscience took hold. "Where are you?" she murmured into the stillness. "Please, I can't see anything. You have to say, or I might not be able to find you."

Silence rang out, and she cursed. Why was she wasting precious time? "Where are you? Can you answer me?"

"Here. I...I'm here."

The voice was barely above a squeak, but Ava's ears were so in tune with the silence that she pinpointed her immediately. Like a bat with sonar, she honed in on the voice. Stumbling forward, waving her arms, she moved with caution. After only a couple of steps, she ran smack into metal.

"Ouch!" she swore, stumbling back. Her hands instinctively reached out to steady herself. She winced, rubbing her knee where it had connected.

Her hands snaked out, making quick work to decipher what she hit.

"It's a car," she uttered. At some point, she had been aware that it was there, seeing the outline in the fragile light, but now, with her mind frantic, the long hours in the dark were all blurring.

Her pulse quickened. How perfect it would be if there were keys in the car. She tried the handle, but it was locked. She pressed her face to the car window but couldn't see anything. She went further down the vehicle, discovering it was a four-door sedan. Her heart plummeted as she tried the back door—locked. Quickly now, she edged around the car, hoping for a miracle. To her dismay, she found all four doors locked.

She couldn't waste more time on the car. She needed to find the other woman and escape.

"My name is Ava. I need you to keep talking so I can find you. We need to get out of here as quickly as possible."

"Ava?" the woman questioned with a scratchy voice. "Ava Mo-Morgahn?"

"Yes. How did you know?" She stretched her hand out instinctively, hoping for some sign of what lay ahead. Her cracked fingertips brushed against a metal pole, cool and unyielding—its surface rough and marked by time. It felt so much like the one she'd been bound to only moments ago. The memory of the ropes biting into her skin flooded her mind, but she pushed it away, focusing instead on the tactile sense of relief that came with this familiar texture.

She slid her hand down the pole, searching for anything that could offer more clarity. Her fingers paused when they encountered something soft and warm. Her heart skipped as she moved her hand further, sensing long, tangled hair. Beneath it, fabric and then a bony shoulder.

"There you are," she whispered, the words tumbling out in disbelief and relief.

"A-Ava," came the voice. It was shaky and hoarse, thick with emotion. "It's me, Molly."

The name hit Ava like a wave, overwhelming her with a rush of panic and confusion. Her heart lurched painfully in her chest as she suddenly found herself tethered to something much larger than her fears. "Molly?" How could it be?

Ava's mind raced, thoughts crashing into one another as she tried to process the voice, touch, and overwhelming recognition sensation. She wrapped her arms around her friend and heard Molly sob.

"Oh, Molls! Don't cry. I've got you." Trying to control her emotions, she said, "We've got to get out of here."

She felt her friend's head bob. Without another second of hesitation, Ava's trembling hands moved down Molly's arms and to the back of the pole, desperate to find the rope that held her in place. Ava's fingers shook violently as she fumbled at the stiff and unyielding knots, the numbness of her fingers working against her as she fought to untangle the cords that held Molly captive.

"Come on, come on…" Ava muttered under her breath, a near-silent chant to coax her fingers to move. Her eyes stung with the effort and the frustration of her frozen, aching limbs. But Molly's soft, pitiful sobs that echoed in the otherwise silent room breathed life into her desperation.

Her breath hitched as she finally succeeded in loosening the first knot, and she moved quickly, feeling the strain of urgency as she struggled with the others. Please let her be okay, Ava thought, hoping desperately that the woman in her hands wasn't beyond repair.

Molly's voice cracked again, this time softer, but it carried all the weight of someone waiting for rescue far longer than Ava had known. "Ava... you found me."

It was a small sign that Molly hadn't been broken by whatever horrors she had endured.

Ava's heart swelled with emotion, and despite the overwhelming relief of the reunion, a new wave of dread and confusion took its place. What had happened to Molly? How had she gotten here?

"I guess I did," Ava forced a small laugh.

"I'm so sorry. He made me do it," Molly sobbed.

"Shh, not now, Molls. We need to focus all our energy on getting out of here." Ava's voice was low but firm, and the urgency was evident as she finished loosening the last knot. The rope fell away, leaving Molly's arms free. Ava immediately placed her hands under Molly's arms, ready to lift.

"There's a rope around my ankles."

"Damn it! Of course, there is." She ran her hands down her friend's legs and worked the knots quickly. "Can you stand?"

Molly's breath was shallow, her voice weak. "I don't know. I barely feel my legs or arms..."

"Lean on me," Ava insisted. She bent down, her muscles aching with the strain of exhaustion. She slid one arm around Molly's waist, the other under her arm. With a grunt, Ava pushed, her legs trembling as she tried to lift her. Molly was so unsteady that her body was dead weight.

For a moment, there was a flicker of success—Molly's feet shuffled across the floor. Ava tried to balance them both, but her own legs barely held under the strain. Their legs buckled at the same time. They fell backward in a tangled heap of limbs, crashing into the floor with a painful thud.

"Damn!" she cursed under her breath, her hands now desperately pressing against the floor to push them upright again.

Molly let out a weak sob, her body shuddering in Ava's arms. "I can't do it, Ava. I can't move... just leave me."

"Don't say that. You can. And I won't," Ava urged, but her voice wavered slightly despite her attempt at strength. "We just need to get out of this room."

Ava's eyes darted around. She was disoriented now, not sure which way the door was. They couldn't waste time wandering around the large, cavernous room trying to find it.

Ava gritted her teeth and pulled Molly back into a sitting position, her own legs still unsteady as she struggled to lift her friend again. This time, she didn't try to get them both up in one go. She had to be more innovative. She leaned into Molly, slowly dragging her up, inch by inch, using the pole as support to brace them.

"We're not giving up. We'll make it," Ava whispered, as much to herself as to Molly, and then added with more determination, "I swear."

Molly's head lolled against Ava's shoulder, her body heavy with exhaustion, but she managed a weak nod. "Okay," she whispered back, barely audible.

Ava moved cautiously, each step like walking on glass, testing the strength of her own legs as she half-carried, half-dragged her friend toward what she prayed was the door.

They crossed the room using the vehicle to steady and guide them partway, but once free of the sedan, the expanse of the room felt like it was a mile wide. Before she could stop, Ava's hand touched the cold concrete wall. She inched along it, clinging tightly to Molly as she felt for the door. Every second that passed, she feared she was going in the wrong direction and that he would return before she could locate the door.

Hinges. She felt them. She was so relieved she let out a little whimper.

She pressed her ear to the cool metal of the door. She couldn't hear any sound coming from the other side.

Her hope of escape ticked up a notch. Had he heard them? Would they be discovered once she opened the door? Did he lay outside in wait? Surely not.

At this point, she didn't care. All that mattered was putting one foot in front of the other. She was prepared to fight him if it came to that.

Ava's heart pounded in her chest as she tried the handle. To her surprise, she found it unlocked.

He must have forgotten to lock it on his way out. Either that or he was so confident he hadn't bothered. It didn't matter either way.

The door squealed open like a stuck pig being slaughtered, sending waves of panic through her.

"We have to move quickly. If he's here, he's bound to have heard that."

The hallway was deep and dark, but it was one step closer to freedom. Ava helped Molly through the opening, her hands shaking with fear and adrenaline. Every step felt like it could be their last, but the air outside that room, however muggy, felt like a promise.

They kept moving, one slow step after another, determined that nothing would stop them now.

"Almost there. Just keep going."

With every step, they moved farther away from the nightmare they'd both been trapped in.

FIFTY-TWO

Dorthea

Dorthea doubled back, trying to evade—not just one, but two —one ahead and one behind. One friend—one foe. Earlier she had moved with calculated caution, slipping away from the warehouse brimming with secrets. As she distanced herself from the building, an unsettling chill ran down her spine—she knew, without a doubt, that she'd been seen.

The streets were dark. And the further she led them away from Broadway, the quieter it got.

Her years in the army had honed her senses to an edge sharper than any blade. She remembered the thrill of the chase—how she'd been trained to hunt, track, and disappear in plain sight. The rush of a successful mission was something she'd lived for, back when every assignment was a game of cat and mouse, with her as the predator, always one step ahead.

Her skills had been put to the test more times than she could count, each mission shaping her into something more than just a soldier. She became a master of stealth, an expert at weaving in and out of danger, blending into the shadows with the ease of someone who had spent years in the dark, both figuratively and literally. Every footstep, every breath, calculated.

But this time, things were different. The weight of years in her body, the aches she'd grown used to, were no longer just a nuisance—they were also the enemy. She moved slower than she should have, her limbs betraying her, not as swift or sharp as they once were. The cold reality stung sharper than it ever had before. She could feel their eyes on her, a heavy pressure that cut through the night. It wasn't just soldiers playing war this time. Something darker, more sinister, was at play. This chase wasn't just about outmaneuvering—it was about survival.

She saw movement to her left and ducked down a backstreet. She wasn't far from her hiding place, her sanctuary. The place she called home when the memories of war became too much. If she could get there, she wouldn't be easily found.

She crouched low and stayed in the shadows of the alley, but felt the presence closing in. At the far side of the passageway, where the buildings ended and the cool grass began, she knew she would be exposed for a few minutes as she made the open trek to safety.

Pressed against the warm bricks of the old building, she sucked in a haggard breath and listened.

All was quiet except for the steady lap of water against the concrete shore and the low hum of the encroaching insects down by the river.

She took a tentative step out of the shadows, her foot on the edge of a pool of light. Her bridge was in sight.

There was a gleam of silver. A glint of a tip. And the pain of a sharp point penetrating between her ribs. It was quick. In and out. Barely more time, mere seconds, than a quick breath of air, but she knew it was deep. And deadly.

FIFTY-THREE

Owen Layne

They walked for well over an hour, and Owen felt like they were wandering through the dark streets of downtown, circling, backtracking, and not making any progress.

Toby had texted him multiple times, wanting to know if he was insane. He hated to admit it, but maybe he was. It was crazy to think this might work. It was crazy to think that his brother's dog, now his, who had been injured, hurt, and broken, could mend and function normally anymore, let alone track a person down without proper training... He couldn't finish the thought.

If only he knew how to get into the cement factory without Dorthea's help he could have gone straight there.

Gunner gave a short, sharp bark—the signal.

The voice came from somewhere in front of him, from the black. "You found me."

Gunner barked again.

"Shut that dog up before he comes back."

Owen gave Gunner the signal, and he released. He'd done it. Gunner had tracked down Dorthea. He bent and rubbed Gunner, whispering, "You did it! Good dog! I owe you a steak dinner!"

"Smart dog," Dorthea said, staying hidden, her voice coming out in breathy waves. "I even doubled back to try to lose you. Guess I didn't fool him."

"Guess not." He looked up. It was so dark down here by the river, the steady flow—a ribbon of ebony velvet behind the grassy edge. "But where exactly are you?" Owen straightened and held out the pink rabbit's foot. "I believe this is yours." He extended his arm, hoping she would come out of the long grass.

"Aye. So it is."

Owen dropped his hand when she didn't step out of the dark toward him. He didn't want to waste any more time. He'd already spent too much tracking her. "Dorthea, what you said earlier..."

"What?"

"That you'd seen Ava at the plant. Is that true?" He stepped toward her. "Please, don't lie to me. She could be in real danger."

"It'd be her."

"Can you take me to her? You said you knew your way in."

"I do, but I can't."

"You can't, or you won't?"

There was a bubbling gurgle in her voice when she answered that set his nerves on edge. "Can't."

"Dorthea," Owen cursed, his voice tight with growing unease. The air down by the river felt too thick, too unnatural. It was as if the very insects that teemed in these damp, moist conditions sensed trouble.

His eyes scanned the reeds, catching a glimpse of movement far above him, but whoever it was, was too distant and indifferent. He knew that even if he yelled, no one would hear him.

Why wasn't she coming forward? A cold knot twisted in his stomach—*what if he had walked straight into a trap?* The air was heavy, with a warning he couldn't ignore.

"Come out," he called, his voice raw with fear. Gunner sensed his apprehension, crouched low, and emitted a deep rumble from his throat. "Come out here where I can see you. Please, Dot."

The words hung in the air, and for a moment, all he could hear was the distant rush of water, the snarl from the dog, and the unsettling absence of an answer.

The air was suddenly filled with harsh, ragged coughing.

Something was wrong. "I'm coming in. So help me, Dorthea... if this is an ambush, I will let Gunner rip you to shreds and not think twice about it."

He lifted his cell and let the flashlight spill over the long grass. He could see where it was trampled slightly, a small path barely big enough for one person, hardly detectable. He guessed that was the point.

Straining at his leash, he let Gunner lead the way. They walked through the waist-high grass with treacherous steps. The light washed over Dorthea. She braced herself against the ground with one hand, her body slumped at the river's edge.

It took a second for his brain to register what his heart already knew.

There was blood trickling out of the side of her mouth. She coughed, and it splattered, dripping down her chin. Her hand pressed weirdly over her gray shirt, and some dark, shiny liquid coated it. The metallic smell registered at the same time as the sight. Blood.

Dot had been stabbed.

The wind picked up and sent a ripple through the long vegetation. "Oh, God, Dot!" Owen squatted in front of her. "Let me help you. Don't move."

"Don't touch me. There's no time. G-go to the cement plant. Back the way you came... Take the fork to the left. You'll enter from behind. There's a hole in the fence, barely big enough to squeeze through. Look for an abandoned skid loader...then a dumpster turned on its side... Follow that street...a hundred clicks...lead you to the... warehouse where she is." She tried to stand up and back out of his reach. "You need to get out of here in case…" She coughed, spewing blood. "Comes back." She stumbled forward, then back. Reached out.

Owen stretched for her hand, but it was so slick with blood that her hand passed right through his grasp. She tumbled backward and toppled into the water.

"Dot!" he yelled as she disappeared beneath the surface.

FIFTY-FOUR

Ava Morgahn

At the end of the hall, a drawn-out screech like an out-of-tune violin scraping its final notes—pierced the silence, grating on Ava's nerves. The sound registered that of a heavy metal garage door lifting, followed by a clatter. The door rolled noisily back down into place.

If she could just get a look, she'd better know who and what she was dealing with…but she wouldn't be able to do it safely while holding up Molly. "We need to hide," Ava hissed in her friend's ear. "He's back."

"But where?"

Ava ran her hand along the wall, looking for an opening. By sheer dumb luck, her hand caught on a knob. She twisted, and the door silently swung open. "In here!" She grabbed Molly's hand and tugged her forward. They stumbled in. It was nothing more than a storage closet, but it was all they had. She lowered Molly onto an overturned bucket. "Stay here, no matter what," Ava instructed Molly.

Ava closed the door behind her with a soft click, praying the sound didn't carry. She heard the slam of a car door, then another.

He wasn't alone.

His voice carried. He was loud and crystal clear, as if he wanted to be heard. Ava knew it was the man behind the light. Ava shuddered, but she crept forward anyway.

She pressed her eye to the crack in the door. He had his back to her and stood over a large wash sink in the corner as the water trickled out and a fluorescent work light dangled above him.

"Son of a bitch," he cursed. "That old bat got blood all over me. I'll probably get rabies or something foul from her. But I showed her. That's what she gets for snooping around. Think she was going to lead the cops here." He laughed cruelly as he scrubbed. "That's about the only way that dipshit Wyatt Lockhart will ever find us."

Ava's hand went to her mouth to cover the sharp intake of breath. Who else had he killed?

He yanked off his shirt, wadded it in a ball, and tossed it in a trash bin. "My frickin' shirt is ruined."

Ava shifted and pressed further against the doors, trying to see who and what else was in the room. Her mind registered items around the large space: a car, desk, stacks of bags of concrete, and tools.

She heard him twist the knobs on the utility sink, and she retreated.

He pushed through the doors and slammed them against the cement walls, his footsteps echoing in the corridor just as she closed the broom closet.

Through the crack in the frame, she saw a light bounce along the corridor.

She pressed back away from the door and tugged Molly with her, putting a finger to her lips to warn. Their breathing was so loud—too loud. It was all she could hear except the drumming of her own heart. The sound was harsh and felt like thunder in this tiny space. Ava raised her hands to cover both their mouths, swallowing back the cry that was about to escape.

She could feel Molly tremble, so Ava risked removing her hands from their mouths to pull her in tight and comfort her. She didn't want to die. She wouldn't be able to live if Molly did, either.

His voice grew louder, a raw edge of anger cutting through the silence, and she caught a glimpse of his shadow sliding past the crack in the door. They instinctively shrank back, pressing themselves harder into the wall behind them, desperate for him to move on. But if he did, he would discover their escape—and that realization cut deep, like a double-edged sword, both a curse and a threat.

What will he do when he discovers they're gone? He was only a few paces past the closet when she heard his phone chime. The tiny ding was like a gong in the vast hall.

He swore as he stopped on the other side of the door, mere inches of wood separating them. She pictured him checking the phone and reading the text.

"I fuckin' swear!" His shadow loomed again, crossing the crack with menacing force, and the heavy stomp of his boots echoed sharply on the broken tile as he retreated, unaware of their presence. They had narrowly escaped, their lives spared by the faintest of moments—saved by nothing more than the chime of his phone.

A tense silence stretched before Ava heard the sharp sound of car doors slamming. The heavy metal door groaned in protest as it ground upward, and the engine roared to life, a deep, guttural growl that vibrated through the air. Then, just as abruptly, the massive door crashed down with a resounding clatter, sealing them back in.

They didn't move. They stood paralyzed, rooted to the spot. Ava held Molly tightly, refusing to let her stir. A minute stretched into five, and finally, Ava exhaled, her breath ragged and heavy. "He's gone."

"What if he comes back?" Molly whispered, her voice barely a tremor.

"We will figure that out if and when the time comes. Right now, we need to get out of this closet. Out of this building." She could feel Molly agree, her head dipping in the darkness.

Ava's heart pounded as she wrestled with the decision: Should she move alone, risking a faster escape, leaving Molly hidden but vulnerable? The thought of leaving her behind, not knowing what he could do, made her stomach twist. What if he came back before she could return? The image of Molly trapped and at his mercy twisted in her mind, each second stretching into eternity. The pressure of the choice tore at her, and Ava couldn't shake the fear of making the wrong decision.

She wouldn't leave her alone. She couldn't.

The decision was made. There was no turning back. Ava released her friend, turned the knob, and slowly eased the door open. She peered into the darkened corridor, determining the immediate area was clear.

"Come on, Molls. We have to keep moving," Ava urged Molly. "We need to get as far away as possible."

They shuffled forward at a snail's pace as every fiber in Ava's body shouted to run, but Molly was so weak that it was all she could do to make progress. After what seemed like an eternity, they reached the end of the corridor and pushed through the double doors into a large empty bay.

"I don't think I can go much further," Molly protested. "I need to stop for just a minute."

There was an old desk with a computer off to the side and a folding chair. Ava eased Molly down. "Sit a minute, catch your breath. I need to see what we're dealing with."

Molly leaned back in the chair and closed her eyes, clearly exhausted. "Ava, I have to tell you how sorry I am."

"For what? You didn't do this."

"No, but I dragged you into it."

"How?" Ava asked as she scanned the cluttered desk. It was littered with empty bottles of sleeping pills, bank receipts, and coils of rope. Ava sifted through the papers, recognizing her and Molly's names and seeing dollar amounts. "I can't believe it." She gasped and lifted a photo out of the clutter. The same photo she had in her car on her visor mirror.

"What?" Molly questioned.

"This photo? How did he get it?"

"It's mine," Molly continued, as if she hadn't heard Ava. "The ad was a trap—a ploy."

"Ad? What ad?" Ava questioned. "And for what, though?"

"The apartment. Money," Molly whispered, her voice trembling. Tears spilled down her face as the words choked out. "He threatened to kill me if I didn't give him money. He already had all my financial information, and he had been able to run it through the paperwork I filled out, but it still wasn't enough. He told me he wasn't the only one that wanted something."

"What did he mean?"

"I don't know. I told him I'd do anything, just to survive, if he would let me go. That's when I sent the video to you—telling you how great it was, hoping you'd come. But it was a lie. I... I was trying to send you a warning. I needed help, but I didn't know how. I'm so sorry. I never wanted you to get caught in this." Her sobs wracked her body, raw with regret and fear.

"Shh," Ava soothed, squatting down to her friend's level. She pushed back Molly's hair from her face, her mind racing to piece it together. "What about your job?"

"I never got to go."

Was it all a lie from the start? The weight of the situation pressed down on her, the confusion gnawing at her like a sharp, insistent ache. Nothing about this made sense. How had he known that's where she worked? She couldn't even begin to wrap her head around it when all she could do was think about escape.

"It's okay. Shh, now. Molls, don't cry. We can talk about it later.

We have to get as far away from here as possible, as soon as you think you can move, we need to. Do you think you can?"

Molly didn't answer, just stared straight ahead. "He's killed others."

It was true. He was the Cumberland Killer.

"How do you know?"

"I didn't know her, but he had someone when I came." Molly cried harder. "He abducted her before me. He did the same thing to her, took her money…" Molly hiccuped, choking on a sob. "I saw her briefly. She was half dazed as he dragged her out of the room. She was delirious, mumbling. She never came back. He said that's what would happen to me."

Ava's heart thudded rapidly against her rib cage. "Did you get a look at him? Do you know who he is?"

She shook her head as tears streamed down her face. "I didn't. He was always behind that damn light."

"He was with me, too. But his voice… I swear, I'd recognize it anywhere. He was at Cognac Creek on my first day." Ava's hands shook as she rifled through the papers on the desk, pushing aside pens, a stapler, and newspaper clippings. Her breath hitched when she saw it. "Here… your name, mine, and the names of other women, all linked to bank accounts. And the newspaper articles…" She swallowed hard, the weight of it crushing her. Looking at Molly, her tears blurred her vision, but she couldn't look away. "Five women are dead, Molly… all killed by the Cumberland Killer."

Molly's face drained of color, and she nodded slowly. "That's what I was afraid of."

"But why? Why us?" Ava lifted the papers and scanned them to look for connections. There was something she was sure of it, but what was she missing?

"I-I don't know."

"There has to be a connection."

"I agree." Molly shifted in her chair uncomfortably. She looked like she was ready to pass out. "But I don't know what," Molly finished quietly, her voice shaky. She ran a hand through her hair, looking lost.

Ava's eyes darkened with a mix of confusion and fear. "But why the money? Why take everything from us—if that's even what's happening? It doesn't add up. This wasn't just about robbing them and us." She paused, trying to piece together a bigger picture. "There's something else...There has to be." Because if it really was just about money... she couldn't even fathom the waste.

Ava snapped her focus back to the present, her pulse quickening. "We'll figure it out later," she said, cutting through the tension in the air. "Right now, we need to get out of here." She scanned the room, anxiety tightening in her chest. The loud screech of the metal door was still ringing in her ears, and someone was bound to hear it if she tried to open it. She couldn't take that risk—not with the killer potentially still nearby. She didn't know how far he had gone or if others were involved. Her eyes darted around the space until they landed on a small window across the room.

"I think I found our way out." Her voice was low but urgent. "Let's go."

She helped Molly to her feet and half-dragged her across the room, praying she could open the window.

A small latch on the inside secured the pane. Once she released it, the window moved up with fits and starts as the old, hard wood warped and twisted. Ava yanked the pane as high as she could, only to be stopped by the humid night air. She peered out, not sure if she should trust the quiet. After all, if he weren't in here, he could be out there—somewhere.

Ava shifted, put her leg through, and shimmed out. She stopped and peered into the night. She deemed it clear and then helped Molly maneuver through the opening.

"We need to move." She didn't want to think about what would happen if he returned. Neither one of them was in any shape to fight him off.

She placed Molly's arm over her shoulders and wrapped her arm around her waist. "Wait. Quiet," Ava warned, her heart thudding against her chest. "Did you hear that?"

"What?"

"Voices."

"I don't hear anything," Molly said, sucking in a deep breath.

"There it is again. They're coming this way. Get back." She pushed Molly back into the little alcove and stood in front of her. "You need to be prepared to run if it comes to that. We can't go back in. We'll be trapped inside with no way out."

Ava put a finger to her lips as a warning.

The murmur of a voice could be heard getting closer. She peered out and saw two figures coming. Wait, one was a dog? She froze, but the dog sensed her and turned in her direction. With a sharp bark, the dog darted toward her. A slick sheen of perspiration coated her skin as panic seized her entire body.

She was frozen in place. Her heart pounded in her chest as the dog barreled toward her. The figure was still advancing, oblivious to her presence, but the dog was fast and on her scent. Her breath caught in her throat as she backed into the shadows, praying the darkness would be enough to hide her and Molly.

The dog's claws scraped against the ground. Ava's mind raced, trying to calculate her options. She had to stay calm. She couldn't outrun the dog, but they couldn't afford to be caught. She was sure Molly wouldn't survive another day.

Thinking of only protecting Molly, she stepped into the path of the quickly advancing animal. His sharp barks turned into a happy whimper as the dog focused on her.

"Gunner?" she mumbled, barely even able to speak as relief

washed over her. She felt faint, falling to her knees in front of the canine. The dog lavished her face with kisses. She buried her face in his fur and hung on tight as his tail thumped out a happy greeting.

"Ava?" Owen questioned as he ran toward her. "Thank God!" He wrapped his arms around both the woman and the dog. "I can't believe it's you."

Ava gently let Gunner go, her heart racing as Owen pulled her close. He wrapped his arms around her, his hands tenderly tracing the outline of her face before gliding down her arms as if memorizing every curve.

"Are you alright?" His voice was ragged with concern.

"I am now," she whispered, her breath soft against his chest as she melted into his embrace. Feeling the warmth of his arms cradle her like a promise, she pulled back slightly, her gaze lifting to meet his. "What are you doing here?"

"Looking for you."

His words were so tender and full of longing that they brought tears to her eyes. "How did you find me?" she asked, her voice barely a breath.

"Dorthea. I'll explain later."

Coming back to reality, panic seized her. "We need to get out of here. If he comes back… and Molly. She can't run."

"Molly?" Owen questioned, clearly surprised.

"My friend Molly," she pointed. "Is over there."

She ran back to her friend and dropped to her knees in front of Molly, her hands shaking as she glanced around frantically. Owen jogged up behind her.

"Wait, no. I already called the police. We can't just—I don't have a car, I don't have anything. There's no way out except on foot, and Dorthea's gone," Owen said. "This place is a maze. It's a miracle we found you."

Her breath hitched, her eyes wild with panic. They were so close to safety, yet so far.

"Stay calm, Ava. We have to stay calm," Owen said, his voice steady but strained. "We're better off waiting for help. Gunner will protect us if it comes to that. We let the police come to us so we don't injure Molly more."

Ava nodded, though every fiber of her being screamed to run, to get as far away as possible.

Owen pulled out his phone, his fingers moving quickly but with no less urgency. He dialed.

It was picked up on the first ring. On the other end, she heard a voice bark, "Well?"

"I found her," Owen said, his voice thick with emotion as he wrapped his arms around her again, pulling her close, holding her like he'd never let go.

FIFTY-FIVE

Owen Layne

"Over here!" Owen called and waved his arm as the car rolled in, parked at the edge of the abandoned lot, and an officer got out. He squeezed Ava's hand. "I'll be right back. Are you going to be okay for a moment?"

"Yes," she nodded. "Go."

He ran toward the officer, flagging him down. "I didn't think you would get here so soon."

"I was in the area when the call came in." Ransick stood next to the car and looked around. His voice dropped low. "Where are the women?"

"Safe," Owen said, pointing to where they were huddled together with Gunner next to the building, some fifty feet away from where they stood. "Do you want to go talk to them?"

Ransick nodded, glancing over. "In a minute. Stay with them. I will return to the entrance and show the ambulance how to get back here. This place is a maze."

"You're telling me," Owen agreed as Ransick walked away.

Owen jogged back over to the women and sat next to Ava on the crumbling curb, protectively draped an arm around her, holding her tight. Relief washed over him—she was back, and nothing else mattered.

Ransick had only been gone for a few minutes when police cars and an ambulance came pulling in, their lights and sirens blaring.

Detective Lockhart was the first to arrive. He jumped out of his vehicle and ran toward them. "Miss Ava Morgahn?" he asked, taking in the three of them.

"Yes," Ava nodded. "And this is Molly..."

"Calhoun," Detective Lockhart finished for her. "I'm happy to see you both. Let's get the paramedics over here and take a look at you." He gave a whistle and flagged them down.

"Molly first," Ava said.

"Of course."

Owen and Lockhart helped the women stand and let the EMTs take over.

Once they were out of earshot Detective Lockhart turned on Owen. "You should have called me sooner. You should have let me know your plans," he stated, his voice a low grumble, frustrated as he spoke to Owen. But then he looked at Ava holding her friend's hand as they loaded her into the ambulance, and he softened. "But I understand why you did it. You're damn lucky you weren't killed." He paused for effect, "or they weren't."

"I know. I wasn't thinking clearly. All I was thinking about was finding her. I hadn't set out tonight to go after Dorthea or use Gunner to track either woman. It just happened."

Owen turned, a rush of emotion flooding through him as he saw Ava slowly making her way back toward them with Gunner at her side. A pang of relief gripped him.

"Everything alright?" Owen asked as he wrapped a protective arm around her to steady her.

She wobbled slightly and leaned into his arm. "Yes, I'm just giving them a little privacy while they check Molly out."

"We need to get you to the hospital," Owen said. "Is there another ambulance coming?"

"Unfortunately, not for twenty minutes or so before another ambulance can arrive. A massive accident on the other side of the city has left dozens injured, a concert just ended at the stadium, and the streets are gridlocked with traffic."

"It's okay. I'm alright. The main thing is that Molly gets there."

"Ma'am?" a young officer came over. "I was told to give you this. Have you drink it so we can get you hydrated again."

"Thank you," Ava said, accepting the bottle of water. She twisted the loose top and took a long drink, wrinkling her nose at the taste.

Wyatt flagged the forensic team down and ushered them into the building as officers sectioned off the perimeter.

"You still need to be checked out. Why don't you go over and sit in the back of my car? It's unlocked." He gestured toward the parked vehicles. "We're sweeping the area to determine if the suspect is still nearby. I'll need to coordinate with the technicians to ensure everything is set up properly. Once that's handled, I've got a few final tasks to take care of, and then I'll personally drive you."

"You don't have to do that," Ava started to protest.

"Don't argue with the man," Owen teased. "Come on. I'll sit and wait with you. You look like you're about ready to fall over."

Ava relented and let him guide her toward the row of cars. As they passed an officer Owen asked, "Which car is Lockhart's?"

"Black sedan."

Owen nodded and steered her between cars. He efficiently tucked Ava into the back of the unmarked car and then slipped around to the other side with Gunner at his heels. He slid in beside her in the backseat, his presence comforting. Gunner was harder to get in. He whined and dug in his paws. Owen gave a command, and Gunner reluctantly curled up on the backseat floor.

Owen pulled Ava gently into his arms, holding her close. Having her there in his arms, her warmth and steady heartbeat ground him as she rested against him.

"Make sure you're drinking that. It could be a little while before he comes back."

"It tastes a little bitter for water," Ava said. She lifted it to her mouth, and Gunner lunged toward her, knocking it out of her hand and spilling the contents all over the interior.

"What the hell?" Owen opened the door. "Gunner out!"

The dog whimpered and scurried out.

"I'm sorry. I don't know what got into him."

"It's okay. He's allowed to be a little frazzled, too."

They sat together in the isolation of the closed car, quiet for a moment as the outside world muted around them. A gentle wave of exhaustion washed over him as if the world had paused just for them despite the frenzy of activity all around them.

Her eyes closed and opened, heavy with fatigue. "I'm sorry, Owen."

"For what?" he asked in a hushed tone.

"For two things."

"One?" He asked, trying to make light of the situation because he could feel her tremble, her emotions brewing under the calm facade.

"I must look awful and smell even worse. And two, I don't think I can stay awake much longer."

He smiled against her head, where his chin rested. "Don't worry about either thing. Go ahead and sleep. I'll be here when you wake."

She nodded. Unable to fight it any longer, she drifted off. He was content to hold her in his arms.

FIFTY-SIX

Ava Morgahn

Ava didn't know when the rain started to fall. The pitter-patter was soothing and relaxing, making her content to just sleep. She was vaguely aware when she heard a slight rap on the window, and she felt Owen kiss her head and slip out of the vehicle.

"I'll be right back," he whispered into her ear.

In her subconscious, she heard the door open and close. In what felt like a matter of seconds, another door opened. Something cold slipped around her wrists. The door closed. The vehicle moved.

"Owen?" she questioned, shifting on the seat, still half asleep. She was jostled around as the car maneuvered through the streets over major potholes and a couple of speed bumps. They were easing out through the concrete plant gate when she sat up and realized she was handcuffed. Panic shot through her like a bullet from a gun. "Owen? Detective Lockhart?"

The officer glanced at her through the rearview mirror, and their eyes connected. "No, sorry. They were a little tied up."

A shot of electricity ran through her, putting her nerves on edge. That voice—cold, calculated, and haunting—cut through the air like a blade. She'd know it anywhere. Her heart slammed against her chest as the realization sank in. It was him.

She knew he saw it the instant it registered in her eyes. She couldn't hide it. It was there, raw and unmasked, painted across her face.

His smile twisted into something darker, more predatory. He knew—he *knew* that she recognized him. And the chill that followed made it clear: there was nowhere to run.

She reached for the door, trying to be slow and unnoticeable. He either saw her or sensed it because the locks clicked when her hand reached the handle.

"Ah, so you did see my face. I wondered."

She swallowed hard, forcing down the fear. "I didn't. It was your voice that gave you away."

He sneered. "So indeed."

She needed to stay calm. Maybe she could reason with him. "Do you think you can drive away with me and no one will notice?"

"Oh, they're sure to notice. Believe it or not, I told them that I would drive you to the hospital so they are aware I have you."

"Then how do you think you'll get away with this?" she demanded, her voice rising slightly with the panic that had begun to bubble to the surface. "Do you think Owen or Detective Lockhart will believe we drove off into the sunset together?"

He was on the main road and took the ramp to I-40, heading away from the city. Where was he headed? The car rolled steadily down the highway, the swish of the wipers and the hum of tires meeting pavement the only noise between them. Ava sat tensed in the back seat, wound tighter than a spring, ready to pounce if given a chance. Her mind raced with questions—each one more unsettling than the last.

"I don't care what they think. In fact, they won't think. I'm going to tell them exactly what happened."

She was only half listening as she looked around the back seat for anything to use as a weapon, but there was nothing but the empty water bottle. Despite her fear, her eyes were uncontrollably heavy.

Her mind fought to stay cognitive. Her hand closed around it, and as the plastic crinkled, the image flashed through her mind. The water he had given her at the warehouse had also tasted bitter. There had been something in the water.

And Gunner knew.

"Why me?" she asked, her voice barely above a whisper. She couldn't keep the fear from creeping in.

"Why not you?"

"Please," she begged. "Can we talk about this? Whatever you think I've done or haven't, I assure you it wasn't my intention to offend you."

"Once upon a time, you thought you were going places, that you were unstoppable, and were somebody." He laughed viciously. "Just a few days ago. You wouldn't even let me buy you a drink. So high and mighty. Now you're begging me to pay attention to you." He checked his rearview mirror to make sure he had her attention. "I guess she was right. You're all alike. Just another number in a sea of steady transients arriving in the city." He laughed heartily. "Except you're number seven in my book and her apartment. My *lucky* number seven. My meal ticket out of this cluster fuck."

Seven? What did that mean? If he was the Cumberland Killer, had there already been six deaths? The newspaper clipping on the desk indicated five.

His hands gripped the wheel with a confidence that unsettled her. He glanced at her through the rearview mirror again, his lips curling into a small, almost amused smile. He picked up his cell phone and called. Whoever it was answered immediately. "I have number seven."

So simple. So quick. It could have meant nothing. But she knew it meant everything.

He was calm, so certain of his success. It was as if he already knew he was untouchable. And maybe, in some twisted way, he was. He had been planning this for days—carefully orchestrating each move, each step.

He turned up the radio, and the static filled the air. Then he turned the air on at full blast and lowered the windows and the wipers on high. The mix of sounds was almost deafening. That's when he made a second call. This time, he spoke loud and quick. "He has Ava Morgahn. I'm following him out of town. Track me!"

Ava screamed, but it was too late. The call had already ended.

She swallowed hard, trying to control the whirlwind of thoughts and fear threatening to overwhelm her. Her chest felt tight, as though the air in the car had thinned.

"You want them to come after us?" she asked in disbelief.

He didn't even look at her. "Yes." His words were ice-cold. "By the time they find us, you'll be dead, and I'll be a hero."

Ava's eyes snapped open, and she fought to push the heavy fog clouding her mind into submission. A wave of dread crashed over her. Dead—it was no longer an idle threat. The way he spoke—so certain, so assured—made her realize he had already anticipated every move, every response. He wasn't afraid of Owen. He wasn't scared of Detective Lockhart.

And worst of all, she was nothing more than a pawn, a means to an end. A number... number seven.

FIFTY-SEVEN

Owen Layne

"I want you to look at this," Detective Lockhart said to Owen as they entered the building.

Immediately, Gunner started barking. He pulled on the leash. "Gunner! Quiet!" Owen scolded. "What's gotten into you?"

The dog whined but still strained at the leash.

Detective Lockhart watched Gunner and didn't seem surprised at his reaction. "Come this way."

"Do you want me to leave him outside?"

"No, bring him. I want him here. I need to test a theory."

That surprised Owen, but he didn't argue. "Okay, but let's make it quick. I don't want to leave Ava for long."

They walked down the long hall and into a massive warehouse. Yellow caution tape that contained a white sedan had already been established around the center of the room. They skirted the perimeter.

Owen followed Detective Lockhart. They swept wide, avoiding the caution tape, while Gunner yipped and pulled hard against the leather leash. It was all he could do to keep control of the German Shepherd.

His eyes shifted from the car when he noticed an officer squatting low to take a photograph of pieces of rope that lay frayed and abandoned on the ground beside a metal pole.

He swallowed hard and asked, "Was that where Ava had been held?"

Detective Lockhart nodded. "I'm afraid so." He motioned for him to come closer. "Try not to look at it. That's not what I brought you in here for." He lifted the tape, and they ducked under. "Where's that bagged evidence I said I would be back for?"

"Here, sir," the young officer said, handing Detective Lockhart the bagged and tagged item.

The Detective took it and turned toward Owen. "Recognize this?"

"I don't know. Should I?" Owen questioned, then stopped cold. "It's a-a blue Jayhawks sweatband."

"Anyone you know wear these?" Lockhart asked.

"My brother did, but I'm guessing you knew that. I gave him a Jayhawks headband with matching wristbands for Christmas during my freshman year in college. It was part of his gift. A gag of sorts, but he actually loved it. He always wore it when he ran."

He looked down at the restrained German Shepherd. "Gunner has the matching wristbands on his teddy bear." Owen rubbed his chin, thinking. "But the funny thing is, when Dylan was found on the side of the road, he wasn't wearing his. It wasn't in his belongings they gave to my mother either. May I?" he asked, holding out his hand.

"Of course."

Owen took the bagged item from Lockhart. "Where did you find this?"

Lockhart pointed to the car. "Under the seat."

"So does that mean..." Owen's voice trailed off, unable to finish the sentence. Emotions swamped him from every direction.

"Won't know for sure until we match the paint with your brother's file. But as you can see," Detective Lockhart pointed at Gunner, the way he whined and pulled, there was no doubt.

"Gunner has already made a positive ID."

FIFTY-EIGHT

Kelleigh Morgahn

Kelleigh couldn't sleep or sit still. The tiny apartment felt suffocating, like the walls were closing in on her, as the rain poured down outside. She had to do something, anything, to escape the monotony. The laundry was done—there was nothing left to do.

So she sorted through more clothes, rewashed a few items, folded, and tucked away Ava's things again in neat, organized piles. Then she put Ava's pictures on the dresser, a small attempt to make the place feel more like home, but there was no trace of her daughter in the room beyond that.

Her thoughts drifted to Cara. She'd been kind enough when she'd been told Ava was missing, but beyond that first initial encounter, she had not done anything to help, and Kelleigh felt that Cara's patience was wearing thin with her being in the apartment.

She understood, especially since it was unclear how long Kelleigh planned to stay.

The thing that bothered her was Cara's odd hours—coming and going first thing in the morning and late at night. It was like she purposely stayed away from the apartment as if she didn't want to be here, or the thought crept through her mind—as if she were hiding something.

And what was it she had come home for this last time? Kelleigh would swear she had been in and out in under five minutes. That's when Kelleigh remembered the scraping sound. Cara had either come home to get something or put something away. Possibly hide it. That thought niggled at her. Until it grew so large that it consumed her every thought.

What could have been so important?

With a frustrated sigh, Kelleigh stood up and paced back and forth in front of Cara's room. She eyed the lock, a solid, simple mechanism that required a key. She had nothing except—maybe there was a way. There had to be a paperclip somewhere in the apartment. Every good junk drawer had one.

If there were a paperclip, Kelleigh could insert the point into the small key hole at the top and wiggle it around until she located the locking mechanism, and then push down. She knew it worked —she'd done it countless times before. After all, she was always misplacing the key to her shed at home.

She reminded herself that that would be an invasion of privacy, but efficiently shoved the thought aside.

Her curiosity was stronger than her hesitation. She needed to know.

In the kitchen, she found the cluttered drawer. Kelleigh sifted through it, located a paperclip, twisted the end, and went back to the bedroom door. After a few attempts, prodding and pushing, she felt the mechanism unlock.

The door creaked open, and Kelleigh froze. The difference between the two rooms hit her like a punch to the gut. Cara's room was everything Ava's wasn't: alive. Pictures adorned the walls, plants sat on the windowsill, and an empty coffee cup perched on the nightstand. It was a space that felt inhabited, lived-in.

She crossed to the dresser—yanked open the first drawer, then another, each motion deliberate, but with an urgency she couldn't suppress. Once she began, there was no turning back. There had to be something here—something that could lead her to Ava. Her hands trembled slightly as she moved swiftly through the room, but she was careful—so careful—trying to make sure nothing was out of place, that nothing would betray the fact that she had been there.

Kelleigh's pulse quickened as she made her way to the closet. The door slid open, revealing a closet crammed full of clothes. The overwhelming fullness of the space made her breath catch.

She rifled through the closet, yanked boxes from the shelves, and skimmed through the clothes, all while desperately maintaining the illusion that everything was undisturbed. The strain of holding back and the rush of panic gnawed at her. She had to find something—anything—before time ran out.

And yet—there was nothing.

Exhausted, she stood in the middle of the room and did a slow three-sixty. She had been so sure there would be something.

Kelleigh brushed against the bed, and a throw pillow tumbled off. She bent over to pick it up, and that's when she saw the corner of the metal box. The sound of metal scraping against wood came back to her. Kelleigh got down on her hands and knees and fished out the foot locker from under the bed.

With her luck, she half expected to find nothing but a pair of sneakers when she lifted the heavy lid, but to her surprise, she found a box full of newspaper clippings.

Kelleigh sat on the edge of the bed and read the first one. It was about a hit-and-run dated six months ago. She scanned the article, gleaning it for pertinent information... *Officer Dylan Layne was pronounced dead at the scene... German Shepherd transported...* Kelleigh gasped and put her hand to her mouth as she realized she was reading articles about Owen's brother.

Several other follow-up articles followed—the funeral, the family, and Officer Layne's career.

Could Cara have been the one behind the wheel of that hit-and-run, the one who sped off without a second thought, leaving a shattered life in her wake? The thought plagued Kelleigh's mind. Or was Cara just obsessed with the case? Why else would she collect all these articles?

Kelleigh needed to let Wyatt—Detective Lockhart, she corrected, know.

She flipped through the remaining articles, her fingers shaking as they unearthed more clippings. Her pulse quickened, her heart racing when she realized it wasn't just more about Officer Layne. Amid the disarray of newspaper articles, official documents were buried—job applications bearing names of different women, their personal information neatly filled out. Among them were apartment listings for this building, with applications from those same women, their lives bare. Detailed bank statements, credit reports, and there, in black and white, Molly and Ava's names. But what made her blood run cold was the stack of articles on the Cumberland Killer and his victims.

A chill crept up her spine as the gravity of her discovery sank in. This wasn't some idle fascination—it was the manic collection of an obsession, the record of the Cumberland Killer himself.

FIFTY-NINE

Ava Morgahn

They hadn't been driving long when the rain tapered off, the heavy downpour leaving huge puddles on the dry, cracked ground. He pulled off the major road onto a small two-lane highway. The headlights swept the rolling landscape, which turned rural quickly.

"Where are we going?" Ava asked.

"You'll find out soon enough," Ransick said. He turned the car down a gravel road that led further away from civilization.

Ava could see the rushing river snaking out along the horizon. They were getting closer. She knew without being told that it was the Cumberland River. The night sky was slowly ebbing toward dawn, and the river loomed large and churned from the torrent of rain that had just passed.

Ransick parked the car and got out. Opening the back door, he yanked out Ava.

"It's about damn time you got here."

Ava heard the voice and turned. "Cara?"

"Surprised? I guess you didn't expect me." Cara laughed.

Cara...Was she friend or foe? Ava's head was spinning, foggy. It was hard to think clearly.

The sun was slowly rising above the horizon. The night was becoming spongy as birds started to chatter, but large thunderclouds still held the sky captive, threatening to let loose at a moment's notice. Ava looked around, trying to get her bearings as they dragged her.

If she was going to die, she needed to know why. "There must be some mistake."

"Trust me, there isn't." Cara scowled at her. "Only unfortunate accidents and the choice you make after. Isn't that right, Officer Ransick?"

Ransick smirked and glanced at Cara. "You got that right."

"I don't understand," Ava murmured, tripping and sprawling in the mud. Ransick jerked her up and pulled her forward to the river.

"One person's misfortune can be another person's opportunity. Wouldn't you agree?" Ransick threw a sideways glance at Cara.

"Shut the hell up, you prick!" Her hand snaked out and slapped him across the face. "I don't want to hear it from you or her." Cara was half-crazed now. She didn't see the shift in Ransick's eyes or how his body tensed. But Ava did.

"You should never share an apartment with your best friend, especially when that friend has money and isn't afraid to flaunt it. Or go to a midnight poker game with a bunch of lowlifes like Officer Ransick here." She jerked a finger in his direction.

"And then be forced to drive home when that so-called friend passes out because she had too much to drink. I had a decision to make: drive or go back into the house with the lowlife scum who just took all our money."

Ransick yanked Ava forward. "She chose poorly."

"I drove home and hit a damn cop and his dog out for an early morning run. I lost everything that morning and haven't had a peaceful night's sleep since."

"Hence the sleeping pills," Ransick muttered. "So apropos, don't you think?" he asked Ava cruelly. "Caught between sleep and awake, she drove home. Right on the edge, where nightmares lurk."

Turning all her fury on him, Cara spoke, "And you! I can't believe you brought her here awake. Don't you know that the poetic justice is to have her half asleep? Like me, she can sleep through the most important moments of her life." She turned a wicked smile on Ava. "Only yours will be your last breath."

"So she'll go in the river, fully awake. Makes no difference to me. You're the psycho bitch that cares."

They were at the river now, down past the rocks where the river was deeper. Ava kicked and writhed, trying to get loose.

"Hold her still," Cara demanded, yanking a hoodie down over her body. Ava recognized it. It was the hoodie Ava had found in the dryer the first day she had arrived. She knew it had looked familiar. It was Molly's.

"I'm about through with you bossing me around, bitch." He clamped his arms around Ava and held her still but spoke to Cara over her head, "A man can only take so much of your shit."

"A man?" Cara spat. "As if. You're nothing but a pathetic gambler trapped in a sick addiction that drains you dry. Every paycheck, every dollar, every cent you get disappears into the next bet, the next poker game, and the debt piles up faster than you can breathe. The loan sharks are circling, closing in. Your phone blows up with warnings, but there's no escape. Every decision you've made has led to this point, and now you're stuck, powerless, with no way out, just like me. Even their money," Cara pointed a finger at Ava. "Hasn't been enough. I should have never listened to you that morning on the road, that cop lying at my feet—barely breathing, the dog snapping at our heels." She sneered at him as she spoke.

"Wait!" Ava screamed, trying to make sense of it all. "What does this have to do with me?"

"Nothing. You are a means to an end. You see, my roommate woke up in the middle of all this. She witnessed the whole thing. The accident and the arrival of Officer Ransick. She tried to blackmail him for talking me into leaving the scene of the crime."

"That was her first mistake," Ransick said, keeping his voice low.

Cara continued as if she hadn't heard him, "After Super Cop drained my roommate's bank accounts dry and dumped her body in the river to cover our tracks, it still wasn't enough. He had me with no witness to corroborate my story... Well," she laughed cruelly. "You get the picture. I had to get more money to keep him happy, so I put out an ad for a new roommate. Thus, the plan was born."

Ava felt trapped as if she were in a straitjacket with the hoodie yanked into place. She took deep, shallow breaths, willing herself not to panic. Ransick grabbed her wrist, pulled a black marker from his pocket, and wrote the number seven on her left palm.

"I don't know why you wrote it there," Cara grumbled. "You said yourself that the detective is worthless. He might miss it."

"Because that's where I want to write it," he growled.

"If she is number seven, what happened to the other one? Did you already dump her in the river without me?"

"No," he said calmly. "She went to the hospital in an ambulance." He again jerked the hoodie down to cover Ava's wrists and hands, clenching the marker in his palm.

Cara screamed in disbelief and stomped, sending muddy water flying. "Then she's number six, you idiot, not seven!"

"No," he corrected her. "You're number six."

SIXTY

Owen Layne

Owen felt sick to his stomach.

His stomach twisted into a tight knot. The crushing realization that they had just found the vehicle that had taken his brother's life slammed into him, drowning him in a wave of grief and rage. His mind raced with questions, everyone more unbearable than the last. He couldn't stay here, couldn't breathe in this suffocating reality. He needed to escape. He needed space. Most of all, he needed Ava.

"I need to get out of here," Owen told Detective Lockhart before he cracked.

"I know this is difficult." Wyatt looked around. "I'll get Ransick to drive you and Ava to the hospital. We need to get her checked out. Now, where did he get to."

It felt like the walls were closing in on Owen. He was on the verge of walking out when the Detective's cell rang, the sharp sound cutting through the tension.

"Ransick, where are you?"

Something in the way he said it made Owen hesitate. Owen saw Lockhart's face morph into disbelief.

Lockhart clicked off and dialed the office. "I need you to track Officer Ransick's phone and send me the coordinates. Then, send it back to his location."

"What's happening?" Owen demanded.

Lockhart shifted into high gear and made a beeline for the door with Owen on his heels. "Ransick is in pursuit of the Cumberland Killer." Lockhart hesitated. "And he has Ava."

"What, how?" Owen challenged.

"I don't know," Wyatt admitted while practically running to his car. "Maybe he was waiting somewhere close by and snatched her right out from under us while we were inside."

Owen swore, running beside him, Gunner in tow. "If you're going after him. I'm coming with you."

Lockhart's phone chimed, downloading the active coordinates of Officer Ransick. "I don't have time to argue."

"Wait."

"What?" Lockhart demanded.

"This is your car?"

"Yes, why?"

"That's not the car I put Ava in." Owen's face turned as pale as a sheet. "Son of a bitch, I put her in the wrong damn car. I gave her to him on a silver platter."

SIXTY-ONE

Ava Morgahn

A fist connected with flesh and cartilage. Cara's head snapped back.

Ava heard the break. Blood gushed. Cara went down like a ton of bricks. Ransick straddled her and uncapped his marker again. She was unconscious. He took her hand and put the marker in her palm. Guiding her hand, he drew a large six right on her forehead.

"No one's gonna miss this number." Then tucked the marker in Cara's pants pocket.

Before Ava could react, Ransick scooped up Cara and carried her dazed to the river.

A sharp and piercing gunshot split the air, jolting Ava into action. She scrambled to her feet, her movements frantic and uncoordinated, the weight of urgency driving her forward despite the difficulty.

"You really gonna make me chase you?" he yelled after her.

Damn right, she was. She may not get very far, but she wasn't going just to lie down and die.

"I am cunning. You'd better be running," he sang out.

The light was returning quickly now, but the ground was uneven and soggy, her legs were weak, and her arms were trapped. She went down hard when he tackled her from behind.

He pinned her to the ground and sucked in a much-needed

breath. "Got ya!"

"Please!" she begged, gasping for air as she kicked and bucked. "You don't have to do this."

"Oh, but I do. I have to follow through with what I started, and you're number seven. That's my lucky number." He laughed as he grabbed her and lifted her into the air. "Old lucky number seven has never let me down yet."

"How do you think you'll get away with this?" Ava asked, kicking out as hard as she could, hoping he would drop her as she squirmed.

"That car you came in, that's Cara's. Everyone saw you get in it. Hell, your boyfriend put you in it. It's the same make and model as the Detective's. I made her buy it, hoping it would come in handy someday, and today it did. But nobody saw it leave except me. I *followed* in my cruiser, which technically Cara drove here."

He pointed over to where it sat. He reached the edge of the river now and stood on the muddy bank.

"Unfortunately, I was too late to stop the Cumberland Killer before *she* struck again. But I shot her in the back of the leg before she tossed you into the river. She fell in, and the current took her. I was more concerned about rescuing you from the water than pursuing her." He shrugged. "The rest of the story writes itself." He angled Ava so she could see Cara lying facedown on the rain-soaked riverbank.

He stared at the dark water churning and bubbling, his gaze cold and unblinking, before locking eyes with her. A sinister smile tugged at the corner of his lips.

"Lucky for you," he said, his voice low and threatening, "the water shouldn't be too cold. But you won't be alive long enough to notice." He hummed the little tune again that haunted her: *Splish, splash...*

Ava didn't even have time to reply. She felt herself fall. Heard the last word as gravity yanked her down. *Splosh!*

The smack of the water. The gasp for breath. She turned. She twisted. Her legs kicked out. The current pulled her forward. She struggled to keep her head above water. She gulped air and went under, squirming against the hoodie. If she could just get it off... She kicked, pushed off a rock, and popped out of the water for a brief second. She saw Ransick pushing Cara further into the water, only to be swallowed whole a moment later.

Ava plunged beneath the surface once more, dragged down by the current. Her lungs burned for air. The current was strong, but she battled against it with her legs, aiming for the shore. She was at the Cumberland's mercy as it tossed and swirled.

SIXTY-TWO

Owen Layne

Detective Lockhart maintained focus on the road and pushed the car beyond the legal limits as they followed the signal, tracking its progress through cell tower pings. With each successive update, the signal's location became increasingly precise.

Detective Lockhart's phone rang, and he patched it in. "Lockhart," he barked.

"Wyatt?" Kelleigh's voice filled the interior of the vehicle.

"Kelleigh?" Wyatt questioned. "Is everything okay? Because now isn't a good time." He spared Owen a glance.

There was a hiccup that stifled a sob on the other end. "I just found something horrible in Cara's room. You're not going to believe it, but I think… I think she is the Cumberland Killer."

Owen stiffened, leaning forward as if the simple act could make him hear better.

"What did you find?" Lockhart asked, his voice full of concern.

"A box under her bed full of newspaper articles, bank statements, apartment applications… seven different women, Ava included."

Gunner paced back and forth in the backseat, peering out the foggy windows.

Owen, his breath heavy and labored, remained tense as Kelleigh filled them in. The tracking dot finally stabilized, pinpointing a fixed location.

"They've stopped," Owen said in a low voice, not wanting to tip Kelleigh off to what was happening. She sounded like she was on the verge of breaking.

"I see that." Lockhart made a turn, hugging the corner at a high speed. Without missing a beat, Lockhart addressed Mrs. Morgahn. "Kelleigh, I want you to sit tight. Don't touch anything else. Hang up the phone and call the station. I want officers over there to go through everything." He gave her a few more instructions and somehow managed to navigate the wet, slippery road as the rain beat down, and he disconnected.

Owen strained his eyes to see as the wipers swished steadily back and forth. "There!" He pointed at the red and blue lights that cut through the dismal rain.

Lockhart came to a screeching halt behind the small sedan almost identical to his own.

Both men jumped out of the vehicle and ran toward the river with the dog leading. They saw blood on the bank and multiple sets of footprints. Then they heard a man's voice yell for help.

They descended the muddy bank, following the river's edge. Stuck out at the far edge of the bank, clinging to a fallen tree, was Ransick.

"Hang on!" Lockhart yelled. "Help is coming! Where's Ava?"

For a brief moment, Ransick lifted his hand in the air and pointed down river before he quickly tried to grasp back on.

"Hold tight! I have backup coming!" Detective Lockhart yelled over the roar of the river. But Ransick couldn't. He lost his grip and slipped under.

"She's in the river!" Owen exclaimed, his voice cracking with terror. "I've got to find her! I can't lose her!"

As he and Gunner ran further down, searching, Owen knew it was a long shot. The river flowed faster at the curve where the

Stone River dumped into it, and Owen was swamped with a sense of hopelessness.

Gunner ran down the bank following the river's edge, slipping and sliding on the muddy bank. Owen had lost sight of Detective Lockhart and the vehicles as the river bent and headed back toward civilization, but he didn't dare slow. Gunner was on to something. The German Shepherd let out a sharp bark. That's when he saw her.

A sapling hung low, bent toward the river. Tethered tenuously, Ava clung to it.

His heart hammered as he maneuvered precariously out to the edge of the wet earth. He was torn between rushing to her and cautiously watching where he stepped. One wrong move, and he would end up in the river with her.

"Ava!" he yelled over the rush of water. "Hang on!" He saw her head snap up. A wave of relief and hope mixed with her expression.

Ava's gaze didn't waver as she struggled to hang on to the sapling despite the strong current.

His eyes scanned the area around him. A long, sturdy branch hung over the riverbank to his right, jutting above the water. It wasn't much, but it might be enough. He stumbled toward it, using the little bit of solid ground he could find. The branch was just out of reach, but he could stretch and grab it. His fingers brushed the rough bark, and he yanked it down, testing its strength.

"Ava!" he called again, his voice trembling. "Grab the branch!"

When she saw the branch, a spark of determination flickered in her eyes. She stretched her arm out, struggling against the current, her fingers brushing the wood. But she could only reach so far. That's when he noticed her wrists were handcuffed together.

He'd have to do better. He'd have to get it closer. He eased further out, bending the branch with his weight. Her hand closed around it. With a final burst of determination, she let go of the sapling. With all the strength he could muster, he began pulling her toward him, inch by agonizing inch. The current tugged at her body, but together, they fought it—he pulled her with everything he had, and Ava used what little energy she had left to kick against the current.

Finally, with one last determined effort, he yanked her within reach. Gunner sank his teeth into the fabric of her shirt, his grip like iron as he pulled. Together, they fought against the current, hauling her toward the riverbank, the water surging violently around them. With a final heave, they dragged her to solid ground, their bodies trembling from the strain. Gasping for breath, they collapsed onto the cold, wet earth, the deafening roar of the river pounding in their ears.

For a moment, neither moved. They lay there, shaking with relief and exhaustion. He pulled Ava into his arms, her head resting against his chest, and held on tight. Gunner sniffed around them, licking their faces and hands, ecstatic to have them on land.

That's where Detective Lockhart discovered them, on the treacherous edge of the muddy riverbank, desperately clinging to each other as the mighty Cumberland River raged by.

EPILOGUE

Three months later

The lights dimmed, casting a soft, golden hue over the wooden stage, and the band eased into the next song, the smooth rhythm filling the air like a slow, swirling dance. Ava shifted on her stool, the familiar weight of her guitar settling against her chest as she adjusted it, her fingers brushing over the strings. The room buzzed with the low hum of conversation, the murmurs fading as the music began to take over.

But it wasn't just the melody that held her attention. She felt his gaze.

Ava glanced over at Owen, her breath catching in her throat. He was standing next to her at the edge of the stage, his guitar hanging casually at his side, but his eyes were fixed on her with an intensity that made her pulse spike.

He grinned, a smile that started at the corners of his mouth and stretched to his eyes, making those dimples deepen into irresistible creases.

Her heart fluttered, as always when he looked at her that way. For a moment, she forgot about the crowd and the music and just let herself be caught in the warmth of his presence. She found herself smiling back, her lips curving up almost involuntarily.

This was it.

One of her wishes was coming true. Right here, right now, as she sat on stage at Cognac Creek. But it wasn't just the stage that made the moment so perfect. It was the man beside her—Owen. Not only was he handsome, but he was also talented, kind, and genuine.

There was a quiet comfort in how he supported her, both on and off the stage. The music they played together wasn't just a performance; it was their connection—an unspoken harmony that had grown between them, blending perfectly.

She was living her dream, yes, but with him beside her, it felt even more real—something larger than life.

Owen's eyes never left hers as the song picked up. There was a spark in his gaze, something playful yet tender, as if he knew exactly how she felt.

They still had a long way to go, but they were working on their dreams as a team—writing songs, playing gigs, and getting to know each other in every aspect.

It was hard to believe that she had been sitting in a booth with her mother only three months ago, watching him perform. The memory of that night was still vivid in her mind, as though it had happened just yesterday. She had been caught in the rhythm of his voice, its deep, gravelly texture, and the way it wrapped around each note.

At that moment, she had never dreamed of anything more than being on stage close to him. But the events that followed had turned everything upside down, changing the course of her life in ways she never could have predicted.

Molly was back in the city after going home, taking some time to heal, not as the hopeful artist she had once been, but as someone still piecing herself together. Molly needed time to recover—physically and emotionally—but being here, in the heart of the music world, felt like a strange kind of homecoming for her. She'd be back, Ava knew, and stronger than before.

Molly, her mother, and Ava's mom had come in for a long weekend. They sat in a curved booth now and watched the set.

Ava's smile widened as she watched Detective Lockhart—Wyatt, she reminded herself, slip into the booth beside her mother and kiss her cheek.

The words rang out between her and Owen, and the meaning of the lyrics they had written rang true as the whole experience came full circle.

Owen finally found closure in Dylan's case when the truth came out. It was confirmed that Cara McCray was the driver of the vehicle that struck Officer Dylan Layne, killing him and seriously injuring Gunner.

Officer Ransick was coming from the same disastrous poker game that Cara and her roommate had just been at. He had lost heavily, and his debts were suffocating him. But when he saw the accident, something clicked in his mind. Cara was vulnerable, desperate, and—most importantly—useful. Ransick offered his help not out of kindness but as a way to escape his own mess, seizing the opportunity to exploit her as his finances crumbled and the threat of loan sharks closed in.

But things didn't go as planned. Officer Ransick had hoped to walk away unscathed and be hailed as a hero for "discovering" the truth and trying to save Ava, but he was wrong to assume that Ava wouldn't survive.

Ransick was pulled from the river that day, and now he sat in a prison cell, awaiting his trial. The stolen money was returned to the victims' families, but his debt remained. If he ever managed to get out, the loan sharks would be waiting.

Cara's body was found in the Cumberland days later, but Dorthea was never recovered.

The song ended, and the last chords lingered as Owen announced a break.

"You doing okay over there?" Owen asked.

"Never better, Cowboy."

He tugged her gently off the stool. "Come with me." He looked down at the dog. "You too, Gunner. You're a part of this."

She let him lead her off the stage and was surprised when he didn't head to the booth with her family and friends. "Where are we going?" she asked, slightly confused.

"You'll see." They went out to the rooftop, where the sun slowly melted behind the cityscape, setting the buildings ablaze.

The air was unseasonably cool for mid-September. The air stirred, and a breeze whipped through her hair. "What are we doing out here? It's cold."

He rubbed his hands up and down her bare arms, trying to warm her. "I have something for you. This will only take a minute."

Stella appeared out of nowhere with a big decorative box and placed it on the table near the railing.

"Great set, you two," she said, giving praise and meaning it.

"Did you have something to do with this?" Ava asked the older woman, pointing at the gift.

She laughed. "Honey, if I had been in charge, this would not have been what you would have been getting. I was only responsible for wrapping, and believe me, it wasn't easy. I told him to go with jewelry, but he insisted this was better." She shrugged. "You've got a good one here, sweetheart." Stella leaned in, hugged Ava, and then walked away a little misty-eyed.

Owen reached for her hand and brought it to his lips, kissing her palm tenderly. "Open it."

Ava gave him a curious look. "It's not my birthday. So what's this for?"

He lifted a shoulder. "Just because I wanted to give you something."

"You didn't have to buy me anything."

"I know, and I didn't." He smiled at her, a heart-wrenching smile that warmed her from her head to her toes. She could see the anxiousness in his face, the mischief behind his eyes. "The top just lifts off," he said with excitement, barely able to contain himself.

"Okay, okay. I think I got it." She chuckled at his impatience. He looked like a kid on Christmas morning waiting to open his gifts. She placed her hands on both sides of the box and lifted the top.

As she peered inside, her hand went to her heart, and she felt a warmth blossom deep in her chest.

A blue Solo Cup with a potted dandelion was nestled deep inside layers of white tissue paper. The bloom was a large, soft white globe.

Ava gently reached in and lifted it out. "How did you know?" she beamed.

He lifted a shoulder nonchalantly, clearly pleased with himself. He took the box from her, set it down, and linked his fingers with hers.

He led her to the edge of the rooftop. "Pick it."

She did as he asked, pinching the stem between her fingers and holding it up for him to see.

"Now," he said, his voice rich as butter. "Make your wish."

She nodded. "Let's wish together?"

"If you're sure?"

"I am. On the count of three."

A fleeting smile tugged at the corners of his mouth. "On three," he agreed.

They leaned in, their mouths a breath apart, and counted. On three, they both blew, sending a myriad of white fluffy seeds out over the city. Ava watched the wind shift and swirl them up and away. Before she could move, Owen pulled her in close, his hand wrapped around her waist, the tips of their boots touching. He placed his mouth over hers, sealing the wish with a kiss and a promise.

She felt a sense of peace, embracing all the joy it brought. She would hold onto this moment, savoring it each day as it came, one wish at a time. There was hope in the future, and she was ready to meet it with an open heart.

"What did you wish for?" he murmured against her lips, just a whisper separating them.

A smile played along her lips. "I can't tell you, or it won't come true."

"I'll tell you mine." He toyed with a strand of her hair, keeping her tucked in close. The warmth from his body pressed into hers. Spreading. "My wish is that I can help make all of your Tennessee wishes come true."

Her eyes sparkled knowingly. "That's exactly what I wished for, too."

Acknowledgments

What can I say that I haven't said before? That is the question, but it's true. So much goes into a story like this, from inspiration to perspiration and inevitable perseverance. And without these individuals always right beside me, this book may never see the light of day.

First and foremost, to my incredible daughter Delaney, whose bravery in pursuing her dreams has been a constant source of inspiration for this story. Your passion, determination, and unwavering support have meant everything to me. Thank you for diving headfirst into the first draft with me—reading, offering thoughtful feedback, and helping me refine every detail. You've been my sharpest critic and greatest ally, pointing out where the plot needed strengthening and whether the twists made sense. Your diligence in content editing has been invaluable, as you tirelessly searched for those tricky plot holes and worked alongside me to make this story the best it could be. I could never have done this without you, Delaney. You're not just my daughter; you're my partner in this journey, and I am forever grateful for you.

To Jess and Liz, my incredible fellow authors—your professionalism, unwavering encouragement, and dedication to Tennessee Wishes have been an invaluable source of both knowledge and inspiration. Every conversation, every piece of feedback, and every word of support, whether said, read in the quiet of the library, or highlighted on a Google doc, has pushed me to grow and improve in ways I never could have on my own. I treasure your insightful comments and even the constructive criticism, as they have all been integral to shaping this story into what it is today. This final version would not have been nearly as rich, as developed, or as meaningful without both of you. I am forever grateful for your partnership and the deep care you've invested in this journey alongside me.

To Kristy—who listens to my endless complaints when I'm stuck, keeps me grounded when I'm convinced everything is falling apart, and steps in with the perfect dose of tough love when I *seriously* consider using Papyrus for my book cover. Your eye for detail, your vast knowledge, and your unshakeable support never cease to amaze me. I am in constant awe of your talent and insight, and I could never thank you enough for being there every step of the way.

To Melisa and Pam, who caught those final, ever-present typos and spelling mistakes—your sharp eyes and attention to detail have truly made a difference in a cleaner final draft! And to the rest of my amazing ARC team—Amy and Erin —thank you for your unwavering support and enthusiasm. Your genuine interest in my books, eagerness to dive in and read, and heartfelt feedback have made this journey so much more meaningful. I am beyond grateful for each of you. Thank you for being a part of this!

To Ryan and Makayla, whom I bounce ideas off of in passing or have them read through a quick passage to see if it all makes sense. I'm deeply appreciative of the unique ways you both contribute to my life and my writing, and I feel incredibly fortunate to have you by my side.

I couldn't have done this without any of you. You have my deepest gratitude, unwavering respect, and all my love.

To my incredible readers: thank you from the bottom of my heart for trusting me with your time and allowing me to be a small part of your entertainment. Your feedback, comments, and questions mean the world to me —keep them coming! You inspire me every day.

Last but absolutely not least, to my family: Your patience as I write and your belief in me—that I can achieve anything—keep me going. You are my rock, and I will forever be grateful for your unwavering support and love. You have my eternal gratitude.

Enjoyed it? Please consider leaving a review.

About the Author

Melissa, a true country girl at heart, grew up in the heart of Iowa. Her childhood was shaped by adventures in the Midwest countryside and long summer days working in the fields. A proud Iowa State University graduate and dedicated Cyclone fan, she later moved to Harford County, Maryland, before settling in Lancaster County, Pennsylvania, where she now lives with her husband and four children.

Melissa stepped into the world of writing in 2020, publishing her first novel and quickly finding her voice in the mystery romance genre. Her books are known for their emotional depth, suspenseful plots, and richly drawn settings —from the haunting charm of small towns to the vibrant streets of cities like Nashville and the coastal allure of Ocean City, Maryland. With five standalone novels under her belt, she writes stories that keep readers turning pages—and guessing until the very end.

Melissa's passion for writing stems from a lifelong love of reading, which she credits as the foundation for her storytelling. She describes writing as "revealing a secret, one page at a time," a philosophy that guides her work and connects her with readers who love a good mystery wrapped in romance.

Whether crafting a new plot or cheering on the Cyclones, Melissa brings warmth, heart, and a bit of Iowa grit to everything she does.

www.ingramcontent.com/pod-product-compliance
Lightning Source LLC
Chambersburg PA
CBHW070833250626
47159CB00003B/759